What People are S

The Salt Mines Mystery

This book has adventure, danger and suspense. A must-read. Can't wait for the next book to come out.

Joshua Potter

The book is an amazing adventure; a whirlwind of exciting action that captured my imagination and kept me enthralled to the very end. It was definitely a page-turner. Couldn't put it down and read the whole thing in two days.

Cindy Burghardt

We found the book a real interest grabber—couldn't wait to see what happened next.

Joan and Ed Hoch

I enjoyed that the main characters were Christians. The family dynamic was a positive one and the brothers had a good relationship—they argued like all siblings do, but they were there for each other. And I liked that Gabe and Alex were always prepared.

Debbie Riddle

Easy to read. Interesting. Realistic. Very relatable story that flows well.

Toby Zeilinski

The Salt
Mines
Mystery

The Salt Mines Mystery

Aaron M. Zook Jr.

Bold Vision Books
PO Box 2011
Friendswood, Texas 77549

Copyright © Aaron M Zook, Jr. 2015

ISBN # 978-0692435366

Published in the United Sates of America

Bold Vision Books
PO Box 2011
Friendswood, Texas 77549

Cover photo by Tomas 1 1 1 1

Cover designed by *k*ae Creative Solutions
Interior designed by *k*ae Creative Solutions

Dedication

I dedicate this book to my excellent wife, Joyce. Her love, encouragement, and support have been incredible throughout thirty-six years of our married life, including 26 years of my military service, three years in full-time ministry, and in particular, during the writing of the Thunder and Lightning book series. She is the joy of my life. May the Lord, to whom all praise is due, bless her abundantly, beyond her greatest dreams.

Table of Contents

Chapter 1
– Fight

Hans Becher threw his skateboard onto the sidewalk in front of my feet.

"The skateboard champion is me, not you." The sixteen-year-old refugee from East Germany strode toward me with determination. "Your words mean nothing."

"My jump was the best, Becher." I pushed my chest forward. "You lose."

Hans' German friends surrounded us.

Pete, my best friend, and twelve like me, laid a hand on my shoulder. "Gabe, it doesn't matter if you're right." He tugged my shirt. "Don't argue with that bully. He's bigger than you. Let's go."

"Pete…" My eyes caught his for a second. "I can handle this."

Hans punched me in the shoulder.

I rocked back to absorb the blow and steadied myself. After Hans threw a couple of jabs, I darted in, fist aimed at his nose, but I missed. I retreated.

"You Americans think you're number one in all the things." Hans circled to his right. "But I'm teaching you different."

Now we were on the grass. Hans' friends dropped their skateboards to form a human wall on the lawn.

Alex, my fourteen-year-old brother, was off to one side, crouching over our dogs, Thunder and Lightning. Both strained at their leashes.

I lunged forward, smashing my fist into Hans' rock hard stomach, and then connected with an uppercut, snapping his head back. While I regrouped for the next blow, Hans muttered a string of German words I hadn't heard before.

He rubbed his jaw, tightened his fists, and circled to his left.

Like a boxer, I bounced away, but he bull-rushed me, knocking me to the ground. I twisted and fell, landing on my hands and chest.

Hans jumped on me, hammering my back to the ground to keep me pinned.

I struggled to breathe. My right cheek felt like it was on fire. My ears rang and I sucked in air and rolled. Or tried to. I didn't move much.

"Polizei." Several boys pointed at a German policeman gazing at us.

Hans let me up. The rest of the boys crowded around us. We brushed ourselves off and adjusted our clothes. The policeman was still on the opposite side of the castle park, looking our way and talking to an elderly couple motioning in our direction.

The circular park sidewalk surrounded a massive grassy area with gardens in the middle divided by smaller wandering paths. Black metal lampposts lining the looping walkway flickered on. The lights' amber glow kept the evening darkness at bay and provided a cheery atmosphere for evening walkers. But not for me.

Alex appeared next to me. "Gabe, check out your right cheek."

I touched the aching area, bringing away red fingertips, which I wiped on the grass. "He scraped me up, no thanks to you."

"You wanted a 'fair fight,' didn't you?" Alex said. "I held the dogs."

"Hans is way older than me. He's sixteen."

"Then pick on kids your own age. Or size. Don't be a twelve-year-old dummy." Alex brushed past me, his shoulder grazing mine.

Pete hurried over with our skateboards. "Take these. We need to leave now or the Polizei will make us answer questions. Don't rush or you'll make it look like we were doing something wrong."

I dumped my skateboard onto the sidewalk and weaved toward the castle, away from the cop. The policeman eyed Hans and his boys. Pete and I scissored back and forth, passing Alex, who had the dogs pulling him on his skateboard like huskies dragging a sled. Alex's dog, Thunder, a black Great Dane mixed breed, did most of the pulling. My dog, Lightning, a small, golden-red Shih-Tzu mix, pranced for show.

I snuck a peek at the Polizei. He left the couple and headed in our direction. I rolled through a park side exit, whizzing under the arch into the busy city side of the castle. I found a bench, stopped, and sat. Pete plopped down next to me.

"Nice going, Gabe," Alex said. "Now we have Polizei chasing us. You can't stay here too long or he'll spot you when he comes out of the park."

"You didn't help at all," I said. "When I beat Hans skateboarding and he shoved me to the ground, you should've—"

"What? Come to rescue my poor, little brother? You would have told me to get lost and let you handle it." He shook his head and narrowed his eyes.

I shoved off the bench and breathed into his face. "Thanks for nothing." I spun around and wiped my cheek. Only a little smeared blood remained. "Come on, Pete. I'm not heading home with this loser." I jerked a thumb in Alex's direction.

"Don't forget your dog, baby brother." Alex stretched out Lightning's leash to me. "And stay on the lighted streets."

"Who are you? My master?" I snatched Lightning's leash out of his hand.

Alex marched away, keeping Thunder close. They crossed the street and merged with the evening crowds as darkness fell rapidly.

"Come on, Pete." I picked up my skateboard. "I'm nobody's baby. We're not following him, but we have to hurry to beat him home." I picked up Lightning and we jogged toward less crowded streets. "There." I pointed to an alleyway. "We can skateboard on the back streets."

"Okay," Pete said. "But I don't like that part of town. And it's not well-lit."

"I don't want to be on the same street as Alex," I said. "He thinks he's a king, ordering me around all the time. Anyway, there are two of us. We'll be okay. I'm not gonna give in to Alex."

Five minutes later, we skateboarded into the area where drunks and druggies hung out at night. Lightning, who was off his leash, darted in and out of corners to sniff everything. The cobblestone paths here made skateboarding worthless. We decided to jog again.

The older section of town had brown, stone buildings. Light orange tiles covered steep roofs. Broken tile pieces littered parts of the alleyway. Odd angles, tiny courtyards, and a few clotheslines reminded me of the medieval pictures I had studied in a homeschool history class about the Middle Ages. A few narrow side passages branched off the main road. Few of the lamppost lights worked. One flickered with a greenish tint.

The muscles in the back of my neck tightened. We slowed to a walk.

"You know how to get us through here, right?" I said.

"Like the back of my hand." Pete stopped, pointed in one direction, shrugged, and motioned another way. "Come on. I know this place during the day. It's a little trickier in the dark."

"Go faster." The tightness spread to my arms and gut. A gate banged behind me. I jumped and looked around. No one was there.

"I have to make sure we're going down the right alley."

"It's been twenty minutes. Shouldn't we be out?" I wiped sweaty palms on my pants. I remembered what happened six months ago. *I don't want anyone kidnapping me again.*

A light fog crept into the dim streets, making it harder to see any great distance. Halos of mist shrouded the lights. Garbage overflowed several trashcans. I plugged my nose. A chill settled between my shoulder blades.

"I may have missed a turn, but we'll get there." Pete faced me. His jaw dropped and he stabbed a finger at something behind me.

"Halt," a deep voice said. A hand slapped onto my shoulder from behind.

I screamed.

Chapter 2
– Foggy Fright

I jerked out of the vise grip, stumbled forward, and whirled to see the attacker.

A pockmarked face of acne scars stared at me. The man's scraggly hair resembled his body—long, thin, and not much there. His clothes had worn spots on the knees and elbows, but looked clean. He grinned, showing yellow teeth with gaping holes. He jutted his chin and tilted his head.

"Geld?" the man said, sticking out his hand. Though his deep tone went up at the end like a question, the thrust-out hand and the glint of his eye told me I had no choice.

"Money," Pete translated. "He wants money."

Lightning raced toward me and growled.

I shuffled next to Pete and checked my pocket. The feel of coins eased my mind. I pulled out a few. "I only have seventy Pfennig—that's not even equal to fifty cents."

The man reached out to take the money.

"Don't." Pete blocked my arm. "Next will be your watch."

The man eased a little closer, bolder now that he had seen cash.

I backed away, still facing the beggar.

Pete followed.

Another step.

Lightning barked, moving toward the man, but I bent down and yanked him by the collar. "Stay here," I said. My hands tingled and my breathing slowed.

The man leaped forward with speed unlike his broken-down appearance. In three steps, his bony talons clamped onto my hand. He pried open my fingers.

"Stop." I tried to tug his hands off mine, but he was too strong. I prepared to drop the coins and take a defensive stance.

But before I adjusted my footing, the man's face changed. He cringed, hands dropping mine as he watched something behind me. His eyes widened. He pushed himself away and scampered into the darkness.

I turned around and dashed right into a man's chest. He loomed over me, the clean smell of aftershave drifting from his jaw.

The hum of a weak, electric light filled the speechless void. My coins clinked on the cobblestones.

The man laughed. He had barely moved when I bounced off him. Over six-feet tall, he had a crew cut, dark slacks, and a light, collared shirt. His face showed no fat. *Two hundred pounds, maybe.* Rock-hard muscle defined the upper body.

A second man, shorter than first, stood next to the guy. Shorty was still a little taller than my five-foot, two-inches, and he smelled like unwashed clothes. He made quick, nervous moves. The guy wore baggy work-pants, black leather combat boots, and a brown jacket.

In a flash, Shorty's hand slapped over Pete's mouth and shoved him against the wall, a fistful of shirt in the other hand. "That's the kid," he said in English. He tilted his head in my direction. "He fits the description."

The tall muscular man cracked his knuckles. "Nice."

"What do you want?" I took a step back.

Muscle man slid his hand into a side pocket, retrieving a six-inch black object. He pressed a button—a blade sprung out, gleaming in the foggy night.

I gulped as the man twirled the blade in his hand. *He's an expert with that thing.* I jerked my head to the rear and mouthed the word, "Run."

Pete's hand chopped Shorty's wrist, loosening his grip. He bolted right.

The man leaped after him, latching onto his belt. He flung him against the wall, pulled out a boot knife and scraped the skin under Pete's quivering chin. "Scared?"

Lightning, yapping and snarling, launched at the attacker who kicked him away. Jerking Pete's ear to his mouth, Shorty whispered something.

"Call him off." Pete's pink skin looked pale. He gulped air. "Quick, or the man says the knife will slip."

"Come here, boy." I patted my leg. "Now."

Lightning skittered over, throat rumbling.

"Don't move," I said.

Muscle man cleaned his fingernails using the switchblade, eying the sweaty man with the boot knife. "Let the kid go," he told his partner.

"But I want to cut him."

"He's not the target. But the other…" Muscle man flashed a smile at me.

Shorty yanked Pete away from the wall, tracing a line from chin to collarbone with his blade. "Walk when you leave or you'll get hurt." He showed his teeth in a big grin. "This is a throwing knife." His lips widened even further as he let go.

Released, Pete massaged his throat and took a few tentative steps.

"Go on," I said with more bravery than I felt. "I'll be okay."

Pete nodded, glanced at his attacker and shuffled the way we had come.

"Faster," Shorty said.

Pete's pace quickened.

"Schnell, schnell," Shorty yelled. In one fluid motion, brown jacket blurring, the creep hurled something at Pete.

Thunk.

The knife's blade sank into a wooden door a foot away from my buddy.

Pete broke into a dash and disappeared.

The two men laughed.

I gritted my teeth and made a fist.

The muscular guy strolled over.

I crouched near a wall.

"Stay." The keyword dog training worked like a charm. Lightning scrambled a little to my right, but kept his body poised for action.

Shorty scooted past us to pull his knife out of the door. His smell made my nose itch.

"You cost me lots of money," muscle man said.

"How?" I balanced with a slight shift, preparing for an attack.

"Don't be stupid. You put Polizei on our trail last year. For that you pay."

"You deserve it, creep." I altered my stance.

Muscle man's jaw tightened. His eyes narrowed at me.

Shorty returned, boot knife sheathed, and stood by his partner's side.

Muscle man's switchblade flipped into a fighting position. "This is no joke. I teach you and your father a lesson. Machete hasn't forgotten you."

His knees bent, eyes inventorying me. He paused before lunging at me, slashing across my belly.

I fell back and sucked in my breath and stomach. The knife shredded my best skateboarding T-shirt. Twirling, I shoved off the wall to the center of the street, side-stepping Lightning in the move. "Jerk." I fingered the tear. The fog made the cobblestones slippery. I repositioned for the next cut.

"Sic 'em," I said.

Lightning leaped, snarling at Shorty, who charged in to help.

Deep barking sounded behind the men. They turned to the noise.

Thunder bounded toward them. Pounding footsteps and Alex's voice echoed in the air.

Muscle man kicked Lightning away from Shorty. He clamped on to his partner's jacket and shoved him into a side passage. Thunder arrived as the gate clicked shut. Lightning barked at the escaping thugs sprinting into the shadows.

Alex ran through the dimness and wrenched the latch. It rattled and banged, but wouldn't open. He shook the gate a few more times, then hurried over to me.

"What happened to your shirt?" He raised both eyebrows.

"Knife cut," I said. "Oh. And I'm glad to see you too."

"We're gonna get nuked when we get home." Alex blew out a deep breath. "Let's go."

Chapter 3
~ Family Fallout

Boys, you're late," Mom said through the open second story window. "Get up here right now." She slammed the window shut.

"Great," I said. "She sounds steamed."

Alex nodded.

We raced the dogs up the stairs and into the apartment.

"What have you boys been doing?" Mom's voice floated out of the kitchen.

"It's a long story," I said. "I'll tell you at dinner."

Mom appeared at the kitchen doorway, wiping her hands on a dishtowel.

"Your dad and I already ate. You're more than half-an-hour late. That's unacceptable. How can you…" She focused on my face. "What is that on your cheek?"

"I got hit in a fight."

"What did you say?" Dad, still in his U.S. Army uniform, stepped out into the hall. "What kind of fight?" He tilted my head, looking at the scraped skin.

"Defensive. Hans Becher, the 'Goeppingen Skateboard Champ,' swung first."

"What did you do to make him want to punch you?"

"I beat him in a skateboard competition."

Dad nodded.

"My scores were better than his. He gathered his buddies and shoved me around."

Dad released my head. "Your scrape needs alcohol and a bandage. Not too bad. What's this?" His hand slipped into my slashed T-shirt and tugged.

"The second thing that happened."

"Are you hurt?"

"No, the switchblade…"

Mom dropped her towel and rushed over. She inspected my blood-smeared cheek and looked at my shirt. "I didn't even notice. What knife?" Her eyebrows drew in, jaw line set firm.

"Dad, can we get something to eat?" Alex covered his face with one hand. "This might take a while."

After saying the blessing for the meal, we ate and told our stories.

Dad nodded during the part about the skateboard fight, but his neck went red when I told about the alleyway scare. He made a fist, his knuckles white.

Mom's olive face drained to a lighter color.

"Okay, boys. I've heard enough." Dad opened his fist and put both palms flat on the table. He pushed to a standing position. "I'm not happy about this."

"Dad, it was self-defense." I raised my hands, palms up, in a helpless gesture. "What…"

"We've told you before, no fighting," he said. "You're mother and I will decide what to do. Now go wash the dishes and get ready for bed." Dad reached for Mom's hand as she stood. He pulled her close and walked her around the corner.

"Looks like we're in hot water again," I said while we walked into the kitchen.

"We?" Alex looked at me. "*You're* in trouble for that shortcut you took. And for not walking away from Hans. I did the right thing by looking for you."

"You think you're an *angel*, never doing anything wrong." I scooped soapsuds from the sink and flung them at his head.

Alex slapped a cupboard shut and chased me into the Great Room, our huge entryway into the apartment. He gave my head a soapsuds bath. I wrestled his hand away and paused.

"Alex, wait. Listen to Mom and Dad." I sat up, straightening my hair.

A muffled conversation came from around the corner.

"I don't care," Mom said. "Our family is in danger. You have got to make this stop. Your special projects at work are the reason."

I made shushing motions and tugged Alex's shirt. We crept close to their bedroom door.

Dad spoke lower, softer. "Hon, calm down. The police are still investigating, clearing the town of anyone connected to Machete. Gabe went into the wrong part of town."

Machete. The terrorist group that kidnapped us at Neuschwanstein castle last year. I knelt next to the open keyhole to hear the details.

"First, it's the wrong part of town, next it will be in the playground, or at the Schloss Park when they are out by themselves. It's too dangerous."

"Okay, okay. I'll see the police chief. And we'll leave until they say the town is safe."

Alex pushed me away, peeping through the keyhole. Then, he stumbled to his feet and sprinted down the hall, waving me to follow. Thunder and Lightning galloped after him.

We flew into our room as the click of Mom and Dad's latch sounded.

Seconds later, Dad poked his head into the room. Alex and I lay on our single beds reading, dogs at our feet.

"Let's go. You're going to tell your story to the Polizei Chief. Afterward, you're coming home to pack. We're going on a vacation."

After telling the Polizei Chief our story, we arrived home and found a note taped to our mailbox from our German landlord. Alex grabbed it and read the broken English out loud.

April 16, 1990.
You have new package.
Pick up in morning. Klaus.

Chapter 4
~ The Package

I woke excited about our vacation. I showered and dressed in a hurry.

After rushing through breakfast, we finished packing. Alex, me, and the dogs bounded down the stairs two at a time to our landlord's shop on the first floor. Dad trailed behind.

Herr Klaus' smile welcomed us into his noisy clock shop. He finished his business with a customer, waved us over, and disappeared into the repair area behind black felt curtains. The dogs sat, tails wagging. In ten seconds the curtains parted and Herr Klaus slid a large, two-foot cube, wrapped in balloon-party paper onto the glass counter.

My heartbeat sped up. *Is this a gift?*

Herr Klaus smiled. "For the boys. Someone came by and left it late last night. You were expecting a package?" His direct gaze caught Alex's eyes, then mine.

"Nein, I…I mean no," Alex said.

"A surprise package?" Our landlord thought hard. "A birthday present?"

"No," Dad said. "No birthdays this month. We'll have to be careful. It seems fine, but I'll do a thorough exam upstairs." Dad thanked Herr Klaus in German and we left.

In the apartment, Dad went to the dining room, pulled out a small briefcase, and told us to go to our bedroom while he did a security scan.

Two minutes later, I heard the dining room door to the Great Room open. I ran from our room to find out the results.

"Checks out okay," Dad said. "But we'll be careful opening it." He nodded at Mom. "Honey, you may want to see it, too."

Dad peeled the paper off with care and pulled the thick cardboard open. A folded note fluttered toward the floor. Lightning snatched the paper and streaked off through the house.

"Lightning," I yelled, "bring that note here right now."

Barking, Thunder chased after him.

I didn't leave. I wanted to see what was inside.

Dad tugged and out came a small bamboo cage, glued to a rocky slab. Hanging from one side of the bamboo cage on hooks were seven keys, each a different color and special shape.

"Unusual," Mom said.

"Hmmm." Dad crossed his arms, tapping his cheek.

Lighting, a reddish-gold whirlwind, burst into the room chased by a lumbering avalanche.

"Freeze." Dad waited until the dogs settled. "Come here."

The dogs sat in front of him, the limp paper hanging from Lightning's mouth.

"Open up." Dad stretched out his hand, taking the note from Lightning. "This is addressed to Alex and Gabe. I'm going to let them read it." He thrust the note into the air.

I beat Alex, snagged the note and read it to everyone.

Seven Keys
For Seven Doors
Open Them All
And the Treasure is Yours

Each Path is Lined
With Treacherous Signs
Carefully Select
What You Will Do Next

To Start the Journey
The Next Clue is Found
Near Walls of White
That Lay Underground

An Island, A Maze
A Prisoner's Face
Are Parts of The Puzzle
To Solve Your Next Case

G

"I wonder if that G stands for Guardian Angel," Alex said.

"During his last mystery, you boys needed all the help you could get." Mom glanced at Dad, a frown on her face.

"Remember the other box that came about six months ago?" I rubbed my hand over the smooth bamboo cage. "G sent that one, too. It had a song for us to memorize to the tune of the sailor song 'Way, Hey, Blow the Man Down.'"

"And the note said the song was for Team Test #2." Alex patted Thunder. "Maybe we'll have another adventure."

"That sounds dangerous," Mom said. "I don't like it. But let's get ready for our trip. We're leaving in thirty minutes." Mom left the dining room.

Dad lifted the first key, a dull white one, from its hook. When he held it next to a light, a golden glow spread through the thinnest parts and revealed a number one etched into its side.

Dad flipped the key over. "I bet this is for the first part of the treasure hunt."

"Can we take our present with us?" I asked.

"No, the cage looks too fragile for our trip."

"But we need to take the first key in case something happens," I protested.

"I guess you can take the key," he said. "It's small enough. But nothing else."

We raced to our room and worked like high-speed robots. In five minutes we straightened the place and took our suitcases and backpacks to the Great Room. Ten minutes later, we drove away in our red minivan toward Lake Chiemsee and the Herrenchiemsee Castle.

I kept silent, mulling over the riddle from the gift. *Sounds like gibberish. And how are we going anywhere near a prisoner? Was this our second survival test from G?*

Chapter 5
– Accidental Disaster

When I opened the van door in the parking lot, the dogs spilled out and bounded toward the hotel. Alex and I chased them down and caught our breath. We walked into the welcome center, nodding our heads at the fancy decorations. But the dogs led us to a new discovery.

"Pete, what are you doing here?" I laughed and ran over to him. He stood next to the fireplace in the Lake Chiemsee Hotel lobby. Dad checked us in at the front desk while we talked.

"Taking a vacation." He smiled. "With you."

The Schultz family, including Pete and his fifteen-year-old sister Jenna, had arrived minutes before us.

In half-an-hour, we all boarded a boat to the Herren Island, home of the Herrenchiemsee Castle. When we had docked, Pete and I raced with the dogs toward the palace gardens and fountains, while Alex and Jenna strolled with hands intertwined.

I beat Pete to the edge of the plaza in front of the castle. "Hey, that's Erik and Dieter." I pointed at the castle door.

Erik Eberstark, a German who was half-a-year older than me, had become a friend after his father joined Dad on a secret project at work. Dieter, Erik's fifteen-year-old friend, stood a full head taller than me. His darker complexion and black hair was the opposite of Erik's blond hair and light skin.

I sprinted, but Erik and Dieter disappeared into the golden-colored palace.

"We've got to connect with them," I said to Pete when he caught up. "Erik might know about the project Dad is working on."

"How would he know?" Pete said.

"At the office, when his father goes to get a cup of coffee, Erik looks around."

"Snoops, you mean?" Pete's eyes widened.

I shrugged.

The palace was incredible, but my mind whirred. *How can I find Erik and Dieter?*

"King Ludwig II loved the Palace of Versailles, which the Sun King, Louis XIV, had built," the tour guide said. "The outside garden is an exact copy of the original. Our first treasure is a gold-feathered, blue enamel peacock monument on a green and red marble base." The guide pointed out the State Staircase, colorful paintings on the walls and ceilings, marble statues and crystal chandeliers.

Each passing moment made me edgy. I had to do something.

In the king's bedroom, our escort directed the group's attention to the Meissen porcelain toilet set.

"Lightning," I whispered, "Find Erik." I shoved him into the next room while everyone crowded around the toilet. He didn't come back. At the tour's end in the gift shop, I still couldn't locate him.

"Lose something?"

Behind me, two friends snickered. Lightning wiggled in Dieter's arms.

Alex, Pete and Jenna joined the group. Talking in hushed tones, the four of us brought Erik and Dieter up to speed on the alleyway escapade and new package. When I got to the song, Dieter snorted.

"Useless." Dieter shook his head. "And I don't know that tune."

"It's an old sailor's song, called a shanty," I said.

"Let's hear it." Dieter led us away from the crowd.

I sang from memory and Alex joined in.

When the roof crashes down, so that you can't be found,
Way, Hey, blow the man down.
Slip to the right, to avoid nasty sights,
Way, Hey, blow the man down.

Ten paces ahead, duck if you like your head
Way, Hey, blow the man down.
Then jump quite a lot, so you don't get too hot.
Way, Hey, blow the man down.

Next, crawl through the mud, 'till what flies makes a thud
Way, Hey, blow the man down.
One at a time, cross the bridge when it chimes
Way, Hey, blow the man down.

Take the tube to your right, where you'll slide out of sight
Way, Hey, blow the man down.
Look for the clock, use the key when it talks
Way, Hey, blow the man down.

"Exciting things, but I have better informations." Erik bent toward us, his broken English making his words seem more confidential. "I know some workings of your father's project."

"What?" I said.

"The notes I am having in my room. A little about sciences and some scary things. I don't understand all, yet."

"Time to go." Dieter's mother arrived and put her arm around him. "Perhaps we'll see you on the lake tomorrow." Dieter and Erik headed toward the island dock to catch the next ship. Erik looked back at me and shrugged.

But we're going to the Salt Mines, not the lake. How will I get to see what Erik has?

Back at the hotel, we decided to cool off at the pool.

"Watch this cannonball." I bounced off the diving board and crashed into the water.

"Bravo." An olive-skinned boy dressed in shirt, slacks, and sandals leaned against a doorway and clapped his hands. "Not too bad."

"Franco, welcome to the pool party." Jenna sat up in her lounge chair.

"My favorite Italian friend." I climbed out of the pool, dripping on the concrete deck. Franco Giovanni, slightly older than me, was a recent home-school group addition.

"May I present," he gave a mock bow, "the lovely Spanish dancer for the party?"

Izabella, a twelve-year-old whose mother taught us dance lessons, curtsied in her sundress.

"We have a lot of friends here." Alex sat next to Jenna. "What brought you two?"

"I must learn to sail." Franco shrugged. "Maybe tomorrow. Where are your dogs?"

"In the room," I said. "Dad doesn't want them near the pool."

"Why don't you come with us to the Salt Mines?" Jenna asked. "It'll be fun."

"Perhaps. My parents are from the island of Sicily, therefore, I must learn to like life on the sea." Franco's eyes narrowed. "But the water, I don't think it likes me."

"It's nothing to be afraid of." I leaped into the pool, splashing Alex and Jenna. When I surfaced, Jenna was on her feet, wiping her face. Alex stood next to her, dripping wet.

"I think he needs to learn some manners," Jenna said.

"I agree." Alex took off his T-shirt and sandals. He took his time, eyes riveted on me.

I swam to the corner ladder, scrambled out, and skittered to the other side of the pool. Alex speed-walked after me. We circled the pool.

"What's the matter, Gabe? Can't take a little of your own medicine?" Alex sped up.

"Catch me if you can." I began to run.

"Stop running," Alex said. "If Mom or Dad sees you, we'll have to go to the room."

"Quit bossing me around." I slowed a bit, anyway. Alex gained on me. Rounding the second corner at the deep end, I slipped.

He grabbed my arm, but I slithered out of his grasp.

As Alex reached over the edge of the corner, I saw my chance to make him pay. I gripped his arm, tugging and twisting while I jumped into the water. *Take that, bossman.* I landed sideways and surfaced with a big grin.

"Alex," Jenna screamed.

My brother floated face down in pinkish water.

The smile drained from my face. In seconds I flipped him over, put my arm under his chin, and swam to the ladder. Pete and Franco waited to hoist him out of the water.

"He is breathing?" Izabella asked.

"I'm not sure," Pete said.

Franco nodded toward a lounge chair laid out flat. "Lay him facedown."

I hurried out of the pool and watched Pete and Franco work.

Jenna placed a towel under his head, turning it to the side. Her hand went to his lips. "He's not breathing. Do something." She glanced at me.

Izabella knelt, pulled his mouth open and put two fingers inside. "He has nothing in his mouth."

I straddled him, two hands on his back and shoved hard. He didn't move.

"Don't stop," Jenna said.

"Come on." I pressed harder with all my weight. And again. I kept pushing, alternating upper and lower back.

Alex's body arched and fluid came out his mouth and nostrils. He coughed and gagged, sides heaving. His head slid to the side, ejecting more yellow junk. He moaned and his eyelids fluttered. A bulge on his right temple kept him from opening one eye all the way. Reddish drops fell from his puffy split-lip.

"Where…" He hacked and spit. "Where am I?"

"How's your head?" Jenna asked Alex. She settled on the bed facing the window. Her hand rested on his. The rest of our friends who had been at the pool stood close.

"My noggin' aches and throbs." Alex rubbed the right side of his brow.

"I can't believe your brother threw you into the edge of the swimming pool." Jenna cast a sideways glance at me.

"I slipped." My neck started to get hot. *Sort of.* "Let's forget about it."

"I should have seen it coming. It's not the first time we've wrestled around the pool." Alex shifted his eyes to me. "Thanks for saving my life."

"Of course." I avoided his eyes. *I almost killed you.*

A loud rap on the door brought me back to the present.

"Ciao." Franco opened the door with a wide sweep of his arm and two boys appeared.

"Erik and Dieter?" Pete's face had a questioning look.

"I see *someone* had an accident." Dieter angled over to Alex.

"How did you know?" I asked.

"We saw doctor come into this hotel on the ground floor and go into your room." Erik gazed at Alex. "That bandage is… almost a turban." He laughed.

"Are you two staying here?" Jenna said.

"Close. Next wing, past dining hall," Erik said. "Rooms 109 and 110. Our parents, they are staying further down the hall."

"Our room is the second floor for you Americans." Dieter grinned.

"We're not that new," I said. "Our first semester on German customs taught us the American first floor is your ground floor."

"We are on the opposite end," said Franco. "On the ground floor, near Izabella's room."

"And we're in the middle," I said. "Jenna and Pete are around the corner from us."

"What is happening here?" Dieter pointed to Alex's head.

"Alex and Gabe were horsing around." Jenna eyed me and told the story.

Good. No pretending for me. While she talked, I zoned out until she elbowed me.

Jenna stood and put her hand on my shoulder. "Alex wouldn't be here without Gabe."

I faced away. *Yeah, right. He wouldn't be laid up without me.* "It wasn't just me," I said, hiding my feelings. "Pete and Franco lifted Alex out of the water and Izabella made sure his airway was clear. We all did something."

"Si, si," Izabella said. "But you were the one who saved him."

A room service cart rattled on the tile floor outside the door. Seconds later, Mom breezed through the door, the bellboy rolling the cart behind her into the carpeted room. The warm smell of roast beef filled the room. Mom tipped the room service man and he left.

"Dinnertime," she announced to the group. "I'm afraid you'll all have to leave. Alex must rest and recuperate. Thanks for coming by." She weaved the cart between them to the bedside.

"Bis morgan." Jenna patted his arm, fingertips brushing his leg as she walked away.

I sighed. *She's going to be a pain now that she has an excuse to hang around Alex.*

I talked with Franco and Izabella for a few minutes. They said goodbye, followed by our other friends. Erik ducked behind the door, pulled me close, and pushed a small business card in my hand.

"For later," he whispered.

Before he left, Pete latched onto my shirt, tugging me back into the room. I stuffed the card in my back pocket to read when Mom and Dad left.

"Gabe, I want you to eat dinner with your father and me," Mom said after ensuring Alex had eaten. "Alex finished most of his food and can rest for a while. Then you can keep him company."

"I wanted to go spend time with Pete."

"Not tonight. Your job is to take care of your brother." She checked Alex's yellowing right eye socket. "We'll see about the Salt Mines." She nodded and walked out.

I touched my pocket with the card in it.

"Well?" Mom stuck her head back in the room.

"Coming," I said, frustrated that the note would have to wait.

Chapter 6
– War Council

W e leave in two minutes." I paced the room.

"Read that card to me again." Alex said.

I pulled the card from my pocket, flipped it over, and read out loud.

Don't forget. War council.

10:30 p.m. My room.

No stairs.

Erik.

The door rattled.

"Yes?" I leaped onto the bed.

Dad came in, closed the door, and looked at us. "Are you boys still awake? You should both be *in* bed, not on top of it." Dad nodded at my shorts and shirt. "Get those clothes off and settle in for the night. Don't forget your prayers. You should be thankful tonight."

I undressed, climbed onto the bed, and slid under the covers.

"That's better. See you in the morning." Dad flicked off the light switch.

I counted to thirty and yanked on my clothes, but Alex moved like a slow motion movie.

"Let's go," I said.

"Give me a break. I have a headache." Alex laced his sneakers.

"We have to use the window to avoid Mom and Dad." I twisted the latch and swung the window in sideways. "Let's take the dogs, but tell them to be quiet." I went over the windowsill and dropped the few feet onto the ground outside. Dim moonlight greeted me. After Lightning jumped into my arms, I whispered a command. He nuzzled against me.

When Alex and Thunder joined us outside, we hugged the stone building, sneaking across a small paved parking lot to get to Erik and Dieter's building. Soon we spotted their light flickering in a second story window.

"Yep," I said. "That's one-oh-nine."

Alex scooped up a few pebbles lying beside the sidewalk. With his good arm, he tossed one at the window. When nothing happened, he threw several at once.

A hawkish face poked through the window's opening. "Wait…" Dieter vanished from the window, then reappeared. "Leave the dogs there. Take this rope. Quick. Climb up."

"Are you kidding?" Alex whispered. He rubbed his right arm.

"You must hold tight with the good arm," Dieter said. "Then we get you up here."

Alex tried several times, crashing into the wall and stifling his cries of pain, but he couldn't make it.

"My turn." Dieter jerked the rope up. A couple of minutes later he lowered a rope seat and a second rope. "Tie this second rope to the belt."

After Dieter dragged Alex into the room, I followed. The four of us gathered at a table lit by a white candle. Shadows danced like ghosts on the walls from the single flame.

"Why are we sneaking?" I asked. "We could have used the stairs."

"Better to be safe," Erik said. "Someone may be watching us. They gave us a warning."

"Warning?" Alex said.

"Something I found," Erik said. "Check the card. The one I gave you."

I pulled it out.

"See." He took the card and matched it to letterhead on a piece of paper he held.

"It's saying 'Salzbergwerk.' These crossed hammers? That's the salt mines sign." Erik laid the paper on the table.

"I still don't get it," Alex said.

"I found this paper on Father's office desk. No classified marking or anything, but it's a case file labeled with a big M." Erik pointed at the typed paragraph beneath the letterhead.

"What's that?" I asked.

"That's getting me scared. I translate the German for you." Erik spoke softer.

Dieter went to the door and pressed his ear against it, listening for suspicious sounds.

"Activities of M have increased near the German salt mines on the Austrian border," Eric read. "Though government has kept this news quiet, six children have vanished there without a trace. Linked to human trafficking and drug smuggling, M threatens well-being and politic stability of Austrian and German people. This new factor in reunification process of East and West Germany might ruin plans for final agreements in fall. Indications are that M plans further…uh…taking of children, especially Americans, to break down reunion and American support for the plan. Small arms have been taken, including Soviet chemical weapons."

"Wow. Are you *sure* this isn't classified?" Alex asked.

A growling sound came through the tiny window opening.

Alex rushed to see what was happening. "Thunder, be quiet."

"We're going to the Bavarian Salt Mines tomorrow," I said. "We leave at nine o'clock in the morning. Is there anything else?" I pointed toward the paperwork.

"The other side is a typed list of last names. The top six are crossed off—they are missing children, including one from Goeppingen, where we live. Look at the next names."

A shiver ran down my spine.

Chapter 7
– The Cover-up

W ell?" I whispered.

Alex paused in the moonlight. We crouched below Erik's window. The candlelight was gone, the window shut. Dieter had left for his room after he lowered us to the sidewalk.

"We're still on Machete's list." Alex slithered along the stone walls.

I kept pace. "Why? What's so important about us?"

"Must be Dad's work," Alex said. "He can't tell anyone what he does—not even Mom."

"One more building to go." I slunk past two parked cars. We needed to cross the parking lot, get past Mom and Dad's window, and climb into our room.

I scurried across the open space. Lightning stayed by me with Thunder following.

"Hey." A deep rumble stopped Alex halfway. He looked around.

Bright lights flashed on Alex, blinding him. He stood exposed while a silver Mercedes accelerated across the blacktop.

I dashed toward him with both dogs in hot pursuit.

The car swerved to make contact.

I tackled him out of the path of the speeding car. We both hit the pavement hard, rolling like we had been taught from years of martial arts practice. The dogs leaped around us, checking us out, but still staying quiet.

I focused on the license plate. I caught the Austrian symbol, but nothing else.

"Ouch." Alex pressed his temple and sat up, taking his time.

I stood, brushed off bits of gravel, and gathered the two dogs. "You okay?" I said. "We've got to get back."

Alex struggled to get to his feet. "My ears are ringing, but I'm good." He tapped me on the arm. "That's two saves today. You're on a roll."

"I hope that's enough." I said. "Tomorrow, when we're in the Salt Mines—that might be another story."

The next morning, Alex and I found Mom and Dad in the hotel banquet room. The aroma of hot eggs, sizzling bacon, and warm hot chocolate made my stomach growl.

"We want to eat outside today." I gave Mom a hug from behind.

She twisted around and put an arm around my waist. "That's fine. We'll let you know when it's time to leave for the salt mines."

"It's a go?" Alex rubbed his forehead. The swelling had gone down a bit, but his bloodshot eye and darkening bruise appeared worse.

Dad laid aside the paper he had been reading, glancing at Alex. He nodded. "That bump isn't too bad. You can survive today." He winked at Mom.

"I guess we're going." She smiled and patted his arm. "But you boys will stay with us in the salt mines. Now go get breakfast. We'll leave in about an hour."

Trailing the two dogs, we weaved through the tables to the patio, settling in at a black, wire mesh table surrounded by four similar chairs. I sat facing the lake with Alex to my right. The patio was set with a typical German continental breakfast.

"I'd like French Toast." I flipped through the menu I had snagged on the way out.

"Can't do it," Alex said. "That's extra money. Mom and Dad said nothing extra while we're here. Part of our punishment, remember?"

I sighed and tossed the menu on one of the empty seats. A warm breeze nudged the few white puffy clouds across the blue sky. The dogs settled near our feet at the table and stayed there while we got our food from the outdoor tables.

Pete and Jenna waved at us. They carried their plates of cheese and meat to our table.

"Frischer Luft," Pete said, arriving at the table. "Fresh air. It's healthy for you."

"We got out in the fresh air last night." I showed off the arm scratches from rolling on the asphalt during Alex's rescue.

"What's that?" Jenna said. She plunked her food and silverware near my brother's. "What were you two doing last night?"

"Were we doing anything last night more than sleeping?" Alex winked at me and looked at Jenna with a twinkle in his eyes.

"Of course not." I stiffened into a British pose of royalty. "Really, my dear. It was nothing. I simply rolled oh-vah in bed." I blinked.

"Out with it," Jenna said. "What crazy things happened?"

"We scaled a wall, had a *war* council with Dieter and Erik, and Alex almost got smashed by a silver Mercedes." I paused. "A jolly good show."

"War council?" Pete slugged me on the leg. "You didn't tell us about a war council? What kind of a best friend are you?"

"I'm beginning to wonder." Jenna's lips set in a line. She stared away, not coming round until Alex's hand touched hers. She pulled it away to adjust her napkin on her lap.

"Our parents watched our every move because of my head injury." Alex tapped the bruise with his right hand and winced. "They kept checking on us. We were late leaving the room. And we thought Erik and Dieter might have invited you, but when we got there, you weren't around. Besides, we had to climb a rope to get in."

"I see." Jenna said, still avoiding eye contact with Alex. "Even though our rooms were on the way, you didn't think to even check? Surely something must be wrong with your head." She took a bite of her scrambled eggs.

"You sure are being picky this morning," I said. "We got there and you weren't around. Simple as that. We had to move quickly or we would have missed the opportunity." I shoved another piece of Brotchen covered with jelly down the hatch.

"Okay, okay." Pete waved his hands in the air. "Stop, already. If you guys want to fight, do it another time. We have fifteen minutes until we have to be in our room. What happened?"

Alex quit eating, swiveled his chair toward the lake and remained silent.

"Hey, I'll tell it." I described what we did. Before I spoke two sentences, Franco and Izabella walked out onto the terrace.

"Ciao. Make room for us," Franco said. "Why so serious?" He glanced at Alex and Jenna. "Enjoy life. It is too short to stay mad."

"Oh, I see." Izabella's head tilted in Jenna's direction. "We have to leave these two alone. There's another table."

"Have you two already eaten?" I said.

"Delicious French Toast," Izabella patted her stomach. "Not like my mama's breakfasts, but tasty."

"Well, I'm not moving yet," I said. "A couple of people here need to grow up." I began the story again while Izabella and Franco shoved extra seats around Pete and me. When I got to the part where Alex and I read our names on Machete's list, Pete grabbed my arm.

"You're kidding," he said. "You guys are next on the list? And the letterhead of that list was the Salzbergwerk? Have you told your parents?"

Jenna brushed off Alex during the story, but faced him when she heard we were on the list. He didn't budge. Eyes fixed on the lake, his jaw muscles twitched.

"Alex," she said.

He ignored her.

"Hey, I'm sorry. I didn't know it was this serious."

He still sat motionless.

"I know a lot of bad things have been happening to you, but this is worse. I don't want you to get hurt." She sniffled and pulled her long blonde hair back from her face. "Are you there?" She reached out and put her hand on his left forearm. "I said I'm sorry."

"Well, there goes my appetite." I tossed my napkin on the table. "I'm going to take a closer look at the lake." I waved for everyone except Alex and Jenna to join me.

We strolled to the patio's far edge and sat on the wall that overlooked the lake.

"I hope I never get like that with a girl," I said. "Too complicated, right?" I patted Pete on the shoulder. "Half the time he's lost interest in practicing baseball or football with me."

The corners of Izabella's lips curved in a smile. She giggled.

"American boys—no heart for the bond between a girl and a boy." Franco grinned.

"Not to change the subject, but we don't have a lot of time," Pete said. "Was there anything else to your story last night? Where did you get the scratches?"

I finished the story.

"You two are in the hot seat, yes?" Izabella said. "Will your parents be saying anything?"

"We're not going to tell them," I said.

Pete's eyes widened. "Why not? They'll make sure the Polizei are on alert."

Izabella stood. "To me, it is necessary to tell the police."

"Our parents told us we had to stay with them the whole time we're in the mines." I shrugged. "If we get separated, we'll stay with all of you." I twisted around and hung my feet outside the wall, facing the lake. "If we worry our parents, Alex and I won't be doing anything fun 'til we leave Germany. And that's a couple of years from now."

"Are you sure?" Pete scratched his head. "This is huge."

"It's like lightning striking in the same place twice. It never happens. They were lucky last time, but this time we'll be more careful and tip off the police if we see them. And we will not go off on our own." I locked eyes with him.

"Well…" Pete rubbed his cheek.

"Besides, we'll tell Mom and Dad after this vacation. No need to worry. Now promise me, you won't tell anyone else."

"It might be okay." Franco waved his hands. "No. It will be easy. Between the six of us, we should be able to stay alert. And who knows, Gabe may be right. We could help capture these criminals by reporting them. But, we must agree to stick together or it will fail. And I agree with Gabe. If they tell their parents, Gabe and Alex will be…how do you say…grounded."

"I'm not sure," Izabella said. "What if these terrible people outsmart us?"

"Our Dad trained Alex and me to avoid danger. We should be able to spot signs of anything unusual." I scooted a little to face Izabella. "If we stay together in a public place, how can the terrorists threaten us, unless they use guns? Even Dad couldn't stop that."

"Okay." She crossed her arms, still concerned. "I guess I will not be saying something."

"Pete." I tapped him on the arm. "Everyone's in. Are you?" I waited, but he didn't answer. "Trust me. I know what I'm doing. Be a part of the plan."

His shoulders slumped as he nodded.

"Thanks, buddy. You won't regret it."

"Boys." Dad's voice echoed across the patio. "Time to get packed and move out. We've got a lot to do today. The salt mines are open."

Jenna and Alex got up, took each other's hand, and walked into the hotel dining room.

"Looks like they made up," I said. "Our secret is still safe."

"It may be safe, but I don't like it." Pete shook his head.

Chapter 8
– The Berchtesgaden Salt Mines

S ize?" the lady said.

"Medium," I said.

The gray-haired woman behind the counter handed me a miner's coverall and jacket and pointed to her left. "You dress there. Go to the next room to get on the train. Your tour starts at 10:00 "

I grabbed the clothes and made for the bench. The wooden counters and heavy coverall suit cloth had a faint smell of crushed rocks. I brushed the dust off and sat.

"Don't sit there," Jenna said. "That's saved for Alex. He's in the bathroom."

"Yes, *ma'am*." I saluted and stomped off.

Most of the seats were full. I took Lightning to the last row, strapped the bib overalls over on, and slid into the jacket. After getting dressed, I shouldered my backpack and wandered over to the train to get a picture taken with the rest of our friends in the last car.

The electric train resembled an adult version of a park's kiddie ride. Dark green panels covered the sides of the cars. Each car held eight people on a straddle-bench. I sat behind, Pete, then Alex and Jenna, and the rest of our friends. Our parents were in the second car.

The photographer told the head engineer to center the train on the trademark—the blue and white diamonds of Bad Reichenhall and the location: SALZBERGWERK BERCTHES-GADEN.

"Perfect. Now, everyone face me." The stout man swiveled to position his lights.

"I'm not sure I want to go on this trip." Jenna leaned on Alex and spoke in softer tones.

"Why not?" he said.

"It seems creepy." She steadied Thunder. "Gabe's breakfast story frightened me." Jenna flipped her long blonde hair and repositioned her head on Alex's chest.

"It'll be all right," Alex said. "We have a plan. We'll stick together."

"All right, we're all set." The photographer counted to three. The popping sounds of the umbrella lights echoed off the rock walls. "Find your pictures at the gift shop after your tour."

"If we return," Jenna said.

The train jerked and we moved into the tunnel.

"Halt, bitte." The command rang out behind me.

The train slowed to a stop. A young assistant spoke into a walkie-talkie in rapid bursts.

"Move forward, please." The man's hand motioned at me.

"Come on, Gabe, tighten it up," Pete said. "Quick."

A blond-haired boy slid behind me and put his feet on the wooden running boards. He gave a thumbs-up. In seconds, we whisked into the tunnel. I twisted a bit, surprised.

"Jonathan, what are you doing here?"

The train accelerated, quiet on its wheels. The first section of tunnel was wide enough for two trains to pass. Overhead and side lights in cages cast dark shadows. We passed a lit sign with two German mining hammers, crossed like battle-axes with the words, "Gluck Auf."

"That means 'good luck' to all the miners who pass by." Jonathan kicked my foot.

"Yeah, dummy. I already know that," I said. The tight space kept me from facing Jonathan to talk. *Why was he here?* He was a sixteen-year-old Dutch kid from the skate park at home.

The walls of the cave became a grayish-white the further we went. Scattered sections looked more flesh or orange colored. The two-track tunnel changed to one-track.

"We're moving faster," Jonathan said when we entered the one-way tunnel.

"Not really," I said. "We're closer to the walls." I ran a couple of fingers against the rock.

"Please keep all hands, arms, legs, and fingers away from the wall while the train is moving." The amplified engineer's voice cut through the soft whispering of the wheels.

My hand zipped back to my leg.

Jonathan laughed.

The engineer continued. "Let me provide you a short history of the Berchtesgaden Salt Mines. They were first established in the fifteen-hundreds…"

Adjusting Lightning, I slipped into a daydream about the old mining days. Images of creaking carts, dusty air, and picks hammering the rock to get the salt out filled my mind.

Jonathan shoved me forward. "Quit leaning on me. You're backpack's getting in my face."

I perked up. The only light was the train's headlight. We were in semi-darkness.

"Where are the lights on the ceiling?" I poked Pete.

"If you had been listening…oh, forget it." Pete elbowed me back. "The engineer told us to save electricity and time running cables, the lighting stops partway into the mountain."

"We have arrived," our guide said. "Please follow me. Welcome to the hidden world of the Berchtesgaden Salt

Mine Caverns, one of the world's largest. We have spectacular presentations of the mine and its operations from the 1800s to now. You'll learn how we extract salt from the ground, enjoy sliding to lower levels, and investigate the machinery we've created to mine salt."

I lifted a leg up and over the bench seat to slide off, inner thighs aching from the cramped position. The apprentice engineers of each passenger car herded us into small groups.

An assistant switched off the dim lights, transforming the scene with bluish lasers. "This cavern is seventeen meters high, three hundred meters wide, and four hundred meters long."

"That's about as big as an American football field stadium." Jonathan bumped into me.

"Pretty big," I said.

The guide continued. "Here we begin our journey into the world of salt extraction. Many believe we use explosives, but using water is a more environmentally correct approach."

Assistants led each group down a winding path. Our apprentice, a young man wearing green overalls and jacket, had us wait until the end.

Jonathan tugged my sleeve.

"What?" I glanced in his direction.

"You wanted to know why I came today." He moved a few steps from the crowd and rubbed his neck. "Poppa dropped me off. He never has time for me. Today he had a business meeting. I saw you leaving and the lady flagged down the train at the last minute."

"We need to go." I motioned at the group. "My parents want me close by."

"Really?" Jonathan said. "A big boy like you? Are they scared you'll get lost?" He snickered. "I'll protect you. I've kept that skateboard bully away from you."

"Not the last time." I told him about the fight.

"Maybe I need to teach him a lesson." He ground a fist into his other hand.

"Lightning," I said. "Here boy."

"Before we reach the group, I have one other thing to tell you."

"Make it quick." I knelt and Lightning trotted up to me.

"Your brother and his friends are telling lies about me." He tapped his chest. "They hate me. And called you stupid and clueless because you hang out with me."

My jaw dropped. *He called me clueless?* I clenched my fists. "I'll fix him."

"Don't tell him I told you. It's a secret." Jonathan's grip tightened on my shoulder. "Don't start anything."

"I won't." I clicked the leash onto Lightning's collar and strode to catch the disappearing group. "I'll give you more freedom later, buddy."

"Freedom, that's what I'm talking about." Jonathan slowed his pace. "There's a subject that requires clear thinking. Not like your group."

Yellow light appeared as we left the initial large chamber and descended a broad tunnel.

"Are you saying I'm dumb?" I said.

"Well," Jonathan said. "I'm older. I've learned that adults tell us what to think instead of giving us freedom to think about the world in our own way. Americans are the worst offenders."

"How?" I said.

"Think about your restrictions. You told me your parents did not want you separated from them." He pointed to the group in front of us.

"Yes," I said. "Because the last time we were underground..." I didn't want to tell him about the kidnapping. We didn't know each other that well—not for that kind of trust. "We ran into a few problems. Mom and Dad care about me. What's wrong with that?"

"If I were in your shoes or should I say, on your leash," Jonathan said, "I'd get my parents to give me a little more slack."

"I'm like a dog on a leash?" I lifted Lightning and hugged him. *Is that true?*

"Parents say they want you to grow up, to think more for yourself. But they'll restrict you to keep you close." Jonathan nodded, agreeing with himself.

"Well, that does make a little sense." I rubbed my cheek against Lightning. "Parents can make life hard. Is that what you mean?" We were ten feet away from our group.

"I think you're getting it," Jonathan said. "Wait and see what they do on this trip."

Our group stood with the others at the top of a huge drop. Blending with the group, I stood next to Alex. Thunder sat next to his feet and Jenna's hand was on his arm. Jonathan wandered over to another group, avoiding Alex.

"In the olden days," our sandy-haired guide continued, "miners wanted a quick way to move from one level of the salt mines to a lower one. Instead of a hand-pulled elevator, at the end of this great salt cathedral, they constructed wooden slides. We still use them today. Watch."

Next to the cave wall stood two ninety-foot slides. Each slide consisted of two wooden rails about a foot apart fixed on a wooden base about as high as a chair. To demonstrate, one assistant sat, straddling the rails facing forward like we did on the train's bench seat. Another assistant sat behind, latching onto the first guide's waist. Low wooden walls within easy reach on either side helped them balance. They lifted their feet up like they were on a snow sled, let go of the walls, and slid over the steep edge, rushing to the bottom. They waved at the end.

"Lots of fun," the head engineer said. "Many families slide together. Some choose the longer walking ramp to the side. Smile for the picture as you pick up speed near the bottom."

Mom and Dad looked at us from their group and motioned us over.

Hmmm. The leash tightens.

"Alex," I said while we walked over, "let's do this on our own. With our friends. We already had a family picture on the train."

"Maybe." Alex cocked his head. "How about the next slide? There's one on a lower level."

"Boys," Mom said, "time for another family photo."

"I want a picture with our friends," I said. "We've got a picture of all of us on the train."

"But we weren't together for the train picture." Dad smiled. "It'll be fun."

"Could we do it on the second slide?" Alex said.

"I don't think you're getting the idea," Dad said. "This will be a simple..."

"But Dad, we never get to do things with our friends like this." I pointed at Pete, Jenna, and the others and spread my arms. "And they're all here now."

The senior engineer overheard our conversation and wandered over to Dad.

"If I might make a suggestion?" he said.

"Yes?" Dad said. "Go ahead."

"I can take a picture of the family here where you mount the slide. The parents can slide down and I'll take a picture of all the youth. Would that work?"

"That would work." I grinned. "Awesome."

"That may be the best solution, Hon." Mom took Dad's arm and hugged him close.

Dad let out a long sigh. "I guess it will work." He patted Mom's hand on his arm. "For now." He lowered his eyebrows at me and escorted Mom to the slide.

Alex and I set our backpacks down and sat on the rails. Right after the engineer took the picture, I jumped off and put Lightning on the ground. I snagged my backpack and ran off.

"See you at the bottom," I said.

"What's the problem?" Alex said minutes later, merging into our group. "You left Mom and Dad like your pants were on fire."

"I want to be free," I said. "You know, free to be with our friends and not hang out with our parents all the time."

"What's gotten into you?" Alex said. "I saw you and Jonathan. He's a bad influence. That's..."

"You know," Jenna said, grabbing his arm. "Gabe might be right."

"About what?"

"I'd like to ride the slide with you and not my parents." She smiled.

Alex let Jenna lead him away, but he scowled at me over his shoulder.

Chapter 9
– Lights Out

Seven groups had completed their slide. We were last.

The tour guides had shut the cavern lights off except for one at the top and one at the bottom. Because of the rock formations, a slider went through eerie semi-darkness before appearing near the end. The other groups had moved out of the cavern to the next stop.

We were together with our friends. Except for Jonathan. He had joined another group.

All eight of us squeezed onto the level entry section of the slide, including the dogs, for our souvenir photo at the top. After the picture, Franco. Izabella, Dieter and Erik pushed forward and lifted their legs. Laughter filled the air as they dropped out of sight.

Alex wrestled Thunder onto his lap in the front. Jenna had his backpack and wrapped her arms around him. Pete rode behind her and I brought up the rear. Arms thrust through the backpack straps, I had one hand on Pete's shoulder and cradled Lightning on top of the backpack.

We pushed ourselves near the edge of the steep drop-off, adjusting for comfort. Our miner's clothes slid easily on rails, like a sled on ice. Alex and I held onto a wooden wall to keep us from slipping away. All we had to do was release our grip and lift our feet to slide to the end.

"Ready?" I said.

Without warning, the lights went out. Pitch-blackness swept over us. Lightning tried to climb over Pete's neck.

"Hey, little fellow," Pete said. His hand touched mine when he reached back. I let go of the wall to keep the wiggling dog from crawling over his shoulder.

"Thunder, cut it out," Alex said. "Gabe, I have to let go."

"You're not leaving me here," Jenna said into the darkness.

Lightning squirmed to get away again.

I caught him and hung on to Pete as he went over the edge. "We're loose."

We accelerated into cool, rushing air, dogs barking and Jenna screaming.

Lightning jerked hard near the end. I tilted toward the open space on the right.

"Don't...tip." Pete clutched my pant legs as we zipped down the rails.

I fell sideways, grabbing for the sidewall and missed. I rolled into the space between the wall and the slide, grinding to a halt. In seconds, Lightning's tongue licked my face. I twisted to get on my knees. Rubbing the bump on my head, I gathered my dog in my arms, and stood.

The lights for the slide flashed on, went off, and flickered to life again. Our guide worked on the electrical box near the main cavern's light switch.

Like bowling pins knocked into the gutters, Pete, Jenna and Alex lay tangled near the wooden wall. Alex shoved Thunder off his chest.

"That dog is getting too heavy to hold," Alex said. "I need to lift more weights."

I plucked Lightning's leash off the ground and surveyed the lower cavern. *Where is Dieter's group?* I hustled past everyone and ran to the exit. I didn't see anyone.

Seconds later, Alex, Jenna, Pete, and Thunder joined me.

"Our friends..." Pete's arms hung slack at his side. "Our friends are..."

"Gone." Alex finished the sentence for him.

"Ich weiss nicht," the assistant said in German for the fourth time. The sandy-haired young man, Frederick Tanner, spread his hands wide.

"Stop telling us you don't know, Tanner." Pete shook a finger at him. "How could you let this happen?"

The guide shrugged. He seemed younger than before, maybe seventeen. Perhaps because he was a little shaken. He glanced away.

"Is maybe the more experienced guides—they play a prank on me," Tanner said. "I'm new. But we are reconnecting with the other groups."

"Can't you call ahead to tell them what's happened?"

"The emergency phones, they are not working. Was an electrical short somewhere. I try the one at the slide landing area."

"We'd better get going," I said. "We're wasting daylight."

"You watch too many westerns," Alex said. "We're in a tunnel. But let's go."

We settled our packs on our backs. But before we got to the bend in the tunnel, Dieter stuck his head around the corner.

"Where have you guys been?" he said. "Your dad, he is right behind me. And mad."

Rounding the corner, I could see Dad in the distance.

"We're coming." I waved at him, but he crossed his arms. I motioned to Alex. "Faster."

"Dad's not too upset," I said to Alex. "We get to stay in our own group." Jonathan hadn't rejoined us, but all our other friends laughed and joked around.

"We'd better stay alert," he said. "It'd be easy to get lost in these tunnels."

We followed the floor's gentle slope, staying with the main marked passages until we came to a dark stretch in the corridor. I stopped. We had fallen behind the other groups. Again.

"Gabe, keep going. We need to catch up." Pete pushed me, but I didn't budge.

"I'm waiting for our guide, 'Sandy,'" I said. " He acts like he's lost sometimes."

"His name's Tanner," Pete said. "And here they come."

Sandy and the rest of the group came alongside us.

"Did the power go out again?" I said.

"You're afraid?" Tanner asked. "Don't worry. Is no trick." He continued with his guide's monologue. "The dark tunnel allows the eyes to adjust. The King Ludwig II monument is a salt grotto containing four great wooden arches, each one smaller as they near the salt picture of the crowned young king. Back-lit translucent salt stones show off a rainbow of colors."

We entered a narrow passage. The stone seemed warm to the touch. The glow of soft, intense hues filled the space. The king's head filled the end of the tunnel.

Sandy sat on a bench, not moving even after we'd spent more than enough time there.

"Something's wrong." I faced the guide. "You're delaying us."

"I'm sure the other groups spent at least five minutes here." Tanner's fingers twined together back and forth. "If we don't stay long…"

"We're leaving." Alex helped him to his feet and shoved him in front of us. "You're moving too slowly, Sandy. Get cracking."

Tanner stumbled.

"Pete, tell him to go faster." I patted his arm. "In German."

"Schnell, schnell," Pete said.

"Don't touch me." Sandy stood straight and arranged his green guide's coat. "If I go fast, I will lose the path. Besides, I have something cool to show you—is a treat no one else sees. But I show it to you since the other guides, they play the prank."

"What's cool?" Dieter said.

"Is kind of an Egyptian relic containing strange looking writing. You'll like it." Sandy stuck his hands in his pockets and waited.

"I'm not doing it." I slashed the air to cut off the conversation. "You've been taking us on too many detours. We need to find the main group."

"I agree," Pete said. "You're stalling. What's going on?"

Dieter and Erik looked at each other.

"What's wrong with a little detour?" Dieter asked. "How long will it take?"

"Is a couple of minutes if we jog," Sandy said. "Anyway, five minutes from here we have our treasure room, our educational center about salt, and the second slide to Mirror Lake."

"Don't you guys see that this isn't right?" I said. "Dad's going to kill us."

"You are upset over a small thing, Gabe." Franco opened his hands. "What is the point?"

"And do you know where the tour goes from here?" Dieter said.

"This guide needs to get us back with the group. Now." Alex stared at the young man.

"But nobody else..." Sandy began.

"Stop it, Sandy." I stepped toward him. "Quit trying to convince us to follow you." I faced the others. "We need to link up with the other groups. Right away."

Sandy sat on a rock.

"Can you take us to the tour group?" Erik asked me. "You didn't answer Dieter."

"I don't know the way around here, but we could follow the main path," I said.

"What main path?" Franco glared at me. "Does this look like a tourist tunnel? And how many turns did we take to get here?"

I glanced around. We were off the beaten path and I didn't know the way back.

"Please," Izabella said. She walked into the center of the group. "We are friends, yes? Why are we fighting?"

"She's right," Pete said. "What are our options to find the tour group?"

"Let us follow the guide a little longer," Franco said. "If we don't join the group in five minutes, we retrace our steps."

"Okay," Pete said. "And Thunder and Lightning could sniff their way to the main area."

"Of course," Dieter said. "The dogs will get us back. This means a few minutes is nothing. We do this quickly. We've wasted already too much time arguing."

"Could be like fun?" Erik said.

Alex tilted his head, lips pressed together.

I scanned everyone's face. "All right, Five minutes, max. Let's jog."

After a minute, the group came to a halt. A split path appeared. Neither tunnel was in good condition. The wooden A-frame entrances sagged and one had support stones missing. The left tunnel rose and the right tunnel dipped into a deeper descent.

"Almost there." Sandy wiped sweat from his forehead. "The easier upper trail meets the lower trail in a few hundred feet. That's the location. Then it's a minute to the treasure room."

"I'm taking this high road," Erik said. Dieter, Franco, and Izabella chose to go with him. "You're not beating us to other side."

"Not if we can help it." I tapped Pete on the shoulder to get his agreement.

"What now?" Jenna said.

"See you." Erik dashed up the trail, disappearing quickly. His group followed.

"Run." I took off at a sprint with Pete and the dogs. Jenna and Alex weren't far behind.

"Wait," Sandy said.

Broken rock and pebbles covered the path. We went through a few switchbacks. Other tunnels intersected ours as we ran. After a minute, I slowed down.

"Where's the rest of the gang?" I blew air out, sides heaving.

"One moment." Sandy held up a finger, face red from the run. "We're pretty…" He sucked in a deep breath, "close. Is the older, deeper part of the salt mines."

"Very encouraging," I said. "It's time to turn around."

"Hey, another guide." Jenna pointed at an indistinct figure half a football field away.

"Jakub," our guide said. "I'm glad he's here. I have difficulty for this one intersection. Of course we must go down to reach Egyptian writings and also meet your friends and family."

Pete grabbed me by the arm. "Haven't we gone far enough?"

"I don't like it either. I'm going back."

"But that's the long way." Sandy invited us to go right. "To search the right path, this is a half an hour for you, even with dogs. We're almost there, but have to move fast."

"Wait," Alex said. He adjusted his backpack. "It's been more than a couple of minutes. We should have caught the tour by now. And the tunnels are in worse shape than before."

"Not fit for tourists." Jenna kicked at a crumbling post. A chunk of rotted wood fell off.

With familiar motions, Alex and I took the leashes off Thunder and Lightning and stored them in the outer pockets of our backpacks.

"Thunder, you and Lightning go find help." Alex squatted and rubbed his chin.

The dogs padded past our guide. Lightning paused, muzzle turned toward me.

"Go on, boy." I clapped my hands together.

Lightning dashed away, Thunder in pursuit. They disappeared around the next corner. We settled into a slow walk.

"There," Sandy said. "Is around the next bend."

On a support beam, I saw a small picture of a laboratory beaker in a battered frame. The arrow pointed in the direction we were going. In big numerals, the sign read: 30 meters.

"That picture looks new, but the frame is a mess." I tapped the guide to get his attention. "Sandy."

"I am called Frederick Tanner."

"Can I call you Fred?" I said.

"Frederick." His hands fidgeted.

"Okay, Fred. What's in the lab?" I asked.

"Is where we see…"

Savage barking cut him off.

Jakub jumped out of the marked corridor, agitated. He pumped his hand and ducked around the corner. The barking grew louder.

I sprinted toward the noise. The others were a step behind. I leaned into the turn, Alex on my heels. We ran into a large cave, big enough to park about forty cars in rows of ten. The ceiling was four times my height. The walls were smooth. A wire mesh fence separated the room, with a third of the room beyond the fenced area. Thunder and Lightning leaped on the fence to get at someone on the other side. Two people grinned at us—Jakub and Hans Becher.

"It is time you are getting here." Becher's lips formed a wicked smile.

We all slowed for a split-second, then came to an abrupt halt. Except for Sandy. He accelerated. Jakub let him through a gate, kicking the dogs away to close it.

"Hans, what kind of a trick is this?" I jabbed a finger in his direction, yelling over the barking dogs. "You're gonna pay."

He laughed. "Really? You're wanting to find Egyptian writings, ja? We'll be seeing how brave you are walking the Egyptian Path of Death."

Chapter 10
~ Cave Calamity

I glared through the floor-to-ceiling fence, pulse racing.

"Who's behind this, Hans?" I balled my hands into fists. *Control. Stay cool.*

"Losing the skateboard championship in Goeppingen isn't worth this much trouble." Alex's words were calmer than mine. Soothing. He inched closer to the gate.

"Skateboard championship?" Hans grinned. "This is nothing. I have new friends who make me a real offer. I'm paid lots of money to lure and capturing the street kids. But you're special." His smile widened. "For Americans, I get good money. And even extra if you're alive."

"Hans, your *friends* don't care about us or you," Jenna said. "What makes you think they'll keep a promise to pay you?"

"They pay me already." Hans pulled out a roll of bills and waved it in the air. "Big money—3,000 Deutschmark." He laughed. "But before I take you in, we're playing a game, a test of bravery. If you win, I let you go. If not, the boss will love to see you. Easy, right?"

"Creep," Pete said. "Jenna and I are German, like you. Why keep us with Americans?"

"Are you a dummkopf?" Hans wrinkled his nose. "You are best friends. You're talking no more like Germans, but sounding just like Americans, being changed without knowing it. Look what's happening in Germany right now. I can know this. My boss, he tells me when East and West Germany complete coming together into one country, my money will not buy as much. And we will being poor, helpless slaves to the United States of America." Hans paced the floor.

"You're nuts. I'm leaving." I collared the dogs and lugged them closer to us.

"Not so fast," Hans said. "As my guests, you haven't playing the game. You must stay. I insist." He nodded at Jakub, who pressed a button in a recessed metal panel in the wall.

A steel door behind us slid shut with a thump.

We all glanced at the closed doorway. Jenna swallowed hard.

"Now we time the first round." Hans locked the gate with a padlock. "Get out in two hours and you win this part. If you are early getting out, you will be set free." He waved and the three hoodlums ducked through a second doorway in the far wall, which closed with a loud click.

"I think Machete's behind this." I sat next to the wall. "Hans Becher's friends."

"Because of what Erik showed you at the war council?" Pete crossed his arms.

"Yes and no." I scratched my head. "That was a cell group of Machete. They wanted to blackmail our Dad for a secret. Erik's father works on that secret project, too. He's also a target. But Hans wants to play games. Maybe he's part of something else. He wants to scare us."

"What can we do?" Pete flopped down beside me. "We don't know where our other friends went. We don't even know where we are underground. How do we get out of here?"

Alex, seated with his head lowered between his arms, came to life. "Remember the last time we couldn't fix anything? We prayed." He rubbed the bruise above his eye.

I stared at the ceiling. "God, we're in another mess. We need Your help. Amen."

Jenna and Pete, to my surprise, echoed the amen.

"How can we get through to the other side of that mesh?" Pete said.

"The lock looks pretty new—like hardened steel," Alex said. "Our climbing equipment won't be able to break it."

Pete crossed to the cage door. He jiggled the padlock. "Hardened steel? How do you know?" The metal lock clanked when he dropped it.

"Police training from Dad," I said.

"Let's go over every inch of the fence," Alex said. "We've gotta break through."

Alex and I dropped our backpacks on the ground.

"Teamwork, remember?" Alex tapped me on the arm with the back of his hand.

I pointed. "I'll climb to the top of the fence. Pete can be the ladder. You and Jenna can check the bottom on the other side."

"All right, you got it," Alex said. He and Jenna both went to the end of the fence and started checking its contact with the floor, working toward the middle.

Pete cupped his hands to boost me. I clung to the fence, digging in my toes and clawing toward the top. Quarter-inch thick staples, about two inches wide, held the fence against the ceiling and sides. I clamped onto one, pulling with all my weight. No give. I checked for loose staples, working across the room's ceiling. Nothing would budge. The sides were the same.

"No way through those staples without equipment. They're all solid." I climbed back down and flexed my fingers and arms to get rid of the aching.

"We can't go through the fence at the floor seam either," Alex said. "It seems stuck in the rock. And there's concrete halfway up the walls."

Jenna lay on the floor. "Are those vents any help?" She pointed to square duct covers in the ceiling. There were two on each side of the room.

Pete flopped on the ground next to his sister for a better view. "They exchange air here with fresh air between upper and lower levels. It creates an air current. But none of us are small enough to get into those ducts to move around."

"Time to try the pitons." I rubbed my sore muscles. "We might be able to pry off the floor staples and crawl under." I went to my backpack.

"We could also chip away the concrete on the side," Alex said. "If it's not too thick."

"I'm glad you're both spelunkers." Jenna sat up. "You carry lots of survival gear."

An hour of work produced little result. I had removed three staples, dug the fence out of the soft rock, and bent it about an inch off the floor.

"The walls are solid concrete, reinforced with iron bars." Alex sighed. "We chipped away a few inches. That's all." He and Jenna came to see our progress.

"At this rate, we'll die of old age before we get out of here," I said.

The door on the other side of the fence swung open.

"We are having fun?" Hans rubbed his nose. A corner of his mouth curled in a lopsided sneer. "Time is up. You lose. I am doubling the stakes from now." Chuckling, Hans went back through the door and reappeared with a red, metal cylinder like a scuba tank strapped on a rolling handcart. A nozzle projected from dials at the top. "This World War II canister has mustard gas. A killing vapor. I will set for one hour, the timer. When it buzzes, the black knob turns and…"

"We're worth more alive than dead," Alex said.

"The money is coming to me either way. And the top man has no care."

"If your boss eliminates people he doesn't need, what about you?" I got a little closer. "You'll be next. When we're gone, any kid could do your job."

"If I do what the boss tells me, I have no worries." Hans pointed at the dials on the cylinder. "I give a five-minute warning before the gas comes out." He left.

I glanced at my watch. 1:15 p.m. *What can we do in one hour?*

Alex talked in soft tones to Jenna off to the side, and her lips began to tremble.

"That can't be real mustard gas." Pete shook the chain link fence. "Right?"

"I don't know." I unzipped my backpack, pulled out an energy bar and handed it to Pete. "You take half. Time to work. We have to hurry."

By 1:30 p.m. we had pried a few more staples off the floor, but I couldn't bend the fence enough to crawl under. Jenna and Alex had no luck either on the sides.

"We're not going to make it." Jenna's puffy eyelids told me she had been crying.

Everyone sat back for a moment while the dogs sniffed their way to the shallow impression Pete and I had dug under the fence.

"What are Lightning and Thunder doing?" Pete said.

"They're scratching at the floor," Jenna said. "Like they're trying to dig out."

"Dig out?" I rubbed the floor and licked a finger. I jumped up, headed to the backpacks. "These are salt caverns. If we wet the floor, the salt might dissolve, or make the floor mushy, making it easier to chip out pieces for a hole to crawl through."

"We don't have enough time to make holes big enough for us." Jenna shook her head.

"Do you have your canteens filled with water?" I asked Alex.

We both pulled out our spare water canteens.

"Here's the plan," I said, each of us taking a sip of water.

I glanced at my watch—2:10 p.m.

The door crashed open. Hans, chest out, stepped into the room. Behind him, the metal door slammed shut. Startled, he stumbled, swiveled to reopen the door, and decided against it.

"What is this?" he asked, hands spread wide. "You have quit?"

We sat on the ground ten feet from the fence, with our backpacks beside Alex and me. "Why waste energy?" Alex said. "You win. But let Pete and Jenna go."

"Good." Becher clapped in mock applause. "But what if you don't give me details? Maybe Jenna and Pete must stay to make you talk." He scanned the room. "Where are the dogs?"

From under a pile of rags on Han's side, Lightning dashed at the teenager, yipping.

Hans laughed. "Well, the little one comes through. Good work."

Thunder's growl came from behind the red canister. Like a panther stalking prey, he moved toward Hans.

Becher's face went white. He ran. Wrestled with the door-knob, but it wouldn't open.

"Told you." Pete said. "You're boss doesn't care about you one bit."

"Hans," Alex said. "We have less than three minutes. Give me the keys."

"The boss, he will kill me."

"Exactly," I said. "When that canister goes off. Open the padlock."

Thunder kept advancing toward Becher, lips back and teeth glistening. Lightning streaked in, nipped at Becher's calves, and ran away.

"Someone will open this door." Becher stalled, kicking at Lightning.

"Two minutes," Pete said. "You're cutting this close."

Thunder's hackles stood on end.

"Okay, okay." Hans threw his hands in the air. "Take them away."

"Keys first," I said. "Open the padlock and hand me the keys."

"A minute and a half." Alex crossed his arms.

Hans fumbled with the keys, opened the padlock and the chain link fence door.

"Thunder, heel." Alex patted the side of his leg.

Snarling, Thunder circled Hans and sat near Alex, eyes riveted on the potential victim.

Pete and I grabbed Becher's arms and hurried him over to the canister.

"About a minute." Pete jerked Hans toward the timer. "Disarm it."

"Gabe." Jenna's knuckles whitened as she clutched at the fence. "Push the button Jakub used to close us in here."

"Great idea." I jammed my thumb into the black plastic. No movement. I slammed the heel of my hand into the metal panel.

"I cannot," Becher said. "I am not knowing the workings."

Chapter 11
~ Timer Trouble

"You don't know how to stop this timer?" I shoved Becher out of the way. "Pete, hold him tight. We have fifty-five seconds."

Sweat beaded on my forehead. I jumped forward, searching for the timer's connections. Metal clamps held the timer in place, attached to a device that would turn the knob. A case surrounded the contraption. Four wires—red, green, blue, and black—protruded from the case.

"Get me a knife." My voice cracked. "I need to cut a wire."

Alex fished a lock-blade knife out of his pocket and gave it a toss. It fell short.

"Hurry." I shifted to a better position, hands extended and shaking. "Thirty seconds."

Pete shoved Hans away and scrambled for the knife. He flipped it to me.

I snatched the knife out of the air and flicked it open.

"Do not." Becher huddled in a corner, Thunder prowling nearby. He held his hands out. "They warned me if a wire is cut, the valve opens."

The knife slid from my hand, landing on the rock floor.

"Do something, Gabe. Now." Jenna's high-pitched shriek didn't help.

"Ten seconds," Alex said.

I clutched at the timer box to wrench it from the knob. My hand hit a latch, jerking it open while I fell. Two batteries clanked onto the metal dolly and rolled to the ground.

Several seconds passed. No one breathed.

Jenna finally removed her scarf from around her mouth.

"No gas." Hans fell to his knees, hands clasped in front of him. "Thank you, thank you, thank you," he said to no one in particular.

I got up, dusted off, and wiped my forehead. I squinted, focusing on the timer.

"Two seconds. That's all we had left." I looked at Hans. "You were going to kill us?"

Hans hung his head, hands trembling. "My friends..." He spoke to himself. "I am one of them. How could they lock me in this way?" His eyes caught mine. "To die with you?"

"Move over there." Alex pointed in the opposite direction of the mustard gas container. "Thunder and Lightning, guard."

Hans eased himself upright. Thunder and Lightning herded him with nips and growls.

"I can't believe they want to kill us," Pete said. "This is bizarre. Do they want us to blackmail our parents for secrets?"

"Whatever they're doing, those two other guys will notice we didn't die." Alex tapped his lower lip. "I bet they're waiting for the air to clear before checking. We have a few minutes."

"This is my job," Hans said. "The boss tells me to hold you five hours. The game now has three. No one will check for another two. Let me go and I get us free."

I ignored the comment. "They left you on your own? I can't believe that. How long have you been with Machete?"

"I am supplier for them, not part of them," Becher said. "They do not own me."

"They won't trust you alone without supervision," I said. "Maybe that's why you were shut in with us. Are the fake engineers part of your cell group?"

Hans edged toward the door. Thunder's ears went up.

Lightning yipped.

Alex cut him off.

"Thunder, watch our prisoner," Alex said. He motioned to Hans. "Get on your stomach."

"You will hurt me." Hans retreated. His jaw muscles tightened and he crouched.

"I'm going to tie you up." Alex signaled for something to tie him with. "On the ground, face down. Now."

Hans rushed forward, kicking the dogs and swinging fists. He grabbed Jenna's hair.

Jenna screamed.

Alex tackled him at the shoulders while I took out his legs. The next few minutes flashed by in a flurry of punching, grunts, and barking. Jenna crawled free. Becher took the worst of the punishment. A little crimson line marked his bulging lip.

"Pete, help me out." Alex ground Hans' face into the rock floor.

Jenna's brother shoved a knee into Becher's back, hands forcing his head flat.

I tossed Alex a length of military-grade 550-cord from my backpack.

Alex tied his hands behind his back and his ankles together. Then, head in hands, Alex stumbled to the wall.

Jenna ran to his side, making him sit. She grabbed his backpack and set it near him.

He rummaged inside, pulled out a bottle of pain capsules and swallowed a few.

Jenna opened a canteen and he sucked down the remaining water.

"How do we get out this door?" Pete asked, working the doorknob with no success. "They locked Hans in here without the key."

"I'm not sure," I said. "My brother's the one who picks locks."

"Pins in door...knock them out." Alex rubbed his forehead.

"Jenna, get a piton and hammer from his backpack," I said.

She grabbed the tools and handed them to me.

I knocked the pins out of the door hinges. "Alex, we're going to need you to finish this."

"Sure. The pain's getting less." With a screwdriver from his repair kit, he pried the door from the frame. The exertion made his face redden. "Help me."

Pete, Jenna, and I braced for the weight of the solid metal door.

"Keep it level or it won't work," Alex said.

First the bottom of the frame popped out, then the top. We heaved the door to a standing position close to the opening.

"It must weigh a hundred pounds." Pete wiped his hand against his forehead.

"Past this door is only way out, a metal room," Hans said. "The doors are like air-locks. The room is with a control section on the left. If we go straight through the opposite hatch, we arrive in the meeting room where we wait for people packages."

Packages. He said it as though people were nothing more than pieces of furniture.

Alex and I gathered our backpacks. I led the way.

The metal room's entry door resembled a submarine. I spun the wheel, opened it, and we climbed in. Pete and Alex wrestled Hans to his feet, had him hop to the entrance, and carried him into the small space. They leaned him into a sitting position against a wall.

Smooth, green tile covered the floor. The ceiling was metal. Round openings like cut-off pipes punctured each wall, two per side, near each corner. The room appeared to be almost twice my height and the walls were shiny stainless steel. A chest-high shelf on the right end had three skulls in the center bookended with two huge ancient diving helmets.

In a science lab, the skulls wouldn't bother me. But after becoming unwilling guests of Hans, the dark, vacant eye sockets made the hair raise on my neck. I glanced down. A hand-sized gap between the bottom of the wall and the floor ran along both sides. *A heating vent?*

"This room's the size of a medium travel-trailer." Alex stood still and studied the space. "There's the exit, the other hatch." He indicated a closed metal plate opposite our entrance point.

"What a weird room." I walked to the far left. "This wall is all glass, including the door. The door has a rubber seal with a control panel on the other side." I yanked down on the bright blue plastic door handle and put my shoulder against the glass, but it didn't budge. "Locked."

"Go this way," Hans said. "We must go to the waiting room."

"Why are you in such a hurry?" Jenna said. "Friends waiting for us?" Her hand rested on Alex's arm. "We need a plan before we open that door."

"Hey, there's a camera in the control room." Pete pointed at the control room ceiling. A red light blinked at regular intervals.

"All right, Becher." I grabbed his arm and swung him toward me. "Talk about cameras."

"They mean nothing." He shrugged. "Sometimes they track us and sometimes not. When green light is on, someone is watching."

"Is there another way out that doesn't take us through the waiting room?" Alex asked. He bent over, running his fingers along the edge of the gap on the lower part of the wall.

A thud caused me to straighten and whirl around. The entry door had shut.

Alex leaped toward the door, latching onto the spinning wheel, but couldn't slow it down.

"Hans, what's happening?" Jenna said.

"The wheel's stopped." Alex said. "Gabe, Pete. Help me open this door."

We tugged. Grunted. Strained. It didn't budge.

Pete, red in the face, quit. "Hans, answer Jenna." He stepped toward the double-crosser.

Thunder began to bark. It echoed off the walls, deafening us.

"Stop." I clapped my hands over my ears.

"We have trouble," Hans said. He pointed with his chin toward the ceiling camera. "The green light is on."

Chapter 12
~ Watery Tomb

Now what?" Jenna crossed her arms, facing Hans. "Your horrible friends are watching?"

He shrugged, his face blank.

"Can this room be remotely controlled?" I said, sliding myself between the furious Jenna and Hans. "And what kind of room is this? Has it been used before?"

"Control is outside for every room with camera to allow turning on whatever is in the room." He paused. "I have not seen this place used since coming here."

"I smell something." Jenna wandered away from our captive toward the walls.

"Yeah." Alex sniffed a few times. "Smells like the ocean."

Lightning's tail waved like a flag in the breeze as he nosed around the gap near the floor.

I knelt close to Lightning. "I feel air flowing out of the room. Is this a vacuum chamber?"

"The pipes near the ceiling are leaking." Pete pointed to one near me.

Jenna cupped her hands and caught a few drops. She took a sip.

"Salt water." She spit it out.

"Quick, open the exit hatch. We must leave." Hans' face had lost its color.

"Are you kidding?" Alex took two steps and knelt next to his face. "We're not going into the waiting arms of kidnappers."

Gurgling sounds behind the walls changed to a deeper, choking cough.

"Sounds like something's stuck," Jenna said. "Hear that sucking? It's like air is being drawn out of those pipes."

The pipes fell silent.

"Nothing's going to happen." I locked eyes within an inch of Hans' face. "I guess your cell's equipment is either broken or clogged."

"They are not cave in this easy," Becher said. Sweat speckled his forehead. "See those skulls? The guys told me stories how they killed intruders in this caves. A friend told me..."

"Friend?" Pete said. "You still call them friends?"

A few beads of sweat joined together and rolled down Hans' sideburn. "Forget it. I thought you are wanting to hear a story about this place."

A deep, throaty groan came from a pipes. A white plug shot out and water gushed.

I picked the white object and sniffed. Tasted it. "More salt. And that water's chilly."

With a series of pops, other plugs flew across the room. Water poured onto the floor, reaching the top of the gaps in the walls in minutes, flowing out faster than it came in.

"Guess they miscalculated the water flow." I faked a chuckle and stepped toward the glass wall. "That control room is the only safe way out."

Thunder and Lightning, oblivious to the danger, splashed and played.

Small metal panels on the inside of the walls creaked like rusty hinges, rose and sealed the gaps. The water flow increased, each hole jetting water like a fire hose.

"We're shut in tight." Jenna got louder.

"Mister tough guy." Hans stared at Alex and adjusted his legs. "In some minutes the waiting room door opens. My buddies will rescuing me and jailing you with the rest of the kids."

"Tough guy?" I left the glass door and poked a finger in his chest. "How would you know? You're a chicken. Didn't you pick on someone smaller than you in Goeppingen?"

Hans sat tall, stiffening his posture, shoulders back. "Open the door now, while you still having a chance. I can give a few *kind* words for you with the top man." Hans wrinkled his nose.

"I oughta…" I snatched a fistful of Hans' shirt and cocked my right fist, raising it high.

"What, little boy?" Hans lifted his eyebrows.

"Hold on, Gabe." Alex waded closer in ankle deep water. "If you hit him with his hands tied, you'd be no better than him. Besides, we need him on his feet or he'll drown."

I lowered my fist. Alex and I lugged him to his feet, but we didn't untie his legs.

Alex tapped the front of Hans' shirt and spoke in quiet words. "Why the change in attitude? You were on edge at first and now you're threatening us."

Hans' eyes twitched.

Alex pressed him tight against the wall. "Did you get a signal from your buddies?"

For the next five minutes, Alex, Pete, and I questioned Hans with no results. He still expected his friends to rescue him at any moment.

The water had risen to cover my belt. Our waterproof backpacks floated in the rushing water. Jenna held Lightning in her arms; Thunder's head was still a foot above the water.

"Quit badgering him," Jenna said. "We need to figure out what to *do*. Get into the control room. Open a hatch. Do something. That water's making me cold."

Pete and I waded to the control room's handle.

"I hope you still feel this confident when the water reaches your mouth." Alex let go of Hans' shirt. "Will your buddies help you then?" He kept an eye on Becher while we worked.

After several attempts, Pete and I abandoned getting the glass door unlocked.

"Use the waiting room door," Hans said. "And untie the legs before I fall. Please." He pleaded with Jenna, eyes darting back and forth from her to the hatch.

"Alex, the dogs can't swim forever." Jenna shivered, tugging her miner's jacket tighter. "Hans is right. We can't survive. Hurry." She hugged herself and jumped in place to stay warm.

I didn't think the water was all that chilly. *Maybe she's sensitive to cold.*

Alex grabbed Thunder and placed his forepaws over Jenna's shoulders. She still had Lightning in her arms, holding his head above water.

"You win for now, Becher." Alex motioned for Pete and me to join him.

"Stop," Becher said. "Untie me."

We ignored him. Each of us grabbed a different part of the wheel-shaped handle.

I took a deep breath, went underwater, and kept my eyes open. Enough light filtered through to let me see the dim, shadowy shape of the door and the handle. I came up for air.

"We'll all have to go down," Alex said.

Our heads ducked under the water. We tugged, faces contorted with effort. No result.

I broke the surface of the water, sucking in air. "Well?" I narrowed my eyes at Becher. "Tell us the secret to opening the door or we'll all drown."

"Make me loose." Hans rotated to show his trussed up hands. He slipped and went under.

"After him," Pete said.

We dove and brought him back to the surface, gasping for air.

I plunged down and untied his feet. When I surfaced, Alex had freed his hands.

I heaved him toward the door. "Do your magic."

A big smile lit Hans' face.

"No magic…only my knowing." Hans swam to the shelf with the skulls and the old deep-sea diving helmets. He lifted the helmet on the left end, exposing two levers underneath—one red and one green to match two slots in the wall.

"Red bar stops the water and green bar opens the door." Hans said.

Hans grunted, working to raise the red lever. "It's stuck."

"Why didn't you tell us about this earlier?" I crossed my arms, splashing water and clenching my teeth. "Jerk."

"My buddies are telling me a story, but I thought it not true." Hans turned toward Alex. "Maybe you can shut off water."

"What are those two tiny lights beside the holes in the wall?" Pete said.

"Maybe this is telling when something is good or bad." Hans said.

"The red lever *is* stuck." Alex's neck muscles stood out from the strain.

"Guys, hurry. I'm freezing." Jenna bobbed over to the shelf. Her teeth chattered. She placed Lightning on top of the second helmet and grabbed onto the shelf for support.

"This light is amber." Hans peered behind the red bar. "Maybe too old to work right. But green bar has green light. This should open the door."

The water level touched my neck. The increasing cold made my feet tingle.

Pete grabbed the slippery helmet shelf, clutching tight to stay anchored.

"Pull green bar down," Hans said.

"You do it." Alex got out of the way to let Hans position himself.

I faced the door. *They are not capturing me.* My heartbeat increased. I coaxed Lightning from the shelf into my arms, rubbing the wet hair on his head.

"Get ready," I whispered. "Attack on my signal."

His ears perked up.

"Here we go." Hans' lips curled into a grimace. He leaned all his weight into the handle.

Chapter 13
~ Houdini Hounds

Becher pulled on the green metal rod. The lever moved an inch, and stopped. The light behind the lever went amber.

"Stupid machine." He lifted the lever back into place. The light changed to green. Using both hands, he braced his feet on the wall and yanked hard. The lever stuck again. Amber light.

Hans switched to German, spitting words out in rapid succession.

"Quit swearing and make it work," Pete said.

"Try again," Alex said.

Water surged through the pipes, stronger than before. The top of the water was over my head. Goosebumps covered my arms. I continued to tread water to keep warm. Jenna climbed onto the shelf with Pete and Alex. Hans had to dive now to press the levers.

"The pipes must be clear now." I managed a few words between strokes. "Every couple of minutes the water rises a foot. That means we've got less than ten minutes."

"Trying once more," Hans said. Salt water drizzled down his forehead. His cheeks flushed with color. He shoved the lever up. Green glow. He yanked down with all his might. The lever moved to the lowest mark on the wall slot.

"The light's still green," I said. I let Lightning dogpaddle to the shelf.

"I did it." Becher shook his fist in the air, water spraying. "It's not so long now."

"It better open." Jenna said. "We're not far from the roof. And I'll be an ice cube soon."

No one spoke. Noise of cascading water pounded my ears. Ten seconds passed.

"How long is this supposed to take?" I said.

We took turns working the handle, but the only progress was a grating sound in the wall.

Maybe the door override gears are broken somehow. We need another way.

The grating stopped.

Hans slammed his hand into the water, spouting a torrent of German words.

Alex shook him by the shoulders. "It's over. It didn't work. You're stuck with us."

Hans rubbed his eyes.

"The camera is blinking red," Jenna said. "Your comrades must think we're stuck."

"There's got to be another way." With my hand on the ceiling, I pushed toward the shelf. As I kicked to stay afloat, my legs knocked the helmet off the other side of the shelf.

Thunder barked and dove after the helmet. Lightning zoomed right behind him, with his tail sloshing water in my face.

Pete and Jenna kicked the skulls off the shelf to make more room to stand. We crammed together on the metal ledge. Two feet of air remained above the water.

Thunder popped out of the water wearing the helmet I knocked over.

"Gabe, get that helmet off him." Alex tapped me. "He can't breathe."

"Not sure how he managed that." I grabbed a paw and drew him close.

Thunder's hind legs clawed at the ledge. He swung the helmet at crazy angles until I freed his head. The helmet flipped in my hands and I saw an arrow drawn on the inside.

"Strange," I said.

"I'm sorry to all." Hans wiped his nose. "We will die."

Jenna pressed herself into Alex's arms to get warm. Our jackets helped a little, but we hunched together to keep the heat from escaping. Hans and Pete stood next to me on the shelf.

I thrust the helmet into Pete's hands. "Look inside."

"There's an arrow pointing down. Do you think something was hidden under it?"

"Maybe." I checked, but came up without a clue. A foot of air space remained.

Lightning surfaced, paws churning. Something hung from his mouth.

I hauled him in and hugged him hard, his face next to mine. *This could be the end.*

A cord rubbed my cheek. "What's that?" Metal dangled from the lanyard.

"A key." I held it up with stiffening fingers. "I've got a key."

"Control room." Alex said. "Quick."

Gulping a huge breath, I plunged underwater, swimming the fifteen feet to the glass door in no time. I touched the wall, going for the lock. The key slipped out of my hand. *Air.* I stroked to the ceiling.

Nine inches of air remained.

I brushed my lips against the roof. *Can't suck in water now.* I knew this was the last chance. In seconds I slipped the key into the lock. It turned, the handle rotated, but even with every muscle engaged, the door wouldn't budge. *The watertight seal.* I swam to the top. Six inches left. "Alex, we need to break the seal. Bring a screwdriver or knife."

Alex gave me a thumbs-up. He snagged a screwdriver and hammer from his backpack and swam to the door. Pete followed. When they arrived, we plunged toward the handle.

Grating of metal on glass created a low vibration as Alex pounded on the screwdriver at one of the edges of the door. Pete nudged me. His muscles tightened.

I missed the signal. Too late. Lungs burning, I swallowed several times to override the automatic throat muscle spasms to breathe.

More grating sounds. Pete tapped me again.

One. *Lungs on fire.*

Two. *Need. To. Breathe.*

Three.

Chapter 14
– The Bad Escape

The door moved a bit, breaking the seal.

I bounced to the surface, gasping for air. But water gushed into my mouth as the swirling current dragged me under, sucking me into the control room.

The water level dropped, but it was still two feet from the ceiling.

I resurfaced, hacking and spluttering, standing on a desk attached to the glass wall. Pete and Alex had been washed into the room and floated nearby.

"Open the exit to the control room," Pete said to Alex. "Quick."

Alex swam over, dove under the water, and rattled the handle.

He surfaced. "Won't open. Locked." Rivulets of water coursed down his face. "Search for a cutoff switch."

We checked as water still rose, but a little slower. We had just delayed the inevitable.

I ducked under again, looking on the back wall. The few electrical gauges and controls had watertight rubberized coverings, including the camera. The room seemed empty.

Pete and Alex investigated the top of the panel facing the room of skulls.

After a quick breath of air, I checked the desk's built-in cupboards. I found three toggle switches with dots below them. The dots were like Braille, but had eroded to smooth patches of green discoloration. I couldn't tell what they meant. I flipped the right switch down and surfaced.

"The water's coming in faster," Jenna said. She swam into the control room and stopped. "Hey, those things could electrocute us." She jabbed a finger at one of the gauges by Alex.

"They're waterproof, like underwater lab equipment," I said. "Otherwise, when the water pulled us into this place we would have been fried."

"I bet it's pretty expensive stuff," Pete said.

Through the glass wall, I saw Hans float to the exit hatch in the other room.

I swam back to the toggle switch and flipped it to the original position. I moved the left of the two remaining switches and rose to the surface to see if that helped.

The water continued to pour in.

Thunder stood on top of the desk where I worked and Lightning had found a metal bookcase that had space near the ceiling. He shook out his coat.

I pointed at Hans on the other side of the glass. "Get him in here and shut the door."

Hans pounded on the hatch to the waiting room, screaming for help.

Alex dragged in Becher. Pete shut the door, but liquid still seeped around the edges.

"Guess that screwdriver Alex used to break the door seal ruined it." Pete slapped the water. "And none of these controls make sense. We'll never make it now."

"I've tried each switch within reach," Alex said. "The water keeps rising."

I lifted a finger and swam to the cupboard, flipping the middle switch. When I returned to the surface, the water level in the control room stabilized a foot from the ceiling.

"That's it." Alex thumbed at the door, balancing himself on the desk. "The last switch tightened the seal. We didn't destroy it." In minutes, the skull chamber was full.

"They have to use remote controls to lower the water since we didn't find them," Jenna said. "I wonder how long those creeps will keep the skull room flooded?"

"The water would have finished several minutes ago if we had not broken into control room," Hans said. "They must know we didn't make it."

"I'm not waiting for them," Pete said. "Time to find the drain." He submerged.

"We'll have to get out of here before Hans' pals find out we aren't dead." I floated over to the control room's metal exit door. "There has to be a key."

"Got it." Pete surfaced, his mouth curved in a large smile.

"Got what?" Jenna asked.

A slurpy sound answered her question as the office began to drain.

In less than five minutes, all that remained of the water was a wet tile floor.

"Way to go." I slapped Pete on the back. Spray flew everywhere.

Alex gave Jenna a hug and Jenna hugged her brother. Thunder and Lightning wiggled their bodies to get rid of the excess water, adding showers to the excitement. Hans trudged to a swivel chair and sat. He frowned and rolled toward the far wall.

A click came from the ceiling and warm air flooded the control area.

I shivered and tugged off the soaked miner's jacket and overalls covering my clothes.

"What are you doing?" Pete asked.

"It's warmer without this stuff," I said. "Drying one layer at a time is easier."

"Good idea," Alex said. Soon everyone was in normal street clothes.

"We made it, Hans," I said. I closed my eyes for a second to feel the heat seeping into my toes and fingers. "Who's gonna help you now? You'd better switch sides for good."

"They didn't know I was with you." Hans' gaze drifted toward the room full of water.

"The green light was on." Pete laughed. "They knew you were in the room."

A loud metal clanking sound came from the skull room. The wall slots near the floor lowered and water drained faster than when the room had filled.

"Unlock the exit door," Jenna said. "They'll be here soon."

With frantic motions, we searched each cabinet on the back wall, looking for the key.

Pete paused. "Gabe, would the key from G work?"

I had forgotten. I lifted the cord out of my shirt, stepped to the door, and shoved key number one at the keyhole. Too fat.

"No dice." I put it away.

"Here's a ring of keys from a cabinet," Jenna said. A silver ring with twenty dangling keys rested on her index finger.

"Open the door." Alex moved toward her. "Gabe, watch for Becher's buddies."

Jenna squished over to the door, putting keys in, jiggling them, and taking them out.

"Hurry," Pete said. "I'm sure they won't be long."

The skull room water had drained to less than a foot.

"I've tried most of the keys." Jenna's voice quavered. "Nothing's working."

"One has to work," Alex said. "Keep trying."

"The door handle on the side to the waiting room is turning," I said. "We need to leave. Pete, lock the control room door." I handed the key to him and shooed Lightning toward Jenna.

"Thunder, get by the door, we'll need to move fast," I said. I grabbed my backpack off the floor where it had floated into the room and slid both arms into the straps.

Alex set his backpack close to the exit. Then he and Pete grabbed Becher's arms.

We crowded together.

"Last key," Jenna said.

The key slid into the door, but wouldn't turn.

"Jiggle it again," I said.

A loud crack caught my attention. The skull room hatch swung open.

"Let me try," Alex said.

Jenna moved out of the way. Alex couldn't make the key budge. He moved away and Pete rammed the door with his shoulder. I wiggled between the three.

"Maybe it's warped," I said. "Pull back hard to ease the pressure on the bolt."

They strained and I twisted the key. With grudging movements, it turned.

Sandy entered the skull room and ran to the entrance into the control room. He tried the handle and shouted at us through the glass wall.

Alex put Hans in a bear hug to prevent him from stealing the key from Pete. Becher kicked and shouted.

"Push," I said.

We popped open the metal-plated door.

"Move." I pointed into the darkness on the other side.

Alex yanked Hans off balance. Pete corralled his legs and helped carry the struggling captive into the tunnel.

Lightning and Thunder bolted into the darkness. Jenna struggled with Alex's backpack, but got it into the tunnel. I shot through last, toting my gear.

I swung the door closed, getting Pete to force it tight with his shoulder. The key twisted a little and stuck with the bolt thrown less than halfway. I clamped on the key with both hands and brought my full weight to bear. "Oops," I said in the dark. No one paid attention.

An instant later, somebody switched on the tunnel lights.

"What kind of escape was that?" Alex groaned. He had Becher on the ground, an arm twisted behind his back. He looked at the path ahead.

"From bad to worse," Jenna said.

Chapter 15
~ The Broken Path

I stepped around Pete to see why this tunnel was worse than being caught by Hans' pals. Mining lights in grey cages illuminated the path. A stone's throw away, a mass of rock and rubble blocked the cave. But a side passage turned right, like a Y. A crack split the usable trail in the middle. The left half ended in a drop. The other side narrowed where the tunnel curved right.

"That's gonna be tricky," Alex said. "We'll have to lean into the wall and make sure we have solid footing."

"No wonder that room was remote control," Hans said. "Is no good way to get here."

"Maybe lack of use is why I had to strain that hard to turn the key," I said. "I wonder if Hans' friends had a spare."

Someone pounded on the door. Everyone flinched, including the dogs. Thunder's barking left no doubt about our location.

"Open the door." The door rattled as our pursuers worked on the lock.

"If they have another key, it won't take them long," Pete said.

"Oops." I held up half of the door key for everyone to see, smiling.

"What happened?" Jenna took the twisted metal from my hand to look closer.

"The other half's still in the lock." I shrugged. "They'll have to break through."

"Let's go." Alex motioned us closer to the broken floor.

"Wait." Jenna pulled on his shirt. "Look at this diagram on the wall."

We gathered around the picture. X marked our position. I dropped my backpack.

"Here's the Y in the path." Jenna pointed. "And I don't see any other way out of the control room except through the skull room."

"The blocked side path we can't use went to a large tunnel and a way to the surface. See the elevator?" Pete traced the path with a finger.

"Yeah, but that's no good," Alex said.

"The path to the right takes us near the waiting room Hans told us about," I said. "Then it seems to disappear for a short distance before joining that corridor on the left through a couple of rooms. What's the section in the middle? I can't make out the words."

"They're German," Pete said. "It says…"

"'This corridor is special project of the boss,'" Hans said. "Then it becomes unreadable."

"That's not unreadable." Jenna rubbed the dust off the plaque, revealing tiny pictures.

"Those symbols look familiar, almost like…" I said.

"Egyptian hieroglyphs." Jenna finished the sentence. "I studied this in history," Jenna said. "The Egyptians used pictures instead of letters to write. These pictures mean something."

More pounding on the door got the dogs barking. They ran toward the sound.

"Can you read it?" I said.

"A little," she said. "Maybe there's something in the next passage that will help us out." She glanced at the door. "We'd better go."

"I've got the lead," I said. "Lightning, come on boy." I threw my backpack on.

My canine sidekick lowered his ears, snorted at the floor, and trotted off.

"I think we should rope ourselves together before you go around that corner," Alex said. "The path's got a big drop-off on one side."

"Thanks for waiting 'til I had saddled up." I dropped my gear, pulled out a length of rope, tied it around myself, and thrust it toward Alex.

"You know we have to be careful," Alex said. "And Pete, stand watch over Hans. I don't want him interfering."

"You'll need to anchor that cord onto something." I jerked on the climbing harness, hooked on the rope, and seated my head lantern, switching it on.

Alex looped the rope around the door handle. He shook his head.

"Use a piton closer to the path," I said.

"I know what I'm doing." Kneeling, he pulled his hammer and a few pitons out of his backpack. He pounded four of them into various cracks in the wall, hooking karabiners to his pitons and threading the rope through each one. He wrapped the rope around his hands and tied the end to the door handle.

"The extra karabiners will give you added protection, in case you fall off," Alex said.

I shook my head. "Thanks for your great confidence in my abilities. Just keep the rope tight."

"Are you sure you trust each other enough to do this?" Jenna said.

"Oh, Gabe's a little touchy today." Alex winked at her. "We've done this lots of times."

Lightning took off around the corner.

"Wait for me," I said.

The walls of the tunnel widened, transforming into a mini-cavern as I traced the curve, tight against the wall. Below me a boulder-strewn hill dropped away into darkness. The wall of the tunnel angled away from me toward the ceiling. I could lean into it when the walkway became nothing more than a foot-wide ledge. I rounded the sweeping curve, losing sight of my brother, who paid out more line.

Lightning stopped about five feet in front of me, putting his paws down and crouching. His tail wiggled with excitement. He was about to jump a large gap in the path.

"Don't do it, boy," I said.

A six-inch wide ledge supported us. The rock wall jutted out at knee height for at least an arm's length. My body would have to resemble the letter C to make it past that spot. *That's not going to work.* And crossing the ten-foot gap to the next section of the ledge seemed ridiculous.

I knelt within arm's length of Lightning's wagging tail. "Come on, buddy. Don't be a hero. Back away." I stretched out to latch onto him.

Lightning looked back at me. But that caused his paws to skitter on the gravel surface, sending a shower of pebbles and a fist-sized rock clattering downward.

I needed a few more inches.

His left paw went over the edge.

I clutched for his collar, and missed. Forcing my other hand into wall cracks, I prayed the grip would keep us from falling and got a hand on his back. *Can't lose you, buddy.*

Lightning slipped through my fingers, like a shaggy orange towel slipping away.

"Stop." I leaned forward on fingertips, snagging his tail. He yelped. But with steady pressure, I dragged him onto the ledge and didn't let go until I cradled him.

"Keep close, boy." His head sunk into my chest. He whimpered.

I dropped a rock and counted a few seconds before it hit bottom. Definitely would have been a bad fall—at least fifty to sixty feet. I returned to the gang.

After I told the group what happened, Pete came over, laughed, and scratched Lightning's muzzle. "You can't jump ten-foot gaps, can you, boy?"

"He's no super dog, except to me." I grinned.

Pete glanced over to check on Hans. He sat, head in arms, on the cave floor by himself.

"Can you put in a second piton for safety and swing over to the other side?" Jenna said.

"She's right," Alex said. "Can you lean on the wall the whole way or does the slope become an overhang?"

"It begins to slope about five feet near the far-side ledge. A trained climber might make it, but not me." I drew a diagram in the dust on the floor.

Alex erased the drawing and sketched his own. "You could climb fifteen feet, go halfway to the other side, and sink the piton there. Then your arc will reach the path on the other side."

"Like Tarzan," Pete said.

"Maybe not that high." I rubbed my chin. "How about ten feet? My legs extend beyond the harness about two-and-a-half feet, giving me a reach of about twelve-and-a-half feet. All I need is seven or eight feet from the halfway point."

"That works. Place the piton in the middle of the gap." Alex's finger tapped his lips. "Make sure you add the height of the piton to the width of the gap. You don't want to be short."

"And pound that piton in tight." Pete slapped me on the shoulder and returned to the tedious job of guarding Hans.

Hans must have felt defeated. His slouch showed the whole picture. He had no way to turn things around. His friends couldn't rescue him. They even tried to drown him with us. If he wanted to stay alive, he would have to come with us and cooperate. I almost felt sorry for him.

I cleared my head, stood, and chalked my hands with powder from my backpack. With smooth, unhurried motions, I climbed sideways, like a spider—high enough over the center of the gap to place a piton ten feet high. The piton sunk deep into a crevice that was full of loose rock. *Seems too easy.* I tugged, but it seemed solid. I looped the rope and clicked it in the karabiner. *Better be safe.* I pounded an extra piton a little lower and right, threading rope and checking for movement. Tight—like I had pounded it into hardened concrete.

"Testing the rope," I said.

"Okay," Alex said.

I leaned back, putting more tension on the rope. It held firm. I inched my left foot out of its toehold, then my right. I swayed in the air. The first piton held. I drove my feet back into the toeholds. "It works. Give me a little slack. Go slow." I clambered to the ledge. "Time to jump."

"Be careful," Jenna said.

"Slack." I measured out an extra eight feet of rope and let it hang over the edge. I didn't want to come up short on the swing. "Make it taut." I bent my shoulders and neck forward to relax my muscles. I took a few deep breaths. The excess rope disappeared around the corner.

"Lightning." I tapped him on the nose. "Stay."

I inched backward, moving him behind me and stretched out the rope to its full length, standing on the rim of the ledge. I closed my eyes for an instant to visualize the swing. *Must get these angles exactly right.* Rope at max tension on the harness, I glanced over the brink. The rubble below reflected the headlamp's light.

I launched sideways into space, body arcing like a pendulum. Momentum brought me up the other side. *Wrong angle.* I touched the landing area, left foot first, but my right side smashed against the wall. Loose rocks sprayed out, rattling downward. I twisted to grasp an outcrop, but failed to gain any grip. I shoved off a lower projection, to rebuild more speed.

"Gabe," Alex said," say something. Did you make it?"

"Missed." I hurtled away from my destination.

Ping.

I didn't like the way that sounded. My body lurched and the piton anchored in loose rock fell past me. I plunged an extra foot.

"We lost a piton." Alex was hoarse with tension.

No kidding, genius.

The line jerked with all my weight bottoming out. My trajectory changed again. I lost a bit of momentum and rotated in a slow spin.

Lightning barked when he saw me on the backswing. He perched on the rim of the path next to the drop off.

Alex's biceps bulged from the increased pressure caused by the jerky motion.

Pete ran close, straining to reach me, but I was too far away.

Swinging to the other side, I kicked my legs out as though on a swing set. I clenched the rope above my head, high enough to land my feet onto the ledge. *Think*. My speed dropped making my approach too low. *Don't panic*. The landing spot was a couple of feet wide. Like a gymnast on the high bar, I leaned back, tucking my knees into my chest at the last second to avoid scraping the ledge. I fired my feet over the rocky outcrop, twisting to land face down.

I landed partially on the ledge, clinging to the rope with my right hand. My left palm jammed against the sharp edges of the rock shelf. I wedged that hand into the wall to stop the rope's pull in the opposite direction.

But I slid forward anyway as I strained to halt my fall into the inky abyss.

Chapter 16 – No Friend Left Behind

I stopped myself half-on and half-off the ledge by spreading my feet, knees dragging on the rocky path. *Don't quit.* If I didn't make it, I would hang in space until the pitons gave way. My right foot caught on a crack and my left foot found a crevice. I hung, right hand re-clutching the rope, and left hand working to find the balance to keep me from the blackness beneath.

I gasped for air. My legs felt like they lay on pins and needles.

Alex or Pete shouted, but I couldn't make out their words.

Is it over? Again, a steadiness overtook me. *Be still.* I controlled my breathing. *Blow it out, draw it in. Slower. Longer.* As normal breathing resumed, the shaking lessened. I relaxed my strained shoulder while tightening my core muscles, thighs, and buttocks. Calves pulling me back, I inched my bruised ribcage onto the ledge. My knees ground into the scratchy surface. I worked my waist past the critical point. In minutes I could sit up, my lower legs quivering.

Sweat dripped off my face and slid into my ears, tickling them. I stared at the six-inch ledge I had abandoned and rested.

"Gabe, you have to answer us," Jenna screamed. "Tell us you're okay."

"I've got slack," Alex said. "Talk to us."

"Another failure." Hans' tone contained a hint of defeat. "He is a weakling."

"Is not." Pete said. "Gabe's stronger than you think."

My toes began to cramp, forcing me to move. Bracing a hand against the wall, I stood, feet inching under me to re-center myself. "Made it."

Lightning yapped.

"Stop it," Alex said. "I thought I heard something."

Throat muscles locked up from the tension and strain, I yanked on the line to respond.

"Gabe," Alex said. "Do that again."

I did.

"He's safe," Alex said. "Pete, go take a look. I'll watch Hans. Then we'll switch."

Pete, clutching the rope, worked his way around the corner. He saw me, grinned, and moved out of sight.

Alex appeared next. He looked me over, then at the situation with the rope swing, and back at me. "Can you talk?" Alex tilted his head.

"Yeah." I rubbed my throat.

"How can we get everyone else over? They can't swing across this gap."

I nodded.

Alex pointed. "What's in that long wooden thing behind you?"

I turned and looked. A two-foot high storage box, made out of grayish wood sat next to the wall. The old crate was about eight feet long and had a lid.

I opened it. "Nothing in here but a hammer."

"Well, that won't help. Let me tell the others." Alex disappeared around the bend.

Minutes later, Pete appeared. "I have an idea." Pete pressed into the wall, his flushed face plastered against the rock.

"Don't be scared, Pete," I said. "You still have a foot-wide ledge where you're standing."

"It could break anytime." He shuffled a little closer. "You have a hammer right?"

I held out a normal looking hammer, claw on one end and a hammer-head on the other.

"Perfect." Pete's fingers dug into the wall. "Let's take the box apart and reuse the wood to build a bridge."

Within half-an-hour, I had torn apart the storage bin for eight-foot, three-inch wide planks. I reinforced them underneath, placing other boards at staggered intervals, nailing them together with the original nails from the chest. To overcome the imbalance of the foot wide bridge on a six-inch ledge, we wrapped cord around the boards, securing the makeshift bridge to the wall with a piton. Alex and I used the first cord I had swung on to act as a handrail.

"Not sure I can do this." Jenna tiptoed to the edge and retreated.

"Pete, you take care of Hans," Alex said. "I'll walk her over and come back for him."

Jenna followed Alex, hanging onto the rope and his shirt.

Halfway over, a slight twitch in the rope caused the bridge to quiver.

"Help." Jenna lurched forward.

"Bend your knees," I said. "You have to keep them flexed to avoid falling."

After a few tense moments, Jenna made a safe passage and Alex returned.

When the group had finished crossing, Alex recovered the cord and pitons. We left the bridge in place. I became Hans' new guard.

"Let's get out of here," Jenna said. "I'm still chilled because my clothes aren't dry. Moving will warm me up."

"In a minute," Alex said.

Alex and I repacked our ropes and gear. He nodded at Jenna and we walked at a fast clip.

"First intersection," I said ten minutes later.

"What is that?" Alex pointed to a bit of cloth hanging on a rusty nail. He removed the silky plaid material. "This looks familiar."

Jenna inspected the cloth. "This is a piece of Izabella's scarf." She looked at Alex. "But she should be safe with the tour, right? They took the high road and we took the low road."

"They should be," Alex said. "Unless…"

"Hans," I said. "What do you know about this?"

He looked away.

"You better tell me what happened to my friend," Jenna said.

Hans wouldn't make eye contact with her.

"Maybe there's another clue around here," I said.

"The map showed a room up ahead. Is that where she is?" Jenna arched her eyebrows and looked at Hans.

Hans hung his head hung low and nodded.

"We should rescue her before we do anything else." Jenna set her jaw. "She's by herself, right Hans?" Jenna's words sounded sweet, but her tone demanded more information.

"If we go left, we are getting to the surface and having the Polizei come to rescue all your friends…I mean her." Hans winced and glanced sideways at Alex.

"All our friends?" I said. "Have all of our friends been captured? If so, are they nearby?"

"We made the plan to catching all of you, but I am not knowing what happened to the other group," Hans said.

"Let's think about what we need to do." Alex dropped his backpack and sat on it.

"Is safer, getting help instead of fighting the guards." Hans put his hands in his pockets.

"Or we could run into another one of your traps trying to free ourselves." I didn't trust Hans. One minute he was mean, the next he seemed concerned. Like he couldn't decide to which side he belonged. "We need to rescue our friends."

"Machete will expecting this," Hans said.

"They probably think we're still stuck in the tunnel next to the control center," Pete said. "They must know that tunnel's a mess."

After a little arguing, we decided, four to one, to rescue our friends.

"I don't even know why we considered *your* vote." Jenna swung her hair to one side, striding away from Hans.

"He's hard to trust, but he agreed to help us get out of here." Alex glanced at Jenna.

"Hey, the door's open." I rushed to Izabella's holding cell, but didn't see a thing.

"Look. Another piece of Izabella's scarf." Jenna darted past me to a hint of blue wedged underneath a bench. "Those creeps moved the whole group." She rubbed the plaid fabric.

How are we ever going to get out of these salt mines with our friends?

"Let's go," I said. "At least there are some rooms to check ahead."

Hans stopped at the next corridor intersection. He rubbed his lips and nose, apparently deciding between the two side corridors. "I am not sure which one is correct."

"There's a sign." Jenna raced toward it. A piece of indigo blue scarf stuck in an old iron grate door. Without hesitation, she flung open the door, and vanished down a dim stairwell.

"Wait," Pete said.

The dogs chased after Jenna, followed by the rest of us. After descending two flights of stairs, we arrived on a square landing. A short dead-end tunnel on one side and a locked door on the other left one option. Straight ahead, an old iron gate was wide open. Rusty orange flakes lay on the ground. Two slippery steps led down to the opening. A damp smell of salt filled the air.

"Pretty drippy here," Pete said.

"Yeah, but which way do we go now?" I said.

"Follow the blue scarf." Alex pointed over my shoulder.

The scarf covered someone's head. Their shoulders stooped forward, quivering.

"Izabella, we're here," Jenna said. But the person didn't get up.

We all rushed inside.

Ropes bound our Spanish's friend's hands and feet to a short pole in front of her. A handkerchief taped around her mouth muffled her cries.

Jenna knelt, hand loosening the tape and brushing her cheek.

"It's a setup." Izabella strained for release.

I stiffened as the door clanged shut.

Chapter 17
~ The Decision

Lightning's high-pitched bark broke into my thoughts. He jumped to get attention.

I tried to open the door. No dice. My little sidekick didn't quit, though.

"What boy? What's up?" I laid him on a shoulder and looked at our new surroundings.

The walls looked grey, but damp. A splash of wetness hit my cheek. Above me, little stalactites dripped water from the ceiling. I swiped the liquid from my cheek and tasted it. Salt.

"It's gonna be okay." Jenna stroked Izabella, who sobbed, hands on her face and ropes tossed aside on the floor. Minutes later, she sniffed and brushed tears from her cheeks.

Alex sat a few feet away on a rock sticking out from the wall. He hunched over, focused on his own thoughts. Thunder, head between his paws, lay at his feet.

"Fine mess we're in now." I set Lightning down and glared at Hans, arms crossed over my chest.

Becher stood against the opposite wall, back against the rock, hands shoved in his pockets. "They will being here in no time." He pointed at the iron door. "When this door goes shut, the alarm is going off."

"We should have gone for the cops," Alex said. "Then rescued everyone else."

"Gone for the cops?" I couldn't believe it. "And left our friends here? You're nuts."

"You just can't stand somebody else's way of doing things."

"Yes, *Mr. Logic*." I oozed with false sincerity and bent at the waist in a mock bow.

"Guys, quit fighting." Jenna let go of Izabella. "The others are here. We can get them out of their cells. Izabella said she knows how."

I stepped toward Alex. "You believe you're always right. And because we've been set up, you think we could've made a better decision."

"Don't take this out on me." Alex stood. "The guy who wants to trap us…"

"Don't change the subject, King Alex. Things would go better if we did it your way, huh?"

"Gabe." Pete's grabbed my shoulder. "Your arguing isn't helping."

"I don't care." I pointed at Alex. "Next time, *you* make the decision, Mr. Perfect, and *you* accept the consequences."

"Enough." Jenna pushed Thunder out of her way, walked past me, and slid her arm through Alex's. She guided him around me to get to Izabella. "We need to let our buddies out of their cells."

Izabella nodded. "They…the cells are filthy."

"Where are the rest of our friends?" Pete asked.

"Oh, I am forgetting. All that fighting…" Izabella fumbled with a pocket in her skirt. She retrieved a wadded piece of yellow paper and held it out to Alex.

"Yes?" Alex said.

"The men who tied me here leave a note."

I peered over Alex's shoulder and saw a title on the page:

RULES OF THE GAME

Chapter 18
– The Final Two
Minutes

Alex hunched over to read the note, not letting me see.

"Let me look at the note," I said.

"Stop," he said. "There's no time. We're in deep trouble. We've got to act fast."

I grabbed the note out of his hand.

"Cut it out." Alex snatched it back. "Let's rescue our friends first. Remember what you wanted to do? We've got ten minutes. Let's go."

Pete shielded Alex as I lunged for the note. "Gabe, calm down." Pete's bulkier body blocked the way. "We'll read the message later. Let's go."

I relaxed, signaling for Lightning to follow and narrowing my eyes at Alex. *You'll wish you had let me read that letter.*

Trailing Izabella, we arrived at an intersection. Straight ahead, a tunnel extended more than a football field's length. On one side was a short passage. We hurried toward the other direction into a wide tunnel, close to thirty feet long. I saw several holes in the right wall—large enough to hold a couple of people.

Rusted iron doors sealed the arched openings. A wooden box at eye level hung on the tunnel's wall at the end.

"The keys." Izabella motioned at the box. "One guy, he stored the keys there while one holds my arms behind my back. The tall man, he slapped me. Twice." Her lower lip trembled.

The box had a simple lock hanging from a metal loop.

"I'll check for the lock-picking kit." Alex set his backpack down and searched.

"I'll take care of it," I said.

I picked up a large rock, took aim, and beat on the weathered, grayish wood where the lock hung. The wood dented, but the metal ring and lock remained secure.

"Try this." Pete handed me a two-foot-long piece of metal rod he found on the floor. One end had a sharpened point.

I shrugged off my backpack and pounded the end of the rod into the metal loop. Like a crow bar, I applied pressure to pop the metal off the wood. Didn't work.

"Make way." Alex stepped up with his tools.

I pounded a few more times. No progress. "All right." Lips pressed together, I tossed the rock and then threw the rod like a javelin the way we had come.

In two minutes, Alex had the lockbox door open. He smiled at Jenna.

"If you throw the keys to me, I can open the locks," Izabella said.

Alex tossed her a set of keys, gave one to Pete and took one himself.

"What about me?" I asked.

"We only have three friends to rescue." Alex shrugged.

"I know another, so four." Izabella unlocked one door. "Those guides bring Jonathan into a cell when bringing Erik, Dieter, and Franco with me."

I grabbed the last set of keys from the lockbox, strolling past Alex. *See, Mr. Know-it-all?*

"Why would Jonathan be captured?" Alex said. "He wasn't with our group when the lights went out."

No one answered him.

We busied ourselves opening the cells, hinges creaking from lack of use.

"I heard you, Alex." Jonathan crawled out of his cell. "I don't know why I'm here, but I bet you're the reason. On the tour, I hung out by myself near the science display. The crowd left. Someone covered my mouth, blindfolded me, and stuck me in here. What did you do?"

"Interesting." Alex raised his eyebrows. He bent down, put his lock-picking kit away, and stretched to full height, yellow note in his hand. He glanced at his watch.

"We've got three minutes to get out." Alex shoved the balled up note into my hand. "Here, you wanted to read this."

I uncrumpled the note while Alex, Thunder, and the gang trotted into the main cavern, veering to our left, away from the iron door. Pete waited at the intersection of the tunnels.

"Gabe, hurry." Pete jogged after the retreating group. "We have two minutes."

I read while I walked.

In jagged handwriting, the note said:

Death is certain if you remain
Or take the door that leads to pain
Ten minutes to decide you have.
If you stay put, you'll make me sad.

No signature, but I knew that whoever ran this organization had written the note.

I reached the intersection. A motion caused my eyes to glance to my left. Thirty yards behind Pete a metal plate glided down from the ceiling at a steady rate.

"Go," I said.

I was fifty yards from the closing gate. I circled, searching the intersection for anything to stop it. Lightning stayed beside me.

Pete was already at the door. "Hurry." His arms couldn't slow the descending door. He staggered under its weight.

I spotted gleaming metal and snagged it. It was the metal rod I had used earlier. I hurled it near Pete. "Jam the door with the rod." I sprinted.

Pete scrambled to get the clattering metal. He ducked under the door to the other side. Falling to his knees, he centered the rod under the door, holding it vertical.

I pumped my arms, running at top speed. Thirty yards to go.

From recessed areas, nozzles popped out of the wall. Steam leaked into the tunnel and rose toward the ceiling.

Lightning zipped under the door. The sliding plate ground to a halt, driving the point of the stake into the rocky floor. Gears in the ceiling whined in protest. The steel trembled.

"It's gonna give out." Pete got down on the ground, part-way under the door.

The metal rod began to bow.

"Get out of there." I gasped for air.

Ten yards. I shifted to overdrive.

Lightning zoomed back under the door toward me, barking. *Wrong side of the door.*

Two yards.

I skidded to a halt, flipping my backpack off, and throwing it at the opening. It wedged between the metal and floor.

I scanned for Lightning.

My furry friend sneezed and wobbled. Green gas flowed from the outlets in jets and it was getting the best of him. Behind him, the vapor floated lower and lower, filling the cavern.

"Lightning." My chest heaved. I glanced at the bar, then at my dog. I dropped to my knees, sucked in two deep breaths from the other side of the dungeon door. Holding in the air, I buried my mouth and nose inside the crook of my elbow and dashed to rescue him.

Lightning collapsed.

Hand under his chest, I swept him up.

"Gabe." Pete yanked my backpack under the door.

106

The door opening shrank as the metal rod bowed even more.

I stumbled, gagging for air through my shirt sleeve. I dove for the opening.

The door slammed shut, snapping the metal rod into two pieces.

Chapter 19
~ Cave In

I had cleared the door by inches. I sucked in clean air, lying flat on the ground. *That was wild.* I checked the seal on the metal door. I didn't see or smell any fumes. *Must be airtight.*

"Cutting it close for fun?" Pete rolled on his back next to me.

"Of course." I slapped his chest, chuckling. I stretched to loosen my stiff muscles and rubbed my shoulder, which was sore after scraping the ground.

Lightning wobbled at first, but eventually shook off the effects of the vapor.

It took me longer to recover.

We caught up to our group as they stopped at a dead end. Rocks half my size lay scattered like tinker toys kicked by an angry kid, piled all the way to a broken ceiling.

Erik picked his way up the slope. He slipped through a narrow gap.

"Wait," Jenna said.

"Why?" Erik reappeared. "The tunnel opens wider on this side. I can stand up straight."

"We found more hieroglyphics," Jenna said. "They might be clues to the path."

"Here is a warning." Izabella pointed toward the etching next to the narrow opening Erik stood in. "The Egyptian symbol of death, he is like an owl. And it also has a falling man holding a staff with a closed half arch over the owl. The closed half arch, he is an Egyptian bread loaf."

"Death?" I said. "Are you sure?"

Izabella nodded and brushed dirt and dust off the carving. "We have studied Egyptian tombs in the last year. It's a curse on anyone who enters the chamber."

"Makes sense," Jenna said. "I'm glad you can read it. We'd better be careful."

"This must be the Path of Death." I glanced at Hans. "Right?"

"Could be," Hans said. "The guys telling me about the Path of Death are not mentioning Egyptian hiero… whatever you call them."

"Let's go back to where we were," Jonathan said.

"And die from gas poisoning?" I sat and crossed my legs. "Pete, Lightning, and me almost died, no thanks to Alex."

Alex's eyes became dark slits.

"If we stay here, we've lost the game." Jenna sat next to Alex, Thunder's head in her lap. She stroked his black fur.

I took a swig from my canteen and passed it around. When everyone finished, I screwed the lid on and rose. "Let's go." I grabbed my backpack and slapped Pete's shoulder, squeezing onto the Path of Death. "I'm not waiting for the boss and his goons to show."

"Can't wait for my decision?" Alex didn't get up.

"We don't really have a choice." I ducked into the gap Erik had found.

I checked behind me. The gang followed me, keeping Hans between Alex and Pete. A slight rumble in the rocks caused me to signal for everyone to freeze. Seconds later, I probed further into the tunnel, wiggling my back to shake out the tingle.

I sensed danger.

"Pete." I paused at a slight right turn, glancing at him. "Do you smell that?"

He drew in a breath of air. "It stinks like a barnyard."

Around the corner, the cave widened into two tunnels built side by side, both with high arched ceilings, separated by a shared middle wall. We stood in the arched entryway that opened into both caverns. The end of the tunnels seemed to be a football field away.

"Disgusting." Jenna pinched her nose shut. "Is this a sewer?"

Lightning surged past my legs.

"Get back here." I lunged forward and grabbed his collar. He yipped and struggled for freedom, but I held him tight.

This section of the cave was man-made with smoother walls, ceiling, and floors. Thirty feet in front of me, a square bamboo cage swung on a rope. The bars were thick as a broomstick handle. The cage was big—a four foot square box. Inside, a hog grunted.

Alex's dog burst past me, barks resonating in the chamber.

"Thunder, stop." Alex's momentum carried him several paces in front of me. Eventually, he obeyed and Alex put him on his leash.

"That hog has to be bait," I said to no one in particular. I knelt and leashed Lightning.

"I agree," Pete said. "It's a trick."

Rumble.

Crack.

The dogs jerked at their leashes. Chunks of plaster and cement crashed to the floor.

"Cave in," Hans shouted. "Get by walls."

Jenna screamed and ran toward Alex, arms over her head.

Small stones broke free from the ceiling and began pelting our heads like hail. Sounds, like gunshots, crackled. And a gash rippled through one of the walls, causing us to split into two groups, one to the right tunnel, one to the left.

My backpack shielded me. Dust filled the air, but I caught a glimpse of Alex who stood flat against the right wall. The entire cavern shook. Large chunks of the ceiling collapsed near me.

"Get closer together," I yelled at Pete and Izabella over the deafening noise. They pressed their bodies tight against me, into a small depression in the wall. Lightning squeezed between my feet. In front of me, Dieter and Hans had hidden under a small outcropping.

Pete shouted in my ear, but I couldn't hear anything over the roar. A wave of rocks, concrete, and stones swept over my backpack. The ordeal was over a couple of minutes later. We were surrounded by rocks, with just a trickle of light making its way in.

Pete groaned.

I coughed, spitting out the dust that filled my nose, eyes, and mouth with a salty film.

Izabella sneezed and began to sob. I gave her a hug.

"Pete, help me push this pack up," I said, resisting the pressure crushing the backpack into my head. "We've got to get out."

"A rock's pinning my leg." Pete tried to clear his throat. "I can't move it."

Izabella, nose covered by her arm, worked around me to take a look. "The rock is jammed into Pete's leg." She shoved the boulder and it rocked.

"Ah…" Pete sucked in a breath. He held it, and then told her to do it again. After five attempts, he was free. He worked to a crouched position beside me under the backpack. "It's bruised, but not broken. If we all push against the backpack together, we might break out."

"Here we go." I coughed. "Ready? Push."

We strained against the backpack. Stones spilled into the space where we stood.

"Again." I adjusted my stance, took a deep breath. "Now."

After three attempts, we pushed the backpack off and a massive stone rolled to the ground. Dust billowed in the air. I hacked to clear my lungs.

Hans and Dieter tugged on me as I crawled out. Izabella, Pete, and Lightning followed, sliding off the rock pile to the floor.

Debris clogged the passageway where we had entered and cut off the connection with the cavern to our right. A haze floated in the air.

"Are either of you hurt?" I inspected Hans and Dieter. Several red marks showed through rips in their clothing. Hans had a big bruise on his neck.

"We are fine." Dieter slapped at his pants. "Nothing broken."

Hans nodded.

"The others?" Izabella pointed to the landslide covering the opening between the two parallel caves.

I attempted to climb the rubble to a gap I saw near the original ceiling. I got halfway up and a loose stone gave way, sending me tumbling to the floor. After checking for injuries, and finding nothing beyond a few more scratches, I clawed higher up the slope to the gap. "Alex. You all right?" The words seemed to die in the thick air.

No response.

I struggled, stretching nearer to the six-inch opening. *What if the earthquake buried them alive?* Sweat dripped into my eyes.

"Alex, answer me." I shouted his name a few more times.

I heard a faint whisper. The lights overhead flickered. I burrowed my toes further into the shifting rubble. "I can't hear you. Say again."

Alex came into view. "We're still digging out, but no problems." Alex nodded, but I noticed a gash on his brow. "You?"

"We're good," I said. "Let's meet at the far…"

A tremor rattled the cave. I ducked, arms protecting my head. Rock and concrete rained from the ceiling. I lost my perch and rolled down the slope.

"There goes the hole," Hans said.

We surveyed the rockslide, but couldn't find any other gaps.

"We have been cut off." Izabella's hands clasped and unclasped.

"We are needing to move on." Dieter strode toward the suspended pig.

"Careful, I bet that's a booby trap," I said.

"Maybe." He studied the cage and scratched his head. "We need to eat. And I have hunger." He grabbed the rope near the pig's cage.

Suddenly, the floor disappeared beneath his feet. He screamed and dropped out of sight.

The pig squealed and Lightning barked.

"Hold on," Izabella said.

I hushed Lighting and glanced down into the hole where Dieter had disappeared.

He had held on. His legs flailed, trapping his lifeline. He pinched the rope between his legs, moving one hand above the other to inch upward like a worm.

"Swing," Pete said when Dieter's feet were above the level of the floor. "We can grab you or the cord and pull you in."

He swung back and forth.

The bottom of the cord whipped near enough for me to touch. Pete and Hans held my legs while I snagged it.

Dieter reversed his climb to maneuver down toward us.

"Stop." I ducked as his foot almost kicked me.

"Hans, I've got Gabe," Pete said. "Get Dieter."

Hans wrapped his arms around one of Dieter's lower legs.

Pete tugged me away from the edge.

"Loosen your hands to slide down." I wriggled my chest onto solid ground and Pete joined Hans, arms circling the dangling boy's thighs.

"I'll fall," he said.

"We have you," Hans said. "Trust us."

"And the pig?" Dieter said.

"Quit the stall and letting go." Hans pulled on his leg. "My arms are tired."

"Here goes." His hands opened and his upper body slammed into the side of the pit.

Pete and Hans fell backward, dragging the black-haired boy with them.

The rope whipped through the ceiling pulley. The frightened hog squealed as it plummeted toward the bottom of the pit.

The bamboo cracked and splintered on the ground. Shortly after impact, the only sound that could be heard was a barking dog.

Hans and Pete lugged Dieter a couple of feet from the pit.

"Quiet." I jerked Lightning's leash. "Guys, grab my legs again."

"And the reason?" Hans asked.

"That pig isn't squealing. I want to know why."

Pebbles trickled over the rim when I shifted over the edge. Below me lay the motionless pig, on its side in the crumpled cage. Metal spikes jutting from the floor had pierced the hog. Encircling the skewered pig were skeleton parts of other animals.

"Gross," I said. "Pull me back."

"What'd you see?" Pete said.

"A dead hog. And skeletons." I dusted off my chest and pants.

Dieter dabbed at his right cheek with a dirty handkerchief. Scratches covered his face.

"Next time, listen." I stared into his eyes.

"I'm have a couple years older than you," he said. "I don't take orders from a kid."

"I know more about exploring caves than you do." I didn't back down even though he outweighed me and was several inches taller.

A grinding noise came from the center wall.

"We've got to keep going." I pointed to the end of the cave. "No telling when the next big cave-in will hit."

Dieter got quiet, but his lips were a straight line.

Chunks of the ceiling covered most of the floor, making footing tricky. The biggest rockslide buildup closed the entryway to the dual cavern. The shared wall between caverns was enough of a jumbled mess that it stretched almost to the outside wall.

Something bugged me about the mess we'd fallen into, but I couldn't figure out what. I fingered the key around my neck and thought of G. Why hadn't he warned us about this?

"We'll have to hike by the outer wall of the tunnel." I slipped on my backpack, removed Lightning's leash, and took the lead. "There are less rocks than on the right-side of this cave, but still enough junk on the floor that one wrong step could send us to the same fate as the pig."

A hush fell over the group. We skirted the pit.

Chapter 20
~ Falling

Crazy rocks." Hans stumbled. New dust particles drifted into the air.

"Pete," I said. "You and Dieter go ahead. I'll stick next to Hans. And stay next to the walls."

We'd covered two-thirds of the cave, moving slow, but safe.

"Dieter Klein, quit pushing me." Pete's stiff face looked like stone. "I'm not stupid enough to rush." He resumed testing the ground to his front, searching for creases, gaps, or lines in the surface.

"But you overdo it," Dieter said. "Watch." He stepped two feet to Pete's right, strolling past him on clearer floor, closer to the center of our cavern.

I straightened up and leaned toward the wall. "We do this together. You saw the gutted pig. Pretty nasty."

"Bloody nasty, the Brits would say." Dieter strolled another foot away from the wall. "But we are near the end of the cave-in. In this I'm no *expert*, but why would another trap come?"

I snagged Pete's shoulder and held him in place. Seconds later I passed him, closing in on Dieter. When I reached him, I latched onto a stone projection with one hand and clenched a handful of his shirt in the other, drawing him toward me.

"That pig pit's less than a foot from the wall," I said. "If there's another pit with skewers, you'll be dead."

"This I don't agree." He twisted his shirt out of my grasp. "Do nothing to stop me." With a shove, he hopped sideways, planting two feet on the surface.

The floor under him vanished as two drop-down panels activated. A five-foot square hole gaped below him. Before he could disappear, I snagged his shirt collar. His hands locked on my arm, causing his upper body to rotate. His shirt bunched up, closing his airway. He grunted and struggled to breathe.

The sudden strain set my muscles on fire.

His eyes bulged. One of his arms clawed at the shirt that was strangling him. He yanked a sliver of the shirt from my grasp.

"Stop moving," I said. I called to the others for help.

Pete leaped alongside me, but without an anchor, his single option was to pull my body toward the wall, relieving part of the tension in my left hand.

"Save him, Gabe," Izabella said.

"Hans." *I'm losing the battle.*

Hans sank to his knees and extended his arm.

Dieter's hand touched the side of the ledge. His thick fingers scrambled to find a grip. He found a hold.

The pressure on my arms eased a bit, but then a portion of the rock in Deiter's hand broke away. He rotated like a doll hanging on a string, causing a searing pain to travel from my arms to my chest. Pieces of his shirt slipped away. *Tighten fingers. Hold.*

"Hang on." Izabella began to cry.

I shut my eyes. *Focus, you can't let go. You can't.*

The shirt tore away. I slammed into the wall like a bowstring released from its firing position.

Dieter plummeted.

Chapter 21
~ The Sailor Song

A scream cut through my daze.

"The leg," Deiter said. "I broke the leg."

"Hang on," I said. "We're coming for you."

Izabella faced the cave wall, tiny fists white at the knuckles.

Hans backed away from the hole, stood, and patted Izabella on the shoulder.

Pete got to his knees and peered into the pit. He wobbled a bit.

Exhausted from holding Dieter, I clung to the stone projection, using both hands.

"I can't see anything," Pete said. "It's too far down."

Releasing first one, then the other hand, I massaged the muscles in my arms, forcing blood into the strained areas. After a few seconds, I leaned out over the pit, but couldn't see much.

"Back up a little, I need some room." I retraced a few steps, then lay on the ground. "Pete and Hans, hold my legs. I need to see." I edged forward.

Dieter sat against a dark grey wall, grasping his leg. Between his knee and ankle was a twist, an odd angle. White bone stuck out the front. A small puddle of red gathered on the floor.

"Anything else broken?" I said.

"Get me out." Dieter shifted his position, groaning.

"We will. Might be half-an-hour, but we'll lift you out." I crept in reverse until I could stand. "We have to get the ropes out and belay them properly."

Without warning, the drop-down panels closed the opening, cutting us off from Dieter.

Muffled shouting under the plate transformed to a loud cry. Followed by silence.

"Nothing we can doing now," Hans said.

I didn't want to leave, but Hans had stated the obvious. I tapped Pete's shoulder. In two minutes we arrived at the end of the cave-in.

Alex and his group were waiting.

I stood in the corner, facing Alex, but looking at the floor. His hands rested on my shoulders. We kept our voices low on purpose. The rest of the gang worked on each other with first aid kits to clean the scrapes and cuts from the cave-in.

"I'm responsible," I said. "And I warned him."

"Gabe, you can't make people do what they don't want to."

"I told him why it was dangerous." I wiped the wetness from around my eyes. "I should have tackled him."

"Well, shake it off." Alex glanced at the group huddled out of earshot. "We have to move on. The gang is depending on us. We can't let them down." Alex patted me on the shoulder.

"But I don't feel like leading now. I lost one person. I might lose someone else." I plopped onto a pile of rocks. I wiped my nose.

"You did everything you could. Besides, we had no warning." Alex took a seat on the ground beside me, next to Thunder and our backpacks.

"We did have a warning." I wiggled one of Lightning's ears. "We had a song from G to memorize. And we got a key to use. Remember?" I lifted the key on its lanyard and traced the surface of the dips and peaks with my finger. It felt soft and slippery, like the salt walls. I held it in the light again to see the golden hues.

"That's right." Alex scratched his head. "And the poem G sent talked about walls of white, a maze, and an island to start our journey toward the treasure. I wonder if the walls of white are salt walls?"

"Maybe. This Path of Death could be the maze."

"But how did that song go? Do you remember?" Alex settled into Thunder, arm on his back. "The first verse had words about a cave-in, right? 'Way, Hey, blow the man down.'"

That's right. I sat forward. "Yes, the sailor's tune."

"How'd it go?" Alex tossed a pebble across the tunnel.

"Let me try." I hummed the tune. "'…roof crashes down …la, la, you can't be found.'"

"'Way, Hey, Blow the man down.'" We both sang the most familiar line.

"What's next," I said.

"'Stick to the right…na, na, avoid nasty sights,'" Alex sang.

"'Way, Hey, blow the man down.'" We sang again.

Jenna stepped next to Alex. "We lost one of our friends and you guys are singing?" She folded her arms and tapped her foot, waiting for an explanation.

"We're trying to remember a song G sent us that might help us out,' Alex said. "It's like a roadmap made of words."

We sang first verse, the best we could remember it.

The others gathered around.

"I think the roof crashes down is the cave-in," Pete said.

"Yeah, we can't be found now, can we?" Erik said.

"Yes. And if we had stayed to the right in the tunnel…" Izabella said.

"We wouldn't have seen the dead pig or Dieter breaking his leg." I shook my head. "We need to remember the rest of that song."

"At least the next verse before we go any further." Alex went to his backpack. "Here." He tossed me a pad and pen from a plastic bag.

After thirty minutes of racking our brains, Alex and I recalled a couple of lines we thought were close, but we were still missing a few words.

> Ten paces ahead, *blank* if you like your head.
> Way, Hey, blow the man down.
> Then *blank* quite a lot, so *blank* don't get too hot.
> Way, Hey, blow the man down.

"I guess we should start to know this part." Izabella moved a long black strand of hair behind her left ear. "Without the missing words, how will we know already what to do? And how many more verses are there to this songs? It hurts me if someone could get killed."

"Four verses. That's all." I stood. "When we get through this verse, we'll figure out the next one." *At least, I hope we will.*

Chapter 22
– Cut in Two

"Ten paces from what?" Pete rubbed his forehead.

I spread my hands. "Maybe there will be a line in the floor. Maybe it means ten steps from the traps. We'll figure it out. Don't worry."

"But we've walked at least ten minutes." Pete drew closer. "I don't want a surprise."

"It'll be a specific point—maybe this wall or some sign." Erik was behind us. "Once we are getting to it, we take ten paces."

"Gabe, come here and look at this," Alex said.

I hurried around Hans, who smelled funky, and Jenna, whose hair fell in a tangled mess.

Thunder and Lightning sniffed the ground in front of Alex. Lightning whined between sniffs. He was onto a clue.

A narrow stream crossed the path. I knelt and touched the water. *Warm.* "This feels like it's heated," I said. "Not sure what that means. And we'll have to get closer to check out the area where the floor is divided ahead, like huge paving stones. Weird."

"We should be careful," Jenna said. "Who's going to lead?"

I discussed the question with Alex and noticed the rag-tag group behind him. Everyone sported bandages and patches, looking tired from our cave-in experience. And they didn't look any better in the gloomy shadows that filled the tunnel. The lights were less frequent here.

"Erik seems to be in the best shape, and there's Hans." I pointed at each, but Alex knocked my hand away.

"It's you or me." He nodded, muscles tight across his cheeks. "We're the reason for this fiasco."

"I'll lead." I jabbed an elbow in his ribs, grabbed Lightning, and walked back to Pete.

"Did you think of any possible answers for the song's missing words?" I said to Pete as we walked forward. I let Lightning lick my unbruised cheek.

"Let's try this one out," he said. "'*Ten paces ahead, shout if you like your head.*'" His lips parted in a smile. "Well?"

I rubbed my nose. "I'm thinking 'run' or 'jump' would work better."

We stopped at the stream.

"If it's ten paces from here, then you won't need this, will you?" He took my backpack and dropped it near the stream.

"That's better." I stood and stretched.

"Why this is the place?" Hans approached the stream, interrupting my preparations.

"Because our dogs act like it," Alex said. "Look at them. They're all jumpy and nervous."

Hans tilted his head to follow the dogs' activities.

"I am not seeing them doing anything different," he said.

"That's because you haven't lived with them." I squatted to pat Lightning's head. "We know our dog's personalities inside and out. And we've trained together for police work."

"Well, do it," Hans said. "Stop this talking."

Everyone in the group watched me.

Guess I'm as ready as I'll ever be. I turned, took a long stride over the creek, and counted.

At the count of nine, I had reached the break in the floor. Step ten would take me onto a square of rock, about the size of a flattened cardboard moving box. There were three of these slabs to cross.

"Come on, Gabe," Alex said. "Keep moving."

With increasing pressure, my toes rested on the rock, muscles tight in case something unexpected happened. I wanted to be ready to leap back to safety.

"Chicken," Hans said. "Is this right?"

I withdrew my foot and spun around.

"Why should I listen to you? You almost drowned us in the skull room."

Lightning sniffed around and walked onto the rock. No magic. No fireworks.

Okay, guess I'll have to take that gamble.

I turned back to the three squares, breathed deep, and stepped onto the rock with both feet.

A light hum tickled my ears, like a mosquito buzzing.

Lightning padded to the front of the slab.

"Stay with me." I bent down on one knee, stretching out to nab my inquisitive friend.

Swoosh.

"Gabe, don't move." Urgency filled Alex's voice.

I tensed up, raising my head to ask why.

Chapter 23
~ Hot Water

"Duck," Izabella said.

I dropped to the ground, cheek banging on the stone as I pressed myself into it.

Swoosh. A light breeze brushed over me.

"What's happening?" I said from the prone position.

"Gabe, without rising up too high, crawl onto the normal tunnel floor beyond the three separate rocks." Alex's steady tone seemed calm, but something still told me I was in danger.

"Okay," I said. "Lightning, here we go." I prodded the fuzzball until he got the message. I pushed up partway, dragging my knees under my gut.

"Lower," Alex said.

I extended my arms forward to keep shoulders and tail low, but moveable. I crawled over the two remaining floor stones, hearing two more swooshes over my head. "Can I stand now?"

"Go a little further...to be sure," Jenna said.

I wiggled ahead several body lengths onto the normal tunnel pathway.

"Stand and look this way," Jenna said. "What do you see?"

"Not much." I wandered toward the flagstones.

"Don't get too close." Alex's right hand shot out to signal me.

"I've got this." I leaned forward to focus better, then sank to my knees. Somehow, I had avoided huge blades that swept over each flagstone. And within each trench below the blades locations, I saw a mixture that made me shudder. "The trenches are full of bone fragments."

The group moved closer, but stopped several feet before the first flagstone.

"Must be pressure-plate activated, from under this rocks." Erik got on his knees. "When you apply pressure, blades sweep across and cut you down."

"Pretty nasty." Pete nodded.

Everyone came across, staying low. Each one activated the sword blades when they crossed, but they knew how to avoid them. The full weight of a person on the stone triggered the light hum and blades. Alex grabbed Thunder's collar to keep his head low during their crawl.

"I bet one of the missing words from the song is 'duck,'" I said when the last person finished. "That fits the first line."

Ten paces ahead, duck if you like your head

"A key word." Pete handed me my backpack. "Are the other words *that* important?"

"We find out at next death challenge." Erik strolled on, whistling the now familiar tune.

"Yes? You have figured out the missing words of the songs for the next challenge?" Izabella touched me. We were sitting next to each other. "I was scared for you at the last spot. You…" She swallowed hard. Tried again. "That blade, she almost kills you."

"I know." I tucked my knees in, chin resting on them. "But I made it." A short silence settled before I spoke again.

"The next part is hard." I sang the words in a quiet way. "'Then *blank* quite a lot, so *blank* don't get too hot.'"

In the gloom, Jonathan's face took shape next to Izabella's frown. "Alex says it's time to move on."

Alex glanced at the three of us. Without a word, he checked that we were behind Hans.

I gave him a thumbs-up. *Guard duty, again.*

Then he led us into the tunnel, which had changed colors to an orange-red mixed with dull white rock in the walls, floor, and ceiling. Gold and green veins exploded throughout walls. We marched under a small archway, down steps cut into the rock, and onto a steeper descent.

"The air's a little misty here." I waved my hand in front of my face.

"That's not mist, it is steam," Franco said. "And did you notice the heat?"

"Yes, I did." Jenna loosened her collar.

At the next light on the wall, steam rose from cracks in the floor.

"We're walking to the center of the earth." I smiled. "Soon we'll hit the lava flows."

"There is no volcanic activity around here," Franco said. "No sulfur smell."

"Then why all the steam?" I wiped my brow.

"Hey, look at this," Alex said from the tunnel in front of me.

We arrived in a new cavern, about three cars wide and six cars long. Cutting us off from the other side, a steaming brook flowed out of one wall into the opposite wall.

Hans knelt at the edge and lowered his palm over the water. "Too hot to touch." He stood. "We cannot cross it either—unless jumping ten meters."

"Mr. Positive, aren't you." Alex wrinkled his nose at Hans. "We'll figure out a way."

Mounted lights stretched out across the right wall about a car length apart. Their dim yellow glow cast a haunting light.

"We're gonna need headlamps the further down we go," I said.

"Ohh," Izabella whispered. "This stream floor is looking like an artist has painted it, like the Yellowstone Park geysers of different colors. I love the deep greens, golden yellows, dark blues, and reds." She turned toward Alex, eyes wide. "This spot has at least twenty feet deep."

"And those are stepping stones." Jenna motioned to the right.

The gang crowded together to see. Seven tiny rock towers poked a foot above the water.

"Well, if they're that far above the water, we can hop from one rock to the other." I jumped right and left to demonstrate.

"If the tops aren't slippery," Alex said. "And the steam won't help."

"I can't jump like that," Jonathan said. "I'm not that coordinated."

"Same for me," Franco said.

So much for that idea.

"How does the song go?" Jenna said.

"'Then *blank* quite a lot, so *blank* don't get too hot. Way, Hey, blow the man down,'" I sang.

"Maybe the song has the meaning you have to jump a lot to get over the rocks to the other side," Franco said.

"But those rocks aren't hot, are they?" Pete said.

"Look, I can do it," I said. "Take the backpack." I stuffed it into Pete's arms and prepared to take my first step. Each landing area on the rocks got smaller and less flat, making the crossing tricky. The first one was about two-feet wide and the last one was one-foot wide. Different distances separated each of them. And the ones in the middle were close to the wall.

"You went first last time," Alex said. "It's my turn."

"I'm lighter than you," I said. "Besides, I did better at jumping in our homeschool track meets."

"He's right," Jenna said. "He's the better choice."

Alex sighed. "You'll need to rope up. If you slip a little, we can try to steady you. If you fall in, you'll be fried."

"Yeah." I looked into his eyes, then broke contact. "I know."

Alex tied rope from his backpack around my waist. He yanked on the knots to ensure they held.

The first landing spot was four feet away, the longest distance between rocks. I prepared for a short run before the jump.

"Don't overshoot," Jonathan said.

"No worries, old chap," I said with a British accent.

Thunder and Lightning sat next to Pete and Jenna, tongues hanging out. Their heads swiveled, following my every move.

I jumped with a high arc, sailing through the air and leaning back to keep from falling forward when I landed. *Success.* Sticky black speckles covered the rock, like asphalt. The second rock took little more than a long step. *Easy.* But my left foot slipped and I rocked, arms gyrating in the air before regaining balance. Fewer speckles covered this rock. I glanced over my shoulder and tugged the rope out of the water.

The dogs were on their feet, barking.

"Gabe." Izabella approached the edge of the stream. "Be slow. Watch out the next step. The water's too hot if you miss."

I shuffled around. "Get Lightning away from the stream and quiet the dogs. I need to concentrate. I'll be safe." I spoke with more confidence than I felt. "And Alex, keep the line a little tighter to keep it dry." I studied the landing spot for the third rock to the right, nearly the size of a baseball home plate. Eyes closed, I cleared my mind. My eyelids flicked up. I leaped.

The dogs erupted.

As my feet hit the step, I swung forward. Too far.

"Stop me," I yelled. I bent forward, chest over the water, arms stretched out.

Idiot!

Chapter 24
~ The Human Pyramid

I closed my eyes for the inevitable searing pain. A stiff tug tightened the safety rope, keeping me upright. I flopped forward like a stuffed doll. Crouching, I regained my balance. Then, like a gymnast standing after an incredible performance, I raised my hands in victory.

"Are you alright?" Alex said. "Do you need to retrace your steps?"

Sweat trickled into my eyes. I rubbed it away but more appeared. The wet heat rising from the water soaked my clothes. "Thanks. That worked. Maybe…" I looked at the larger rocks going back and the smaller steps I still had left to cross, stomach churning. "Maybe…"

Rumble.

The stream bubbled and the rock projection I stood on trembled.

The dogs barked, but not at me. They seemed to sense that something was wrong.

The water level in the stream dropped a foot, revealing a pathway near the opposite cavern wall. The steam pouring out of several vents near the floor of the cavern ceased.

"We can cross there." Hans pointed.

"Not unless you do it now," I said. "This could be like a geyser and change any minute."

"I'm not moving," Alex said. "Gabe's tied to me."

"I will trying the other way." Hans hustled to the new rock-ridge path

"Don't rush or you'll slip," Jenna said. "That path is still wet. Is it wide enough?"

Hans nodded and took more deliberate steps. The loose surface crumbled a bit as he inched along at a snail's pace. Arms level on each side, Hans looked like a tightrope walker.

At the third step, the rumble sounded again.

The water level began to rise.

"Hans, get back here now," Pete said.

Hans lost his balance briefly, waving his arms in the air. His first step to retreat landed on dry ground, but his second splashed a thin sheet of scalding water into the air. His next stride landed him in steaming liquid that covered the tips of his shoes. He screamed and flung himself on the stream's bank, rolling on his side. He groaned and reached for his feet.

Everyone ran to help him, except Alex, who signaled Thunder to stay, and Izabella, who held Lightning tight.

I acted fast, jumping to the fourth stepping stone as the water rose past its original level. The fifth spot, not quite the size of first base, poked out of the water three-and-a-half feet away. I gulped. Swinging my arms to build up momentum, I crouched and sprang like a coiled snake.

"Gabe, straighten up." Alex kept the tension on the rope.

Arms flailing like a windmill, my toes dug into the rock's edge. I stretched sideways over the gap between the rock and the wall, grasping an outcropping, but unable to stand upright.

"Don't panic." Jenna said over Hans' moans.

Concentrate. You trained for this. I ignored my aching back and quivering arms. My mind flicked into memories of my oriental martial arts instructor when I was ten years old. During an exercise that had put me in a similar position, he had coached me how to escape.

"Move your feet away from the wall," he had said. "Half steps."

I remembered putting my training to use, achieving a thirty-degree angle to the wall.

"Now focus on relaxing one side of your body at a time," he had instructed. "Work your way up the right side, loosening the muscles of your ankle, the calf, then your knee."

"Gabe, are you listening?" Alex said.

His question jolted me into the present. The water, inches from touching the toes of my shoes, rose fast. I stole quick glances at Alex when I shifted my weight from hand to hand.

"I'm changing places to get a better angle," Alex said. "You'll feel the rope move around your waist till I'm right behind you. Don't zone out. Stay with me."

"Wait." Franco drew a picture in the air. "If you tug on him now, your rope is too low and he'll fall in the water. But if the rope is higher than him, we could lift him up toward us."

My aching arm and back muscles screamed for attention, but I kept my sense of humor. "Take your time, I've got all day."

"You're sagging," Pete said.

I willed myself into a straighter position. The relief lasted mere seconds.

"We can't raise the rope to the roof, this is too high. But we can build a human pyramid to help." Izabella gathered the gang together and explained her idea.

"Hey," I said. "The pain is killing me." Changing hands to relieve the strain, I snatched a glance to see what was happening.

"Hans, stop groaning and get over here," Pete said.

Pete and Jonathan, joined by a limping Hans, got on their hands and knees behind Alex. Jenna and Izabella crawled onto the backs of the boys. Alex, without creating slack in the rope, moved in reverse, detouring around the group. He clambered onto the kneeling girls, holding the rope taut, but staying balanced.

"Brace yourselves," Alex said. "I'm going to pull." Alex steadied himself on his knees and adjusted his hands on the rope.

The pressure eased. Distance widened between the wall and me. In a moment, the rope held me suspended at an angle, but I couldn't balance yet. Water began to seep into my running shoes. "My toes are burning."

"I'm gonna yank hard," Alex said.

"Do it. Now." Fiery pain shot up my legs, but the extra tug pulled me upright. The rope went slack causing me to twist. I glanced at the group to discover that the pyramid had collapsed.

Izabella rolled to her knees. Her right hand traced the sign of the cross on her chest.

"Gabe, jump," Pete said.

In spite of pain and fear, calmness came over me. *Relax. Trust.* I judged the gap, leaped, and cleared it, bouncing off one rock to the next. And I landed in an inch of boiling water. Agony exploded in me. I sprang to the bank and collapsed, yelling and tearing at my shoelaces.

I heard shouting, but couldn't make out the words. I ripped off my shoes and tossed them, rocking on the ground. Tears streamed down my face.

Minutes passed. More voices.

I ran my hands over my bright red feet and toes. I winced, pressing and prodding. Blisters began to rise on the tops of my feet—bubbles of sensitivity. I wiped the tears from my eyes and answered the group's questions. "I'm okay, but this hurts like the dickens."

Pete and the rest of the gang reassembled on the far side. They brushed the dust and dirt off their clothes. Izabella still knelt with her head bowed.

"And how the rest of us to getting over there?" Erik said. "We can't stay here."

I spotted a six-inch ledge on the cave wall near me, running knee-high partway to the side I had left. The water had stopped rising, staying within the banks of the creek.

"Look, there's a ledge on the wall where I crossed." I pointed. "If we run a rope over the brackets that are holding the lights in place, the person crossing could hang onto it for safety."

"I see them." Alex moved to the wall. "There's no ledge on this side, but there are toeholds that look solid. If the lights are bolted in, the rope could support a person's weight."

A light swayed on its wall fixture above the middle of the creek, about seven feet above the water. A black metal base with a metal arm thrusting up supported a lantern.

Gritting my teeth from pain, I untied the rope on my waist, gathered a little slack, and tossed it over the metal arm of the lamp. Pete swung the rope over a second light on his end. I copied him and tied the rope around me. Alex did the same with the rope on his side.

"Don't forget Lightning," I said to Pete.

Pete grabbed my backpack and stuffed Lightning into the bag to make it easier to cross. He took his time, wobbling every now and then. The others began to follow.

"Hans, your turn," I said.

"My feet are sore." He sat and massaged them.

"Mine are too," I said. "You don't have a choice. We all have to cross."

"Get up." Alex hovered over Hans. "Or are you a chicken now?"

"I can doing this better than anyone." Hans worked his shoes on and hobbled to the wall. He wedged a shoe tip in the first toehold, grabbed the rope, and steadied himself. "See? Pretty easy." But, few toeholds later, his lead foot slipped. He clutched at the safety line. "Help."

The rope tightened in spasms, dragging Alex and me toward the creek.

"Pete, Erik, Franco." I tensed against the uneven pulses. "Give us a hand."

They scrambled to grab and tighten the line. With all our weight, the rope straightened.

"I'm losing my grip." The pitch of Hans' tone was higher. Words spilled out like a flood. "I'm not wanting to boil in the water, to die this way, I…"

"Shut up," Alex said. "And quit tugging or you'll haul Gabe and Pete in the water with you." Alex nodded at Jenna. "Tell him where to put his feet."

Jenna guided Hans from one toehold to the next. In minutes, he completed the crossing.

Alex relaxed and approached Jenna. "Can you make it over?"

"After that?" She sat. "Give me a few minutes."

"Izabella?" Alex looked her in the eyes. She gave a slight nod and crossed herself.

"Jenna," Alex said. "Maybe it will help if you guide Izabella."

Without a word, Jenna rose, hugged Izabella, and walked her to the beginning.

Izabella bit her lower lip.

"Let's keep moving," Jonathan said. He'd been hanging in the background. He assisted Izabella in finding the first toehold.

Her foot slipped once, but she didn't panic. She arrived, minus the color in her face.

Jenna shook her head as Alex talked with her. I couldn't hear anything, but Jonathan and Erik joined them. Her shoulders heaved, and she placed her head on Alex's shoulder.

"Anything I can do?" I said.

Alex hushed me.

A few minutes later, Jenna and Jonathan latched onto the rope, Jenna going first.

"Gabe, Pete, Hans," Alex said. "You guys get on the rope. Erik and I will hold this side."

They made a few stops, but not for long. When Jenna was safely across, she focused on those who were left on the opposite bank.

"How is he going to get Thunder over here?" Jenna folded her arms.

"Fireman's carry?" I bent down and rubbed the tops of my bare feet.

Alex gave the end of the rope to Erik, who tied it around his waist.

"Thunder, this isn't going to hurt." Alex bent over to settle Thunder on his shoulders. He balanced him, tying his paws together with a small cord.

Thunder whined and licked his muzzle.

"Shh." Alex patted Thunder, wrapping another rope around the dog and tied the ends to his belt loops. "We're gonna make it, boy."

"Ready?" Alex said.

"On belay," I said.

"On belay," Erik said.

Alex drove his fingers into tiny wall crevices. He forced Thunder forward on his shoulders. He scaled the wall sideways until he could reach the rope. Unable to look straight up, his left hand searched for the rope while clinging to the wall. His arms glistened with sweat.

"Alex, reach higher," Jenna said.

"Erik, slacken the rope to make it sag on your side," I said.

We watched, faces tight.

Alex closed his eyes and clenched his teeth. His fingers touched the rope. With a final effort, he stretched and caught the rope in his hand.

"Easy," I said to Erik. "Don't tighten up until both his hands have the rope and his feet are on the ledge."

A few minutes later, Alex stepped from the ledge and fell to his knees.

Pete rushed to lift Thunder off his shoulders and untie the dog's legs. I followed. He wagged his tail with gusto. He ran to Alex, barked, and rubbed against Alex's leg.

"What about Erik?" Pete said.

"I'll get him." I limped over to put my shoes on.

"Don't." Alex looked at me, massaging his arms. "You're already hurt. I'll help him."

"But you're exhausted," Pete said.

"I need five minutes to recover, then I'll go." After a few moments, Alex stood, stretched, and grabbed the rope. "This time, I'll do it the easy way." He moved onto the ledge and back to the starting side.

I went back to controlling the rope, this time sitting on the ground.

Erik clung to the cord, testing each toehold, but didn't slip or pause. He was quick.

Alex made the final crossing. He didn't have a fixed safety line. Instead, he tied the cord around his waist and climbed toward the light. Clinging to the wall, he gave the signal. "Slack."

I let out a little rope until he could swing it over the black light holder.

Alex bungled his first attempt. His right foot slipped off the rock face and his left toehold crumbled underneath him, causing him to hang by one hand.

"No," Jenna said.

I leaned into the rope, yanking hard.

Alex slammed into the wall, left hand and toes feeling for any grip possible. A few seconds later, he found what he was looking for and he rested.

Jenna didn't take her hand away from her mouth until Alex had cleared the first two lights and tip-toed onto the shelf. When he touched the ground, she rushed over to him and gave him a hug, tears streaking her cheeks.

Thunder barked at Lightning, chasing him around the group while Alex recovered.

I sat on the ground and heaved a sigh of relief, smiling at the rowdy dogs.

"Safe again." Jenna squeezed Alex.

Izabella grabbed the first aid kit and began to patch me up. We punctured blisters to relieve the pressure, sterilizing the needle by putting it into a match's flame. Next she applied antiseptic cream, moleskin, and bandages. Then she took care of everybody else.

Teeth clenched, I eased on my damp shoes.

"I'm glad that's over," Erik said.

"We still have two more verses to go in the song." I gripped Pete's helping hand to stand.

"Does that mean two more obstacles?" Izabella asked.

I took a few steps, slow at first. "I don't think so. Each verse has two challenges. I can't figure out how G knew all this stuff."

"Me either, but he hasn't been wrong yet," Pete said.

"Four more trials?" Hans said. "I'm not making it."

Jenna ignored the bully. "What were the missing words to that verse?"

"Then *jump* quite a lot, so *your feet* don't get too hot," Alex said.

"The last part doesn't rhyme like it should," I said. "I think it's 'Then *jump* quite a lot, so *you* don't get too hot. Way, Hey, blow the man down.'" I wiggled my toes. "At least I didn't get burned too badly."

"Yes," said Franco. "Good job."

"I believe it was God's job," Izabella said. "I prayed hard and He answered."

"This is not right. God is having nothing to do with this." Hans startled me by slinging a rock into the cave wall. "Gabe has the luck."

"Stuff it," I said. "How would you know, anyway?"

"Keep going," Jonathan said, cutting off the argument. "Otherwise, we won't get out."

"Then let's go." Alex walked into the next tunnel.

"What's the next verse in the song?" Jenna fell in beside us.

Neither Alex nor I could remember.

Chapter 25
~ Muddy Mess

Trekking through the mountain, the floor of the cave took a slight downward slant. We had walked a couple of minutes when the first inkling of our next trial came.

"There's water coming out of the side of the wall." Pete's fingers came away wet when he rubbed his hand against it.

"And notice what's on this side of the tunnel." Erik touched the rocky boundary.

The tunnel, the width of a two-lane highway, had a floor with a heavy coating of dust and bare rock. One tunnel wall was different—a dark, dense material that felt like coarse wood. Few wall lanterns lit this passage, creating pools of darkness between bright spots.

"Stop." Alex, who had been leading the group, held out his arm to keep anyone from passing him. "Look at our shoes. We're getting mud on them. That's in the song."

"Yeah." Tapping my lips, I thought hard. "Let's see. 'Next, crawl through the mud, till what flies makes a thud, Way, Hey, blow the man down.'"

Alex hummed the tune, trying out the words.

"Sounds right. We need to crawl through the mud."

"I will *not* crawling," Hans said. "My clothes are dry. They are not getting wet again."

"You're crazy," Pete said. He walked a few feet to dry land and took off his shoes and socks. "I'm going to crawl, but I'm going to keep this stuff dry."

A cool breeze flowed into the cavern where the water flowed into the tunnel. The gang went to where Pete sat. Each of us removed our shoes and socks, tied the shoestrings together with a knot, and hung them around our necks. With one exception. Hans.

"We should have kept the miner's clothes," Jenna said. "This is my favorite pair of jeans." She rolled her jeans over her knees to keep as much of the mud off them as possible.

"Yes? Better to be safe, than sorry," Izabella said.

"Are you ready?" Hans' lips formed a sneer. "You are being scared of a silly song."

"It's not silly, Becher." I stood and crossed my arms. "Every verse has come true for each test on this Path of Death."

"This whole song is only nonsense," Hans said. "Almost anything could be fitting these strange verses. But you are having faith in the mystical G." He made air quotes with his fingers and shook his head. "You make me a pain in the stomach."

"Hans Becher," Izabella said. "That is terrible to say. Why you don't believe G's notes?"

"You are not knowing the man. Have you ever seen him?"

Izabella brushed dirt off her shirt. "Is that a problem? I believe in a lot of peoples I haven't seen. You have heard about Bach? Homer? Moses? You're talking really about trust."

Hans shrugged. "Maybe. But it's not right this receiving notes and packages from an unknown person."

"Maybe he could be an angel," Izabella said. "You see them when they want you to see. Like God." She tugged her left pant leg over her knee, stood up, and ran her fingers through her dark locks. She stared at Hans.

He looked away. "Whatever." Hans walked toward the muddy sludge covering the floor.

"Hans, wait." I leaped ahead and tugged on his arm. "Think. Even though you don't believe in G, let one of us go first to see what happens."

"Okay, but I'm walking, not ruining these clothes."

"If you insist." I turned around. "Who's going first?"

"Me." Franco smoothed out his shirt and pants. "I can crawl in the mud with the best of them." He stepped with confidence into the slippery mud, fine as silt. It covered the entire floor.

Franco slid his fingers into the goop. "Cold." He inched forward on his hands and knees.

Pete and Jenna watched the sides of the tunnel. Alex's eyes locked on the ceiling.

I crouched for action, taking shallow breaths. My heart pounded.

"Halfway there." Franco paused and looked at us.

The salty, dank air reminded me of a muddy beach from a vacation years ago.

"Keep moving," Pete said.

"See what I mean?" Hans shook his head in disgust. "You being chickens." He strode into the mess, splattering mud onto the rocky walls.

"Hans," Jenna said. "Don't do it."

The dogs rushed to the edge of the mud, paws stiffening as they backpedaled to a stop. Thunder barked once and Lightning whined, tilting his head.

Chest stuck out, Hans took several steps before we heard it.

Thud.

"The song," I said. "That's the sound." I scanned the tunnel's sides to find any clue regarding the danger. "It came from behind the walls."

Hans waited.

"Hans, use slow motions," Jenna said. "Did you see anything?"

He glanced to the rear and shook his head, his eyebrows furrowed and lips clenched. He shifted toward Franco, who had paused to watch him. He took another step.

Click.

A puff of air split the quiet.

Hans swore, dropping to his knees.

Chapter 26
~ Hallucinations

"Hans, get lower," Erik said.

I couldn't hear over the dog's racket. "Stop barking." I tapped Thunder on the nose and Pete grabbed Lightning by the collar. Thunder's ears were straight up and his head cocked to one side.

Thud.

Click.

Hans yelled and fell face forward into the mud. Random whistling sounds and thuds echoed in the passage. It quieted for a second or two and another volley erupted, followed by more thuds.

"Franco, keep going," Alex said.

"Get on your elbows," I said. "Stay low."

"Heading right." Alex dove chest first into the mud and crawled toward Hans.

"Going left." I followed his lead. Mud flicked into my face, flowing through my wide-spread fingers. I wiggled through the cold mess, shivering.

Hans was swearing in German when we reached him.

"Enough," I said. "We're going to get you out of here."

He howled.

Alex thumped him on the side.

"We're here," Alex said. "We know you're hurt. Stop yelling.

Hans' vocal outburst quieted to groans and moans.

"He's got a dart in the right thigh," I said. When I touched the shaft, Hans cried out.

"Another dart in the right arm, above the elbow." Alex signaled the others. "You're going to have to crawl to get through this. Erik, we'll need our backpacks."

"I'll take Gabe's backpack," Pete said. "And Lightning."

"Try to keep the backpacks clean," I said. "We can use the bandages inside to patch him up."

"We'll sit them on our bellies and worm through on our backs," Erik said.

"Thunder," Alex said. "Crawl."

His dog plunged into the mud, tail wagging. Lightning escaped Pete's grasp to join his buddy. They both slid and crawled over each other, playing their way to the other side.

Alex and I grabbed Hans by his belt and shoulders to pull him to the other side. He used his left arm and leg to move, but he struggled to move his right leg and arm.

"Erik and Pete, move it," I said. "He's going into shock."

We reached the edge of the mud and dragged Hans by the wall, propping him against a boulder to get his heart higher than the punctures. I examined the wounds. His upper arm had a small shaft, six inches long, sticking out of the skin. The dark color of blood mixed with the brown mud on Hans' shirt at the entry point. His mud-caked pants showed no traces of blood that I could see.

"You're lucky," Alex said. "I don't think either of these darts hit an artery or major vein."

"A mistake. Another bad misss-stake." Hans rolled his head backward. Straining, he brought it forward again. "It'sss bad. Made too many bad…"

"Keep fighting, buddy," I said.

Erik and Pete hurried to bring the backpacks. I told them where to find the medical supplies. Jenna and Izabella arrived as Erik found the first one.

"We can't see anything with his shirt and pants like this." Jenna moved Hans' arm with caution.

"Help me." Beads of sweat formed on his upper lip.

"Quiet. We are here to help you." Izabella wiped his forehead. "Relax."

"S-s-s-sorry." Hans gritted his teeth.

"He's getting loopy," I said. "We need water to clean off the mud and wash out the punctures. Alex, did you bring any antibiotics?"

"I hid them, but we need water to clean his wounds or whatever we do will be useless," Alex said.

"Further down the tunnel I heard a splashing sound," Franco said.

"Great," Alex said. "You and Gabe fill the canteens—they're all empty. We'll use that water to wash out the wounds. Jenna and Izabella can make Hans comfortable while I get the antibiotics."

Franco and I dashed away, sprinting a short distance. Water spilled into a pool where the tunnel opened up.

"Did you see that?" I stopped at water's edge and fell to my hands and knees.

"What?" Franco said.

"That rock over there moved—like there was a mouse or a small animal."

"No time to think about that now." Franco rinsed his hands with the running water, which ran in a diagonal trench through the bedrock of the cave floor. I washed in the pool's elbow-deep water. It widened enough to hold a couple of people. The pool stayed clear because of the constant water flow.

My arms were covered with goose bumps as I dunked them, rinsing them off. We filled the canteens.

Hans was worse by the time we returned. His head listed to one side. He slurred every word. Izabella patted one of his hands.

I nudged Izabella out of the way, and began washing the mud off. "Hans, talk to me."

"Sh-should have listening." He gazed at me before his head drooped.

"Hans, it'll be okay." Alex shifted on his knees to tap his shoulder. "We'll get you medical help."

"No, no." His left arm smashed into Alex's face, sending him to the ground.

I fell on my tail.

"He's hallucinating," Jenna said.

"And he's shaking pretty bad." Alex rubbed his jaw. "We need to pull those darts and sanitize the punctures in his skin."

Hans shrieked toward the ceiling, rising to his feet, then collapsing in a heap.

"Franco, Pete," Alex said. "Grab our backpacks." He jabbed his finger at the pool. "Meet us at the water."

"Hurry," Jenna said. "He's fading."

Seizing the backpacks, the two boys sprinted away.

"Wait," Jenna said, calling out to them. "It's too late."

Chapter 27
~ The Other Cheek

Izabella knelt by Hans.

I shifted around, drawing nearer.

In silence, Izabella made the sign of the cross, lips moving. She finished and slipped away, hand over her mouth. Her shoulders shook.

Pete touched Hans' eyelids, closing them.

Jenna's hands covered her face. She bowed her head and sobbed.

"Alex," I said.

He didn't answer, but stood behind Pete, viewing the still form of the brown-haired, fair-skinned boy.

Thunder and Lightning lay on either side of Hans' legs, forepaws out and heads between their legs. Thunder's low rumbling sounds mixed with Lightning's whimpering noises.

I placed the back of my hand on Hans' forehead. Cold as ice. My skin prickled, hair standing on end.

Alex knelt, head bowed.

"He's gone," I whispered.

"Yeah." Alex stood and walked to Jenna.

She sniffled, her body quivering. She laid her head on Alex's shoulder. His arm supported her.

My eyes stung. I made a beeline to the opposite side of the tunnel, blotting my damp cheeks. I found a rocky perch and sat.

Pete and Erik settled in silence on the ground next to me. Lightning, hair caked with mud, came over and lay near me.

After a few minutes, Erik broke the silence. "How are we to take care of this?"

"I don't know," I said. "There isn't much we can do, except …"

Jenna, Alex, and Izabella wandered into earshot.

"Except what?" Jenna said.

"Except pray," Izabella said. "I prayed for his soul, but we should pray together. I don't pray out loud."

"Neither do I," Pete said.

Jonathan joined the group. His face looked clean, the brown silt washed away.

"I don't pray at all," Jonathan said. "He made the wrong choice, and now he's dead. That's it."

"I don't believe that's true," Alex said. "There is a lot more to life than what we can see."

"I've heard it all before," Jonathan said. "No one's been able to prove it to me."

"If you choose not to see, that's your problem." Alex scratched his chin. "We were raised in a home in which we pray out loud. Gabe, you pray for him."

"Me?" I clenched and unclenched my hands, eyes bouncing from face to face. I stared at Alex. "How can I pray for him? He hated my guts and wanted to prove himself bigger and smarter than me. Not once, but all the time."

Alex gave a little shrug. "You can do it. You're the one who has all the words. Besides, Mom and Dad say you're supposed to forgive people. And he's not going to fight anymore."

I made a chopping motion. "I'm not going to pray if you don't pray."

"Guys." Izabella placed a gentle hand on my shoulder. "Don't fight. Please, say for him a short prayer—together, if you know."

"Well, we know the Lord's Prayer," I said. "We learned it in Sunday school."

"Then say that one," Izabella said.

I sighed. "Okay." My eyes met Alex's.

He nodded.

I shut my eyes. "God, I don't know what to pray. We warned Hans—Oww."

Jenna poked me in the ribs.

I rubbed my side. Everyone glanced away and waited. Most lowered their heads.

"Anyway, we know You're in charge and we're sorry this happened. Our Father, who is in heaven, holy is Your name…" One by one, everyone joined in, praying with me—except Jonathan. When we got to the "forgive us our sins as we forgive others" part, I hesitated, struggling to breathe. *I want to forgive him. But he was mean to us. A traitor. And now he's dead. Lord, help me. I can't do it myself.*

The gang waited.

Finally I could get the words out and kept going. We finished the prayer together.

"…for Yours is the kingdom, the power, and the glory forever. Amen."

I raised my head. Izabella bit her lower lip. Alex and Jenna stood in silence. Pete, Franco and Erik drifted toward the pool. Jonathan, waited down the tunnel, his head resting against the wall.

"What do we do with Hans…I mean his body?" Pete had returned.

"We can't bury him," Alex said. "When we escape, we'll have the police come and get him."

Satisfied, Pete nodded.

"Come on, Lightning." I patted my leg. "Time to go."

Lightning licked my cheek as I carried him. I grabbed my backpack and trudged toward the pool.

"Gabe, wait." Pete tugged my muddy sleeve and we walked in silence for a brief moment. "You tried to tell him. He should've listened to us. He should've followed the song's directions."

I swallowed to remove the lump in my throat.

"He didn't believe..." Pete said. "You know. In G."

"Yeah." I shuffled a little further.

"Gabe?"

"What?"

"We're not done. We still have more of the song to go."

"That's why we have to remember the rest of it." I slowed the pace even further and plowed my fingers through Lightning's mud-matted hair. He squirmed and nuzzled me. "And right now, I don't remember anything." I shook my head, eyes blurry.

"It'll come." Pete patted me. "It'll come."

Chapter 28
~ Bridge to Nowhere

Jonathan slouched near the diagonal channel in the tunnel floor. Seeing Pete and me, he pushed off the wall toward us.

"Is everyone feeling better now?" His tone was neutral.

"Is that a joke?" I said. "If it is, it isn't funny." I unloaded the backpack and set Lightning on the rocky floor.

"Relax." Jonathan ran his hand through his hair. "I meant now that you've said your prayers, maybe you'd feel better. I don't feel like prayer does anything. At least not for me."

"Our parents taught us to talk with God about what's important to us, especially to give Him our problems, tell Him when we're hurting or ask for His direction," I sighed. "You can think whatever you want. It's your business." I glanced around. "Pete, why did everyone stop?"

He went to find out.

"It's sad that Hans didn't listen to you." Jonathan folded his arms, but his face remained unreadable. "You're pretty smart."

"He'd be alive if he had." I arched my back to stretch out. *And if I'd listened to Pete at the Chiemsee Lake Hotel and told Mom and Dad, we wouldn't be here either.* Guilt washed over me for Hans' death and our capture. I rubbed my jaw to distract myself.

The gang approached. Pete trotted, getting to me first. Jonathan faded behind me, leaving Pete and me alone for a moment.

"Jonathan's dangerous." Pete scratched Lightning's head. "He's not wired like us. No feelings and no respect. Be careful."

I nodded. His experiences must be different than mine. *Wouldn't hurt to listen, would it?*

Alex and Jenna arrived, with Thunder, Erik, Franco, and Izabella several paces behind. Jonathan had joined Franco and Erik.

"I'm not moving until we know the next part of the song," Jenna said. She separated herself from Alex to get a cold handful of water to drink and to wash her face.

"Is that why you stopped?" I said.

"Of course." Franco tapped his head. "To avoid danger, we must know the next verse."

"And we need fresh water supplies," Alex said.

Izabella's lips curled into an angelic smile. "And to cleanup. Plus we need to find a place to, you know, do the basics."

Erik snickered.

A little life crept back into the group.

"Right," Pete said. "It's been a while since we visited the bathrooms in the gift shop."

"Maybe there's a 'pink' room for girls and a 'blue' one for boys," Jenna said.

"Let's clean and refill the canteens with water first." Alex motioned for me to get mine. "Then we'll find a side cave to use for a bathroom."

"Yes? We don't have any paper for the toilet." Izabella frowned.

I pointed at our backpacks and grinned.

Izabella patted my arm. "I'm glad you came prepared."

"You never know what can happen on a spelunking trip," I said.

Izabella and Jenna accepted the toilet paper, retraced several steps, and entered a "pink" cave. Seconds later, a screech came from the cave and the girls rushed back into the tunnel.

"There's a rat in there," Jenna said.

I nodded at Franco. "I told you I saw something move that rock."

"Well, don't just sit there." Jenna plucked at Alex's shirt. "Go get rid of it."

Alex went into the cave and made lots of noise.

Jonathan smirked.

"All clear," Alex said. "I scared the little thing to death." He chuckled.

"Thanks." Jenna patted his shoulder on her way into the room.

Izabella followed.

"What about your song?" Erik said. He grabbed the canteens from me and filled them.

"Hmm." Alex scratched his neck after rinsing. "'Bridge' was one of the words."

"That's right." I crouched, selected a sharp stone, and scratched the ground. "'Slipping' was another." I sang out loud, throwing different words and phrases together.

Alex pitched a few suggestions.

Everybody else got involved, adding and subtracting words. While we brainstormed, each of us splashed mud off our bodies and slipped in and out of the cave toilet.

After the bathroom break, I scrawled a few lines on paper and held up my hand. "Listen to this. It's missing a few words, but I don't think they're important."

"Let's sing it, to see if it rhymes," Jenna said.

We gathered around the piece of paper and sang the words together.

Next, crawl through the mud, till what flies makes a thud
Way, Hey, blow the man down.

One at a time, *blank* the *blank* when it chimes
Way, Hey, blow the man down.

Take *blank* to your right, where you'll slide out of sight
Way, Hey, blow the man down.

Look for the clock, use the key when it talks
Way, Hey, blow the man down.

"That'll do," Alex said. "Everyone have enough water and snacks? Bathroom business done?" He made eye contact with each of us, waiting until each person nodded. "Okay. Let's go."

Alex took the lead, with Jenna and Thunder alongside him. His backpack looked fresh and new against his muddy pants and shirt.

Our faces were clean, but none of us washed our clothes in the freezing water.

The tunnel curved to our left. While we walked, I pulled one of the backpack's zipper cords around my waist to fix it, not paying attention to anything else. I smacked into Franco.

"Watch where you're going," he said. He shoved me and rubbed his elbow.

I gave him a half-hearted shove in return. Past Franco, the tunnel's narrow walls widened into a huge, well-lit open space. We could see a stone bridge in front of us. The air was humid. Warm. The scent of rotting wood and wet dirt tickled my nose.

Alex barred us from going ahead.

"We have to be careful. This…"

A flash of orange-gold fur interrupted Alex's speech as Lightning squirted through my legs and dashed ahead.

"Lightning, slow down," I said.

I pushed around Franco and Erik and ducked Alex's outstretched arm.

"Gabe, stop." Alex snagged my backpack's carrying handle. "This is our next challenge."

"Let him go," Jonathan said. "It's not a worry. He's a big boy."

"I'm not going to lose my dog." I wrenched the backpack out of Alex's grip with a jerk of my shoulder and followed Lightning's path.

Thunder growled.

Lightning had raced thirty feet to a big drop off. Nostrils flared, he checked out a crumbling lower level outcrop, forepaws testing the footing and drawing back.

"What do you see, little fella?" I stroked his back, removing dried clumps of dirt from the knotted mess. I dropped my backpack. On my knees, I stretched out on my hands on the lower ledge and eased myself out. A couple of shelves lay below us, with a huge drop beyond. Jagged edges lined the sides of a stream at the bottom of the deep, V-shaped crevasse.

"Don't lean out too far," Pete said. His shoulder touched mine as he joined me. "What is that on the rocks? Turtles?"

I focused on the boulders below.

"Those aren't turtles." Jenna said. "They're rats. I *hate* rats."

Erik hurled a stone into the stream, spraying water and causing the rats to scatter.

"They're coming here," Izabella said.

"You're imagining things," Pete said.

"Yes? Then what am I seeing there?" Izabella lay by my left side and thrust her finger at the wall on our far left, a good forty-five feet below. Five or six rats zigzagged up the hill on a gentle slope at the edges of the cave.

"Those rats are huge," Erik said. "I hear bad stories about these sewer rats in London."

"They make me nervous," Franco said.

"We've got to get away," Jenna said. "I can't stand the thought of them next to me."

"Our only way out is that broken-down bridge." I slid backward, scrambled to my feet and covered the short distance to the arched walkway with rapid paces. Scattered pieces of the bridge crunched under my feet.

Made out of stone steps, the graceful curve rose to twice my height at the highest point. The other side was about eight car lengths away. Wide enough for one person to walk on, the stones would take two strides apiece to cross. I counted ten steps up, a jumpable gap, and ten steps down. Several steps had eroded. Wide stone columns rising from the crevasse floor supported the bridge, two columns for each stone slab.

"Look at that huge clock." Pete pointed. His stared, eyebrows knitting together. "Like a Bavarian cuckoo clock."

A twelve-foot tall German cuckoo clock dangled by a bolt in the ceiling, centered on the highest point of the bridge, but out of reach to the right. Like most cuckoo clocks, a stage below the clock's hands jutted from the body. On the stage little mechanical people dressed in traditional German costumes posed in several positions of work. To one side of the workers, a chime about Alex's height hung suspended on a small chain linked to a metal rod.

"Very unusual," Izabella said.

"Is it working?" Franco asked. "The clock should chime every quarter of an hour, with a full 'cuckoo' on the hour. I haven't heard any chimes yet."

Two giant slabs of rock jammed into an A-frame formed the cavern ceiling. Opposite the clock, level with the bridge hung a wooden turnstile, similar to one that knights used to train their jousting skills for tournaments. At the end of each spoke of the turnstile, a carved fist clenched a different weapon a knight might face in combat. One had a length of chain mail—a thick metal mesh, another had a club, the third held a mace, and the fourth wielded an ax.

"Ridiculous." Erik pointed toward the spokes. "Does your song saying anything about jousting? It's like a history lesson of the Middle Ages."

"Nothing in the song," I said.

"We have to cross that bridge soon," Jenna said. "The rats are halfway up the hill."

"Rats won't bother us." Jonathan shrugged. "They'll scurry into holes and hide."

"But London rats attacked streets kids," Erik said. "Waking them with bite."

"Stop it. You're making Jenna nervous." Alex narrowed his eyes. "Back to business. I'll go first." Alex stepped onto the first bridge stone. The rock grated, dropping a little. The turnstile swung from the wall until it fit between the bridge's two center stones. The spokes of the turnstile whirled in a circle a few feet above the top steps, the weapons in each fist slashing the air. German music played from the clock while the figures on the stage twisted and twirled.

"Those fists won't let you cross that gap," Jenna said.

"Right." Alex jumped off the step and the turnstile returned to the wall. The little people stopped and the music died. "How'd that song go again?"

"One at a time, *blank* the *blank* when it chimes." I said.

"It must means when you are crossing the bridge," Erik said. "The next challenge."

"We can't talk all day," Jenna said. "Those rats are getting closer. Scare them off."

Pete and Franco selected several stones and jogged toward the cliff.

"I'm gonna try to get close to the top of the bridge," I said. I stepped on the first rock, which sank. The spinning fists took up the middle part of the bridge.

"Gabe, watch the mechanical people work," Franco said. "The peasants stack up gold coins, lifting them from one pile to make another pile. They have ten coins to stack."

I balanced myself, passing over broken steps on parts narrower than my shoes. The clock figures and fists kept moving though I had left the first rock. Happy music played. Near the top step, I tossed rocks at the chime to make it ring, but instead heard a dull clank when I hit it.

"The coins are nine high, one left to go on the stack," Pete said.

Distracted by Pete, I didn't see the chain mail as it swept out and caught my left leg, knocking me onto my face. I fell inches from the gap in the middle of the bridge. The turnstile whisked around, fists punching through the air. The chain mail scraped across my body, but couldn't pull me off the stone step.

"Gabe, stay down," Alex said. "And wait. Take your time."

"The tenth coin is stacked," Franco said. "There's a knight with a sword."

I moved down a step and gazed at the action. A felt-covered rod withdrew from the hollow chime. The knight had emerged from doors beneath the clock face. Mounted on a carved white stallion, he advanced toward the chime. In his hand, he held a large broadsword. At the chime, he swung his sword, and a mellow tone floated in the air. The fists slowed to a stop.

The turnstile moved to its original position, opening the way to jump to the other side.

"That's the secret." I stood, brushed my pants off, and turned to make the leap.

But after a slight pause, the turnstile swept into position again, arms sweeping through the air. I dropped to my chest, hands breaking the fall. I inched back. *How do we get past that?* When I was out of range of the whirling dervish, I rose and waved Pete to join me.

"Pete, I need your help." I studied the peasants. The stack of ten coins, minus one, had been moved back to the original position. The workers were now restacking them near the chime. "Hurry." I pumped my hand faster.

After a moment's hesitation, Pete joined me.

"Gabe, the fists are going to stop again," Alex said. "Can you get to the other side?"

I glanced at the three steps I had to cover. "Yeah, I can do it."

"The knight's riding toward the chime. Get ready." Alex held his hand in the air.

I wobbled for a second, hands touching the next step, and I prepared like a sprinter in a track meet getting ready for the starter's gun.

The chime sounded. The fists moved left.

"Now." Alex's hand dropped.

I rushed forward.

The turnstile pulled away and paused.

I jumped.

The turnstile returned, fists slashing the air. The chain mail caught me again before I landed, twisting me like a pretzel stick at the shoulders, feet too far in front of me to land well. My martial arts training took control.

"Gabe, you must reach out for the step," Franco said.

"You can do it," Alex said.

I strained to stop the forward motion. *Must hang on.* My sneakers slid off the rock surface, sending cascades of pebbles below. My chest and head slammed into the rock and my cheek scraped against the surface. Both knees skidded off the edge of the stone step.

"Grab the rock," Erik said.

I scrabbled for a solid hold. My scraped and torn fingers wrapped around the thinner edges of the stepping stone. *God, don't let me die.* My belly rested on the rim of the step, legs and hips hanging into space, all held in place by sweat drenched hands.

My grip failed.

Chapter 29
– Rat Attack

A widening of the step halted my slide, providing a better handhold.

Neck muscles quivering, I clamped down harder.

"Hang on. I'm almost there." Pete crouched a fraction of an inch beyond the reach of the spinning turnstile, peering around its arms to see me. "Don't give up. I'm waiting for the chime to ring." He glanced above me at the mechanical figures. "Three coins to go."

I couldn't talk. I shifted my weight, inching forward while my muscles screamed for relief. One bicep cramped into a knot. I slipped a fraction.

"Two coins."

Pete's head became a blur. *The pain's too much*. I adjusted again. My hands slid a bit more. *No*.

"Gabe, you can make it," Jenna said.

"One coin." Pete said.

Blood and sweat made a sure grip impossible. Gravity tugged at me, arms now fully extended. My belt buckle caught on the rock. The chime rang out. *Hurry, Pete*. A spasm shot through my left arm, causing that hand to lose its hold. My head sank onto the rock and my belt buckle skidded past the lip of the step.

"Oh, no, you don't." Pete's insistence sliced through my exhaustion. "You're not leaving me behind in this mess." Pete's sneakers appeared in front of me. He heaved my dangling legs onto the stone surface and fell on me.

"Uhh." I couldn't breathe.

"Sorry about that," Pete said. The pressure lifted. "I had to avoid the fist with the mace." He crawled to the end of the stone, crouched, and jumped onto the next step.

"Okay, Mr. Macho Man, now that we've made it across the gap without falling, it's time to escape those fists," Pete said. "Push yourself toward me. Hurry."

I shoved away from the turnstile, feeling for the ragged edge of the next stone step.

"Faster." Pete tapped my legs hard.

Without hesitation, I thrust up onto exhausted arms and moved back to make that second step. Hunched over, I swiveled toward Pete. "What's the rush?" I said.

"Rats." Pete pointed at our stranded friends.

Five or six rats darted past the far end of the cavern wall. Several more disappeared into cracks in the wall. They were two shelves below our group's ledge. Jenna, Izabella, Erik, Franco, and Jonathan occupied the stone steps, ready to cross the gap. The girls, Erik, and Franco huddled close to each other. Jonathan balanced alone.

Facing the rats, Alex perched atop a large flat stone near the steps. Thunder and Lightning stood by him, next to his small pile of stones.

On the clock's stage, the workers stacked the coins. The final coin brought out the knight, who struck the chime. A worker in a red shirt and green lederhosen took the top coin, turned and placed it into a slot in the wall. A conveyer belt slid the remaining coins to the original position.

Seven coins piled up. The chime sounded. The turnstile swung away. Music filled the air.

I held out my hand and Jenna leaped across. The steps were too narrow to pass each other. We rushed down two steps to avoid the twirling turnstile's weapons.

"We'll have to switch." We grasped each other's forearms. Like slow motion dancers, we changed positions, stepping between each other's feet to avoid tripping.

"Not bad for no dance lessons," I said.

Jenna balanced on the stone step, arms extended to keep her balance. "You did well, but I prefer your brother." She smiled and with tentative steps, made it to the other side.

I moved to the ninth step.

The workers placed the sixth coin in position. The chime sounded again.

Izabella jumped across. She stumbled a bit when she landed, falling to one side.

I bent forward and caught her under the armpits, breaking her fall, but swaying down a step in reaction. Afraid of losing her, I sank to the rock with her in my arms.

"Thanks." She gave me a quick hug and pushed away to stand. She brushed her hair behind her shoulders, which lifted and dropped in rapid succession.

"Breathing hard?" I got to my feet.

"I'm frightened." She dabbed at her left eye and sniffed. "That's a big drop."

"You've done the hard part. We have to switch positions fast. Erik is next."

I placed one of her hands on my forearm. She let go and wrapped me in a bear hug.

"I would like this easier way," she said.

My arms encircled her and we rotated. She let go, eyes connecting with mine.

"There. That wasn't so bad, yes?"

A look of amusement came and went in her eyes. She teetered over to join Jenna.

"If you're done dancing, you can let me through." Erik, who had jumped the gap right after Izabella lost her footing, flashed his white teeth. He waited on the ninth step, coming down to join me on the eighth step. Grabbing forearms, we switched.

Lightning's head popped out of my backpack that Erik had strapped on.

"Hey, take care of my dog," I said.

A quick yip from Lightning let me know he was fine.

"Next." I returned to the ninth step.

"I cannot do this." Franco's hands flailed for balance.

"Crouch down," I said. "Don't let the fists hit you."

Shaking, Franco got lower, staying centered on the two-foot wide stone.

"Even lower."

Franco got onto his hands and knees.

"That's it. But get ready to jump." I crouched to see past the rotating turnstile.

Five coins. The chime sounded and the turnstile moved out of the gap. I climbed onto the final step and reached across. Franco's hand reached out, but he drew it back.

"Duck," I said. The swirling turnstile returned.

Franco clutched his head between his hands. His sides shook.

"It's okay. Relax a minute. We still have a few more coins. But you've got to act fast."

"Alex, there's a rat behind you," Jenna said, yelling across the chasm.

Thunder bounded toward the rodent, barking. It burrowed into a hole in the cave wall.

Alex threw a few rocks at the pack of rats, but they scattered.

Thunder chased them, then halted and sniffed. He moved toward a crevice, growling.

"Thunder, come here right now," Alex said.

The chime rang as the fourth coin hit the stack. I missed it. The opportunity vanished.

Dummy. Pay attention.

Franco still had his head down. Jonathan towered over his quivering form.

"Franco, we don't have much time." I licked my lips. "When this next chime rings, you have to get over here. I'll catch you. All you have to do is take a little jump."

"I am not good at rock climbing or playing of sports. A teacher told me…"

"What your teacher said doesn't matter. You can do this."

Three coins. The chime sounded and the turnstile swept away.

"Out of the way, wimp." Jonathan smashed Franco into the stone, stepping on his back. "Stay still." Jonathan took his last step on the stone bridge to jump the gap and he piled into me.

I absorbed his forward momentum, stepping backward with one foot. I grabbed his waist to save him from falling. He lurched on impact.

"Let go." Jonathan steadied himself, pushing my hands away. "Quick, I have to get past."

What a jerk. I glared before switching with him in time to duck the whirling fists.

"Thunder, no." Alex's shout caught my attention again.

His dog, a couple of feet from the dark opening in the cave wall, approached it low to the ground. In an instant he was fighting for his life.

A cat, twice a housecat's size, shot out of the cave. Hissing, its claws raked Thunder.

Alex leaped from the stone rock, throwing off his backpack. He found a utility knife in a side pocket. He jammed the knife into his jeans, scooped up several rocks, and raced to help.

The cat leaped, paws slashing, ears flat on its head.

Thunder snarled. He retreated, then attacked the wildcat again. Snapping, teeth bared.

"Alex, look out," Jenna said. "Behind you."

A huge rat, avoiding the cat-dog-fight, skittered close to Alex's leg. Alex shifted his weight and tripped, landing near the raging battle. He fell in a heap, hands breaking his fall.

The cat slunk towards its lair and eyed the new target on the ground. Two kittens popped their heads into sight, but the cat hissed and lashed its tail. The kittens vanished.

"Alex," I said.

The cat charged.

Chapter 30
~ Rescue or Ruin

"Help," Franco said.

His cry jolted me back to my immediate concern. *Focus. Don't panic.* I stared at the clock. The knight prepared to strike the chime. The clock's lively music bothered me, clashing with our life and death struggles. I was running out of options.

Think.

"Franco," I said, "when the chime sounds, stand and grab my arm."

"I might fall." His hands clenched the step.

"I'll steady you. Get ready."

The chime sounded. The turnstile swept away as the second coin topped the stack.

Franco rose to a jittery stance. He extended wobbly arms, working to keep balanced.

"Grab on." I leaned over the edge, stretching to the limit.

Franco made a tentative try, but pulled back.

"Do it now." I raised my voice. "Quick."

Franco's hand touched mine.

"Jump." I clamped onto his forearm and yanked hard.

Franco's clumsy leap got him across the gap, but pulled me toward him.

He stabilized his position while I fell forward toward the gap. I let go of him and launched, landing chest first on the side Franco had vacated. I kept from falling off the step, rotating my legs to swing them out of the gap. The swirling air of the juggernaut fists streamed past my face. I coughed, chest aching. I extended my feet to touch the next step.

"Gabe, I have let you down." Franco's form seemed to hover over the rock.

"Forget it. Get to safety." I stood, facing him.

He pointed. "Only one coin is left. The time is short." His shoulders hunched, eyes darting toward the chasm below.

"Go all the way to the other side. I'll take care of Alex." I pointed behind Franco to the safety of the ledge. "Go on. We'll make it."

Franco's head bobbed. He hesitated and moved toward safety.

Yeah. We'll make it. But how?

The mechanical workers grabbed the final coin. They danced a different pattern than before, parading the coin from one worker to the next. That would give us more time, but we couldn't both get across with Thunder during the absence of the turnstile. *And what's going to happen when there aren't any coins left?*

The German polka music continued to waft through the air. Happy, jolly. But I wasn't. I took a deep breath. *Don't look down.*

Sprinting, I leapt from step to step until I stood ten feet from the cat, breathing in deep gulps. I found two stones. In rapid-fire, I threw them at the cat's head, trying not to hit Alex or Thunder. The cat dodged the rocks with little effort.

Thunder had charged the cat when it attacked Alex, but paid the price. Blood dripped from his muzzle. And the cat had batted him away, but landed opposite its lair.

Alex lay on his side, knife open, blade pointing at the cat. The cat had clawed his arm, leaving his shirt ripped. He acted sluggish.

"Alex, I'm here," I said.

"We've got to take out this cat."

"That's a mother cat defending her babies."

"What?"

"When you fell, I saw them." I approached Alex, but the cat arched its body, hair on end. "Crawl toward me, or slide this way. If I come closer the cat will attack. Quick. We have to cross the bridge."

Thunder stood guard over his master as he squirmed toward me. When Alex got to me, I helped him stand.

I threw a few rocks at the cat. Hissing, it faded toward the den's entrance.

We hurried toward the bridge.

"Alex," I said. "Faster. They're getting ready to place the last coin. Can you make it?"

"Yeah," he said over his shoulder. "Let's get moving."

"You go first." Ruffling Thunder's rich black fur, I pushed him toward Alex, who was already slinging his backpack. "And take your dog. He won't go without you."

Alex nodded. He rubbed his head, jumping half-heartedly onto the stone bridge, and motioned for his pet to follow.

Thunder took a few steps and paused to look at me.

"Let's go, boy," Alex said. "He's coming."

Thunder surged from step to step, his pace increasing as Alex became steadier.

While I watched their progress, I kept my eyes on the cat. It had crept along the wall, tail twitching. I snagged a couple of broken pieces of the bridge stone. Taking careful aim, I fired away and scored one hit. The cat loped away, but now I was ten seconds late.

The worker deposited the last coin and the chime sounded. The whirling fists moved aside. Alex jumped the gap, followed by Thunder.

The juggernaut swung into the middle.

I didn't make it.

Chapter 31
~ Bridge Collapse

Alex peered at me through the turnstile. Thunder barked and the cheery, polka accordion played on.

"Go to Jenna." Alex pushed his dog away.

The barking continued.

"Do it. Go." Alex swatted him on his hindquarters.

"What happens now?" I said.

A loud cuckoo sound poured out of the clock. Ten times the cuckoo chirped. Classical music began to echo in the cave—loud enough to burst eardrums. Orchestral instruments—tympani, other drums, trumpets, and swelling strings filled the space with harmony. After the last cuckoo, the fists moved out of the center of the gap.

Ah, that's more like it. I prepared to jump, then dropped. The swirling fists glided toward me. The juggernaut stopped and lowered itself to a six-inch clearance between the fists and the bridge's top stone step. I slid backward while it lowered the height of the swinging fists. The turnstile advanced on me at a steady, slow pace.

"Alex, think." I crawled in reverse, preparing to run.

"Get ready to jump," he said. "Go a little further."

I hurried away from the menacing fists. I crouched and my muscles tensed.

"Grab this rope and jump to your right," Alex said.

A rope weighted with a C-ring on the end sailed over the turnstile.

I caught it, flicking the excess to the right. The slack went under the spinning machine and the bridge. I tied a slipknot in the rope, re-clamped the C-ring, and inserted my hand through the rope's loop at the end. I pulled most of the slack out of the line, ready for anything.

"Now," Alex said.

"What are you anchored on?" I couldn't see how he tied off. "I'll pull you over."

"On the rock. Don't worry." He crouched on the narrow stone bride. On the far side ledge, most of the gang and our two dogs watched the drama. Pete had moved behind Alex.

I jumped to the rear and to my right, but couldn't make the rope taut enough. As it tightened around my right wrist, my left hand tugged hard to keep most of the weight off the loop of rope. Like a roller coaster racing down the tracks, I swung twenty-five feet straight down. The first column of the top step on the other side loomed in my face. I pulled up my feet to cushion my collision. The column wobbled when I hit. *The bridge must be collapsing.*

"Get me up quick," I said.

Alex lifted me a couple of feet.

The column's swaying caused the supported stone step to twist. The structure made grinding noises and a chunk of the first column toppled to my left.

I felt a tug, and gasped. The falling step had grazed my right ribs, scraping the skin. Fragments crashed into the stone littered landscape below. The rope dropped three more feet and stopped. I remained suspended twenty-five feet above the floor of the crevasse, now swinging near what had been the second top step of the bridge's far side. Alex peeked over the edge.

"What's happening," I said.

"The steps aren't solid," he said. "The one I'm on is moving, too. It's 'cause you're swinging too much. I need to get you higher." He heaved on the rope. "Climb hand over hand."

Pete stuck his head over the edge of the third stone step. "Erik, Franco and Jenna are going to anchor Alex and me while we get you out of this mess."

"Do it quick." I couldn't climb. "My arms are killing me."

"We have to loosen the rope a bit to help," Pete said.

"Don't all stand on the same stone step." Alex waved them away. "The bridge was built for one or two people at a time."

"Hang on," Pete said. "We have to undo the part tied around the stone."

"No, that's our anchor," Alex said.

"We tied another rope to this one and wrapped the end around the others." Pete said. "If this step collapses, we can guide Gabe around the pillars to solid ground."

The rope quivered. The second stone started to shift.

"Get off the step now," I said.

In slow motion, the second stone tilted forward. Alex fell backward, grabbing the rope with both hands. His legs wrapped around the rope, which dropped five feet. The stone step crashed into the first two columns, sheering them off above me. Crashing sounds of rock echoed in the cavern. Dust fell onto my face.

I sputtered for a moment. Blinked my eyes to clear away the itchy grit.

Now Alex dangled above me.

"Pete, go all the way to the ledge," Alex said. "Move one stone at a time. Anchor man goes first, followed by the other two."

"We're getting tired," Pete said.

"You're tired?" I said. "I've been hanging on for ten minutes."

"Gabe, save your strength." Alex climbed toward our friends.

I slid to the end of the rope, arms and hands feeling useless. The noose pinched my right wrist and after a little bit, that hand felt numb. I closed my eyes.

Chapter 32
– Tunnel Trials

Someone grabbed me by the arms and lifted. I flopped against the edge of the ledge. *It's the far side. I made it.*

"Get him all the way up and keep him still for a few minutes," Jenna said.

On top, I rolled onto my back. I opened my eyes, but couldn't focus, so shut them.

"Gabe," Alex said. "Wake up."

"Hey." Hands shook my shoulders.

I cracked my eyelids again. Pete's face seemed upside down above mine. Off to the side, Izabella sat, hand on my chest. Tiny furrows creased her forehead and her eyes were misty.

"I'm okay," I said. "But tired."

Pete and Alex lifted me to a sitting position, leaning against the wall.

I rubbed my right wrist where the rope's noose had left a red imprint. My hand tingled like it had gone to sleep. I couldn't make it do anything.

"That was close," Pete said. "We'd have lost you if Alex hadn't invented an escape."

"At least I'm here." I adjusted my position. "Guess you saved me, bro."

"Forget it," Alex said. "You saved me a couple of times already."

Lightning buried his muzzle in my face. Every few minutes he'd give me a lick.

"Hey, buddy." I stroked his hair. "You're the best." I winced when he touched my ribs.

"Let's gather round and talk about what's next," Alex said.

Erik, Franco, Jenna, Izabella, and Pete stood or sat in a circle around me. Jonathan stood in the shadows a few feet from the group.

"What's the next part of the song?" I tried to use my right hand, but I didn't have control over it. Tingling sapped the strength from my forearm. "Pete, I wrote notes and stuffed them in my right pocket. Can you get them for me?"

Pete retrieved the paper from my pants pocket and read the verse.

Take the *blank* to your right, where you'll slide out of sight.
Way, Hey, blow the man down.

Look for the clock, use the key when it talks.
Way, Hey, blow the man down."

"Two more challenges to go," Alex said.

"Let's do it," Jenna said.

"Can this happen for you, Gabe?" Erik asked.

"Sure. Yeah. I can do it." I braced myself and stood, threading my useless arm through one backpack strap and shouldering it one-handed. I motioned for Lightning to go in front of me.

"I'm going first," Erik said. "You and Alex need a tiny break."

The tunnel walls had a soft glow from the dim lamps on the ceiling. White cables ran between the normal mining lights, spaced about forty feet apart. The tunnel had narrowed from the great hall of the bridge to a space the size of a hallway in a school building. Underfoot was a mixture of coarse rock and pebbles that crunched when you walked on it.

"It has got to be around the next turn." Franco swept his arm in a large arc.

Erik paused, letting Franco catch him.

"The floor, he is slanting more." Izabella stopped to extract a rock out of her shoe.

The floor surface had changed to a silt type of substance, like what we had crawled through when Hans got killed. I bent over and rubbed a little between my fingers.

The music from the great hall faded. Our conversation dropped to normal levels.

"A pipe here sticks out of the wall, and water comes out." Erik stopped, cupped his hands and sipped the fluid. "If this is a spring, it is only salt."

"And another one." Pete pointed it out the rusty metal twenty feet ahead.

We found four more pipes, each trickling water. The silt surrounding our feet became slick. The floor tilted more than a ramp in a skateboard park.

"Hang on to the wall," I said. "It's almost too steep to walk."

"Another corner," Erik said.

The tunnel bent to our left. Erik, still in the lead, eased around the curved wall.

"Instead of a water park, we're having a mud park," he said.

Alex peered around Erik and he motioned to me. "We've found the *blank* in the song. Lava tubes. The missing word is tube. We're supposed to slide down the one to our right."

The tunnel floor made a steep drop in the next forty feet. We stood at the top of a mud-hole slide. The passage ended with two man-sized arches, larger than water park tubes, separated by a rocky middle section about the width of a large tire. A sucking noise came and went.

The dogs stuck their heads between our legs to find the noise. Thunder rumbled.

"I'm thinking this is tricky," Erik said. "Have we a slide to the tube?"

"We should at least check it out." I wedged in closer. "Who's going first?"

"Not you two." Pete peeked around me. "One of us guys."

"Let's regroup and talk it over," Alex said. He pushed the dogs away and motioned for Erik, Pete, and me to move. Alex's left foot slipped on the floor and he went down onto the incline. He rolled to his stomach, trying to stop his momentum.

"I've got you." I extended my right hand, though my wrist still tingled. "Grab on."

Alex's hand surrounded mine, but I had no strength.

"I can't hold on," I said.

He dropped away, braking with his arms. He slid to the left, searching for a hand-hold.

"Go to the middle," Jenna said.

Alex struggled to get control.

"We'll throw you a rope," I said.

Alex angled his slide toward the wall on his left. Once he got there, he used his feet to kick his body to the middle. He ended on his stomach in the center, feet in the left lava tube and head drooping into the right one.

The sucking noise got louder.

Alex pulled himself toward the opening on the right in order to balance on the middle part separating the tubes. "Must be a wind tunnel. I'm being pulled into the hole. I'll...chopped... bits. Can't...long. Hurry."

"What?" I said.

"I can't stay here long."

"Pete, give me a hand." I eased off my backpack.

Pete got onto his knees. He yanked open the main pouch, pulling rope out.

"Something's grabbing..." Alex's foot lashed out. "It's tugging me the wrong way. Gotta get away."

Pete and I dropped the rope to watch.

Gray tentacles wrapped onto Alex's pants. He kicked and beat at the waving tentacles, but lost his balance. He disappeared headfirst into the right tube, legs thrashing.

Chapter 33
~ Tentacle Tragedy

He's gone. I've failed again." I buried my face in my hands. "Hans and Alex are dead because of me."

"Gabe, it's not over," Jenna said.

"You heard him. He may be cut to pieces." I spread my hands.

"If you don't go, I'll go." She crossed her arms.

"It's my turn," Erik said. "How is this slide working?"

I sighed. "We'll lower you on a rope." I picked up the rope we had dropped earlier. "If you find Alex, get him out of that tube. But you have to hang on tight to the line."

"Why do we want to rescue Alex?" Jonathan drifted toward us. "Aren't we supposed to go into the right tunnel anyway?" He raised his eyebrows, glancing at me.

"This I hate to admit, but Jonathan is correct," Izabella said. She shot him a grim, tight-lipped stare. "That's what the song said."

I ran the song's words through my head. *He's right.* "Okay. We all have to go down the right side, but I want everyone to use the rope. That way we can guide you."

"I'm the one." Erik patted my shoulder. "I should have been gone first, anyway."

"We can't use a harness because you have to let go," I said. "But you must hold on tight. Otherwise, you'll go down the wrong side. And who knows what's in that tube."

"It doesn't look pretty." Jenna shook her head. "Looks like a giant squid lives there."

"Here's how you hold on to maintain a good grip." I wrapped the rope around my left wrist once and grabbed it with the left hand. "You do the same for the right." I wanted to use my right hand, but still couldn't use it. "Franco, you try it."

Franco demonstrated with both hands that he had the idea.

"Good. Make sure your strongest hand's on top," I said. "Questions?"

When no one spoke, I nodded at Erik. "You wanted to go first?"

"I'm ready." He held out his hands, used the grip I had shown him, and sat on the floor.

The sucking sound from the tubes kept me alert. I lowered Erik at a steady pace.

"The rope's getting slick," Erik said.

"Try to keep it out of the mud," I said.

"How?"

"Roll on your back. It'll keep the rope taut." I lifted the rope to keep it high and tight.

Erik rotated, hanging a few feet above the two holes, closer to the right side.

A grey tentacle shot out, touching his leg.

"It's got my foot." He thrashed on the end of the line.

I lurched forward, but Pete and Franco stopped me from following him down.

"Don't let go," I said.

Six grey tentacles from the left tube snaked around Erik's waist and legs. Erik tried to climb the line, punching and kicking with savage intensity. The line flexed in a violent jerk.

I fought to hold on, but the tentacles' irresistible strength dragged Erik to the left tube.

The dogs bounced around, barking at Erik's struggles.

"Quiet," I said.

"Get off me." Erik wrestled the monster's coiling feelers, yanking a tentacle off his neck.

"Hold the rope," Jenna said.

Erik's feet disappeared.

"Pull," Izabella said.

"I'm trying," Erik's face contorted, jawbone stiff and twisted. "The pain…"

Chapter 34
– Stolen Goods

Erik's body slid deeper inside the left tube. Only his head and hands remained.

"Fight with all you've got," I said.

A final feeler circled his neck, tightened and gathered him in. His eyes bulged wide. His hand, covered in dark red goo, clutched at the rim. But one finger at a time, his hand went limp, leaving a trail of red as it disappeared. We fell backwards when the rope went slack.

Silence.

Izabella prayed. Jenna's hands covered her face. The rest of us sat stunned.

"What next, leader of the pack?" Jonathan stepped close and sat down by me. "How do we get into the tube on our right without getting eaten by the monster in the left one?"

"I don't know." I shook my head.

A deep belch sounded. Rotten fumes rose from the area of the tubes.

"Yuck. Smells horrible." Jenna squeezed her nostrils shut. She coughed several times.

"I can taste that smell." I spit at the wall. "Reminds me of food rotting in a dumpster."

"Come on," Jonathan said. "You're the idea man. The leader guy. Go ahead. Lead."

"Do you have a good idea?" I stood. "We have to go on. There's no other way out."

"I'd burn that thing with fire," Jonathan said. "Have you got kerosene?"

"What thing?" I said.

"The wiggling tentacles are like a squid." He wiggled his fingers, then an involuntary spasm convulsed his neck and shoulders. "I hate those things. They disgust me."

"Fire might work." Pete said. "Alex told me you carry flares. True?"

"Yeah." I unzipped the bottom pocket of my backpack and pulled out two flares. In an outside pocket, I located the metal cylinder of waterproof matches. "And?"

"You can drop us on the right side of the tunnel, yes?" Izabella said. "Maybe those snakes-like arms, they should not be long enough if we stayed against that wall."

I got on my feet and checked out the tube from the top of the incline. "I've got a plan. We'd have to pound metal staples into the wall to hold a rope in place. That should keep us from sliding too far left." I dug deeper into the backpack. "This is what we have. Five staples."

"And the dogs?" Franco said.

"Let's form a chain on the wall and pass them by their collars," Jenna said.

"Good solution." I handed Alex's backpack to Pete. "You'll have to carry this."

We gathered the rope at the top into a coil. I cut it in two, donned my climbing harness, and wrapped one half of the rope on my arm.

Pete and Franco lowered me several feet at a time. Each strike of the hammer on a staple sent electric shocks pulsing through my right hand, but it felt closer to normal. The soft rock made driving in the staples easier. *Hope these hold.* If we lost a staple, we wouldn't get close enough to the right tube to be safe.

"Pete, lower me a few more feet." I stowed the hammer in my belt loop, holding onto the last staple. A tentacle shot out, slapping against my shoe. I jerked my legs out of reach. "Whoa."

I kept dropping.

"Pete, stop," I said." Lift me back up." Legs raised, I slashed the tentacle using the final staple, ripping its skin, and causing it to twitch. I almost lost the staple.

The gang reversed their direction, and pulled me up the incline several feet.

"Enough," I said. Out of the tentacle's reach, I secured the final staple, looping the end of the stapled rope through my belt with a quick release knot. "Okay. Send the first person down."

Soon, Pete used the other half of the rope coil to allow Jenna to slide next to me.

"Sure you want to be first?" I asked.

"The order doesn't matter. We all have to do it." Jenna braced herself against the wall.

"Go under my rope when I let go." I pulled out a waterproof match and the flare. I struck the match. Its light blazed for an instant and died. The air suction from the lava tubes killed it.

"Jenna, hold this flare." I thrust it into her hands.

I struck the next match, cupping my hands to avoid the suction. A little flame flickered. The smell of burning sulphur filled the air.

"Good," I said. "Light the torch."

Jenna dipped the fuse into the flame. It caught. The flare blazed into a brilliant pink light.

I tucked the matches away and shouted to the guys at the top. "Lower away." I held the rope that I had wrapped twice around my weakened hand and the flaming torch with the left. I maneuvered myself toward the middle section of the tunnel, near the area where the tentacles had captured Erik. The tentacles popped out, but wiggled away from the heat.

"It worked," I said. "Go, go, go."

They each took positions near a staple in the wall, Franco above me and Izabella above him. Jenna slid on her back under the rope and vanished into the tube.

Thunder tried to walk, but slipped to his belly with a splat. Izabella grabbed his collar in an awkward way and swung his heavy body around to slide tail first. The muddy dog barked, trying to get on his feet.

"My wrist," Izabella said. She cried out in pain and let go, the canine cannonball sliding sideways, tail headed toward Franco.

"Franco, grab him," I said above the noise. The barking deafened me in the confined space.

Franco stretched out with his left hand to latch onto the collar. His hand swiped, but missed. "Too muddy."

Thunder's rear slid toward the left tube.

"Grab my shoe." I stabbed my left foot in his direction. "Don't let go."

His sharp teeth closed over my shoe, but not hard enough to break any skin.

The tentacles surged around Thunder's body. His feet kicked and scratched to get away.

I almost dislocated a shoulder to get the flare over the dog's body, but it worked. Again the slimy tentacles drew away.

"Thunder, help me out." I dragged him to the hole. His hind legs dug into the middle section and he launched into the escape tube, dangling from my foot.

"Let go." I shook my foot hard and my shoe came off, sliding out of sight with the dog. I swiveled back into position, thrusting the torch into the tentacles.

Franco, Izabella, and Pete went past. No Jonathan.

"Jonathan," I said. "Hurry. This flare won't last forever."

"I don't want to be near that thing." Jonathan peered down the slope.

I climbed toward the top. "There's no other way out of here. You *have* to do it. Now." I yanked on his right arm, but he shoved me.

"I told you, I hate slimy tentacles."

"This flare is almost out. But we have enough if we go now."

The pink light's intensity dimmed.

"I'm not going anywhere." Jonathan sat.

"Suit yourself." I zipped the open pockets and put on my backpack. "Five minutes or less and this flare is gone." I went to the ropes and gave him one last look.

"Bye." I slid to the last staple.

The tentacles seemed to have grown longer. And the flare sputtered.

A brilliant white light appeared above me, filling the tunnel like daylight. Jonathan lowered himself on the rope attached to the wall.

"Where'd you get that flare?" I said.

"From your backpack," he said. "I took it after Pete stowed it away."

"But that's our last flare," I said.

"Does it matter? I need it now. I'm more important than having an extra flare, right?"

"Don't you look ahead?" I swiped my faltering flare at the exploring arm of the squid, or whatever it was. "We don't know what's next. We might need to signal for help." A tentacle slipped around my leg. I thrust my flare at it, but the flame sputtered and was gone. A slimy feeler encircled my leg. I snagged the staple, higher up the rope, but it gave way. "Jonathan, help."

"It's not coming near me." His hand shaking, he held out the blazing light to ward off the monster.

"Jonathan, we can both make it." I kicked the tentacle with my shoeless foot. "Come closer. It won't get you."

"Not if I can—" Jonathan shouted as the last two staples pulled off the wall and he plunged into the tube on the right.

Chapter 35
~ Underground Pool

As he fell, Jonathan knocked me to the ledge between the tubes. The tentacles coiled around me as the white flare flew into the left tube, leaving me in darkness. *I tried, God. I tried.* As two coils tightened around my midsection, light flashed from an explosion. Flames rushed out of the left tube housing the beast and its tentacles writhed in the heat.

I yanked myself free and fell face first into the pitch-black right tube. Water cascaded on my face and into my nose. I sped down the winding chute, hands covering my face. I crashed into a wall. The jolt caused me to suck in more water. I coughed, gulping for air. The chute bottomed out and rose into a slight incline.

The tube ended, throwing me into a dim space. A fresh breeze brushed my face as I plummeted to a pool below. Seconds later I smashed head-first into warm water. I surfaced under pounding water, took a quick breath, and dove, swimming away from the falls. I counted to estimate the time underwater.

Before I reached twenty, hands behind me clamped on my arms. I attempted to jerk out of their grip, but failed. Someone dragged me out of the water, and I collapsed on a cold, rock-hard floor. I kept my eyes closed to fake near unconsciousness, in case I had been captured.

"Is he dead?" Izabella broke the silence.

"Nah," Pete said. "He fought us when we pulled him in from the water."

A shoe poked me in the ribs. I coughed.

"Hey. Sleepyhead."

Alex?

The toe kept digging. "I can tell you haven't been knocked out."

I twisted sideways, coughed, and looked around. Izabella and Jenna knelt beside me.

"You are safe," Izabella said. A smile lit her face.

"Great work, buddy. Lose something?" Pete lifted me to a sitting position and dangled my missing shoe from his finger.

"We didn't all make it," Alex said. "Erik didn't come out of the other tube. What happened to him?"

"Gabe thought we could lower him onto the right side without protection," Jonathan said. "Like you." He sat cross-legged on the rocky floor, away from the rest of us.

"Don't start, Jonathan." Jenna stood and walked over to Alex. "Erik wanted to go next because he thought we had lost you. Gabe tried to keep him away from the monster in the second hole, but Erik couldn't hold on."

"What did you try to do?" Alex said.

"Let it go." I belched, getting rid of the extra stomach gas from almost drowning. I rolled to my knees and let a couple of the others help me stand.

"It could've happened to any of us." Franco spread his hands. "At least the rest of the gang is here."

Thunder thumped his tail on the ground.

"Who has Lightning?" I swiveled around to see him.

"I don't have him," Alex said. "Jenna?"

"Not me either." Jenna shrugged.

No one knew anything about Lightning. I sloshed into the pool.

"Gabe what are you doing?" Pete asked. "He's not paddling around anywhere."

"He's got to be here." I kicked the water, whirling to glare at my friend. "I can't lose him." I waded toward the waterfall again, calling him. "Lightning, come here, boy. Come on."

The falls originated from the escape tunnel, arcing like liquid poured from the spout of a pitcher, spilling into the wide pool. A dark object floated near the opposite side.

"Gabe, wait," Pete said. He tackled me as I dove in to swim toward it.

"That's gotta be your backpack." Pete reeled me in. "And walking the edge of the pool is faster." He patted my shoulder. "Lightning's okay. You find him in the weirdest places sometimes. I think…"

"Pete, quit trying to cheer me up." I shrugged off his hand, sloshing out of the water to sit on a rock. "Lightning's my best pal." My nose dripped. "We've lost two people, and now this."

"He'll turn up. I know he will." Pete sat by me. "Hold it together. We're not home yet."

I wiped my nose. I didn't respond, but studied the area.

The uneven cliff-face behind the waterfalls looked dark and grim. The few lights on the sides of the pool cast dingy shadows on the huddled forms of the gang. Beyond them, the lights' glow faded into inky darkness.

"What's next?" I said.

"Your backpack, then a bath," Pete said. "After that, we make plans for how we'll break out of here. Come on, let's go." He slapped my knee.

With my legs and arms feeling like lead, I swayed to my feet and trudged behind Pete to get the backpack.

Chapter 36
~ Drowning Isn't for Cowards

I tramped toward my backpack floating in the shallows, Pete keeping pace in silence.

Five feet from the bobbing object, Pete stopped. "Hey, you're backpack's moving."

It jerked left and right. Muffled noises came with each twitch of the bag.

"Lightning?" I said.

"Careful." Pete grabbed my arm. "After messing with that squid and those rats, anything might have crawled into a pocket."

"Take the other side," I said. "Use a rock to smash whatever comes out."

Pete selected a fist-sized rock with jagged edges. He nodded.

I wrenched the backpack onto the rock, breaking the watertight seal on the top pocket and unzipping the opening.

A streak of orange flashed onto my chest. Lightning's sandpaper tongue brushed my chin and neck.

"Hey, fuzzball. How did you sneak inside the backpack?"

I hugged him, held him in the air, and ruffled his ears. "Who cares? You're alive." I laughed a while, then joined the group.

After taking time to pile up rocks and pray for Erik, we washed off in shifts, eating snack foods to reenergize. Jonathan walked off and Franco went to wash his hands. The group continued to talk about our escape from this endless maze of caverns.

Franco rejoined our impromptu planning meeting. "Did you figure out what we will do?"

"Maybe," Alex said. He drew a diagram in the dust on the floor. "We can't tell how big this place is, but we're on a shelf shaped like half of a plate jammed into the wall, with the pool at the plate's center. And our shelf's above water, enough to be a lake. Imagine a ten-meter high diving board, which is more than thirty feet from the surface. That's how high we are."

"And there are lights here, and those lights across the water are along a lower ledge, maybe ten or twelve feet high." I took over the drawing. "Almost straight across from us is a small inlet that cuts into the ledge. The inlet has a wall I can't see behind. And there's land between us and the other place. But from our location we can't see far enough in any direction to tell if this huge cave extends even further."

"That land could be an island." Pete shrugged. "We'll check it out."

"But there is no boat," Franco said. "We must have a boat because I cannot swim."

Jonathan joined us. "You'd learn if someone threw you in. I can't swim either, but I can hang onto a good swimmer."

"You? Throw me in?" Franco smiled and stretched out his chest.

"Think I can't do it?" Jonathan cocked his head.

"Boys, stop." Jenna cut through the chatter. "No fighting."

"I shouldn't bother," Jonathan kept going. "You're afraid to try anything. Like the bridge crossing. A few of us could've been stuck there."

"Jonathan." Izabella darted forward. She tugged at his arm.

Jonathan relaxed and after a second, smiled.

"It's a joke." He pried Izabella's fingers off his arm.

"It didn't look like joking to me." I motioned at the rest of the group. "Nobody else thought it was a joke."

Jonathan's expression didn't change. He drifted toward the rim of the cliff.

"We're not too high above the water," Alex said.

"Thirty feet's high to me." Pete shook his head.

"I jumped off a high dive a couple of times," I said. "It was fun."

"Forget that. We don't know what's under the water. Too dangerous." Alex drew an X on the ground. "We'll lower everyone on a rope here since our shelf drops straight down."

"There's a flat beach by the lower shelf," Jenna said. "I should take the lead. I'm a strong swimmer."

"The island, she looks closer than the beach." Izabella pointed. "You should swim there first, yes? And I'm a great swimmer, too."

I glanced at Alex. "I think Izabella's right."

"Sure." Alex nodded. "I'll lower Jenna first, then Izabella."

While Jenna and Izabella got ready, Alex made a simple seat with a loop in the rope.

I went over to look at the drop. The brim of our platform faded back under the edge enough that whoever went down the rope wouldn't be able to put their feet against anything to steady themselves after a couple of steps. They'd have only the rope. I laid a small towel on the cliff edge to keep the rope from fraying when Alex lowered Jenna. Franco anchored him.

"Because of the wall's angle, after a few steps these will be the only brakes you have." Alex tapped Jenna's karabiners. "Pull up on the rope and they will slow you." He finished telling her what to expect.

Jenna pushed out hard with her feet on the edge, straddling the towel I held in place.

"That's good." Alex kept the tension on the rope. "Controlled descent means you control how fast you lower yourself. Balance the tension on one leg, and move the other foot lower. Adjust after each step and keep doing that until you have cleared the edge."

Jenna moved lower, picking out her footholds with great care.

"I'm going to have to swing." She tilted her face toward me.

I had inched forward, chest extended beyond the rim. I relayed her message to Alex.

"I'm touching the water," Jenna said four minutes later. "You can let loose now."

"She's down." I glanced at the rope. "The drop is twenty feet."

Alex and Franco released the rope tension and peeked over the cliff's edge.

"Hey, what's the tug for?" Alex leaned over the rim.

"I'm going to the island. It's not that far." Jenna wiggled out of the rope, waved, and began her swim.

Alex and I waved at her, but a growing disturbance caught our attention.

"Do not push me," Franco said.

"I'm not pushing," Jonathan said.

Jonathan and Franco faced off against each other close to the platform's rim.

"Look at the water from the edge. It won't kill you." Jonathan motioned toward the rim.

"I do not like getting that near to empty space." Franco stepped back and folded his arms.

Jonathan grabbed Franco and forced him to glance over the edge. "Look." Jonathan aimed Franco's head toward the water. "Nothing to be afraid of."

"I'm falling." Franco's hands clutched Jonathan's shirt for safety. "Let me go."

Franco's foot slipped on the rock and hit Jonathan in the shin. As Jonathan shifted his weight, Franco tried to break free. Both boys fell off the cliff.

Barking, Thunder and Lightning rushed to the spot where the boys had gone over.

Franco and Jonathan hit the water together, separating upon impact. Jonathan came to the surface in seconds. His wild arm motions splashed water everywhere.

"Help. I'm drowning." Jonathan went under.

"Alex, I'm going." I ran to the dogs, stripping off my shoes.

"You find Franco, he's smaller. I'll handle Jonathan." Alex tossed his shoes aside and rushed toward the cliff.

Thunder and Lightning danced at the edge, waiting to go in.

Jenna was halfway to the island when I hit the water, Alex right beside me. The dogs followed us. The water felt good—a bit on the cool side, but it got my heart pumping. I kicked to the surface. Lightning met me with a slurpy welcome. "Thanks, pal." I kept treading water while rotating to search for Franco, glad that my right hand was working like normal again.

Alex swam behind the flustered Jonathan. In a minute, he had his arm locked under Jonathan's chin.

"Lightning, where's Franco? Find Franco." I splashed water at him.

He paddled toward the island and dove. Seconds later he burst onto the surface, yipping.

In two strokes I got to Lightning, took a deep breath, and plunged deep under the surface. I swam in the gloom, able to see shades of dark and light. I spread my hands, grasping, feeling for a body. No luck. I went further down until a hand grabbed my throat.

Chapter 37
– Lights Out

I broke free of Franco's clutching fingers and propelled myself deeper to discover why he hadn't risen to the surface. Plant fronds had wrapped themselves around his left leg. I jerked at the plant, but it didn't budge.

Air. My lungs ached, but I gulped, suppressing the urge to breathe. I explored his foot. Several roots had captured his shoelaces, which had tangled in hopeless confusion when he struggled for freedom.

Franco's free leg slashed in all directions. His arms swept at the water to drag himself upward. It didn't work.

Fending off the kicks, I unwound the root and tugged his leg clear of the mess. Spasms wracked his body.

My chest burned for oxygen. I shot to the surface with Franco in tow.

We broke the surface, and I sucked in air. But Franco went limp.

"Franco, breathe." I rolled him face down, using one hand to keep his face out of the water and the other to pound on his back.

He didn't respond.

Treading water, I stayed behind him, arms supporting him. I made a fist with one hand against his gut, locked on with my other hand, and leaned back, pulling up into his stomach with a modified Heimlich maneuver. It wasn't much pressure, but the best I could do.

Nothing.

I did it again.

Franco's head moved.

Another go.

Fluid spewed out of his mouth. He hacked, coughed, and spit out brownish-junk.

Ugh. It stunk. I changed arm positions to keep his face out of the water.

When Franco could breathe, he grappled behind his head and seized a handful of my hair. He tried to roll me over. We thrashed for control.

"Hey, I'm right here." I wrestled with him. "I've got you."

Franco continued to cough and struggle.

"Kick your legs." I began to drag him. "I'll take you to land."

His legs moved in response. Finally, he calmed down and we gained momentum.

I switched to the rescuer position, cupping Franco's chin in the palm of my hand.

"Help me get you to shore by kicking like you're swimming." I fluttered my feet faster, stroking my free arm with more strength. His leg kicks helped a little.

Beyond Franco's head, I saw Pete throw our backpacks off the cliff and jump in behind them. Izabella dove last.

I focused on my stroke technique.

Franco kicked stronger, allowing us to reach shallow water ten minutes later.

"Franco, can you stand?" I loosened the grip on his chin.

He twisted to make contact with the bottom. Staggering, he latched a hand onto my shoulder. "Thank you." He was hoarse from the experience.

"No problem." I swung an arm around his waist and looped his arm around my neck. We waded onto the beach where I lowered him to the sand.

Pete and Izabella swam, towing the backpacks behind them. They were halfway to the island. I waved at Jenna, Alex, and Jonathan further down the beach. Everyone looked okay.

I turned to say something to Franco and the lights went out.

Chapter 38
~ Trapped In the Current

Where are you?" a girl's voice said.

"Over here," I said. Jenna and Alex also answered.

"I can't tell where you are," Izabella said. "I'm treading water."

"Turn on a flashlight." Pete's words were clear, but faint.

"It's in my backpack," I said. "Alex, do you have one?"

"No," he said.

The darkness seemed colder to me since I was wet. I shivered and rubbed my arms. I couldn't even see my hand in front of my face when my palm touched the tip of my nose.

"Help us." Pete's command floated on the salty air.

"Hang in there, buddy," I said. "Alex?" I faced in his general direction. "Let's have one person call out at a time to avoid confusing anyone."

"Okay," Alex said. "Jenna will call first. You and I can walk out into the shallow water a little to locate them that way."

"Alright." I touched Franco on the shoulder. "You stay here and rest. I'll wade in waist-deep and come straight back. Be ready to guide me by talking to me."

I tensed as I entered the cold water, sliding each foot forward with care. When my right foot couldn't find the bottom, I went under. I shot up to get a breath, located the bottom again, and stood. *Am I oriented in the right direction?* I rotated in a circle as Jenna called out.

Something hit my forearm.

"Hey." I grabbed at the object, ready to battle a water snake.

"Hey, yourself," Izabella said. "Help me out."

"Gotcha." I pulled her toward the shore. "Jenna, Izabella made it here."

"Good," Jenna said. "One more to go. Pete, are you there?"

"Hello?" Pete sounded weaker.

"Pete, you're moving at an angle—toward my right, your left," I said.

"I'm in a current, I think," Pete said.

"Swim harder toward us. Swim toward Jenna's voice." I finished leading Izabella to the sandy beach, taking the backpack from her and setting it on the ground. "I'll take out a headlamp and see if that helps." Moments later, the headlamp's light pierced the darkness.

The first person in the light was Alex. He grinned. I swept the beam of light over Franco and Izabella sitting next to me, and then toward Jenna.

She stood ankle deep, hands by her side, looking in the distance. Behind her in the dim glow, a sandy beach extended into a hilly, rocky center of the island.

"Over here," Pete said. He was over a football field off shore, drifting further to our right.

"Come on, Lightning." I dashed past Franco. When I passed Alex, I tossed him the headlamp. "We'll lose him if the current takes him around the corner of the island."

"Gabe's coming," Alex said, positioning the headlamp on Pete.

I dove, bracing for the frigid impact. Surfacing, I swam with steady strokes. Lightning had latched onto my shirt when I passed him in the water. He worked his way onto my back. I concentrated on strokes and breathing. *Gotta keep moving. Can't lose Pete.* Every ten strokes I checked my progress. I had intentionally swum to my right to intercept Pete while the current pushed him toward me. He had maneuvered himself a bit closer.

At the end of the protection of the island shoreline, the current tugged at me. I reversed direction, swimming into the current for about five strokes, then tread water.

Pete approached me, but still floated several car lengths away.

"Grab this line." Pete threw the end of a rope toward me. It fell way short.

"Good idea, but you need a weight on the end of it," I said.

Need a rock or…yes. "Lightning, football time."

Lightning jumped into the water.

"Pete, you're drifting closer. I'm going to throw Lightning at you. Tie the rope around him and throw him to me."

"He weighs too much," Pete said. "He's over ten pounds."

"Think of him like a shot put." I snagged Lightning. "You did well in sixth grade, right?"

"That was a few years ago," Pete said.

"Try," I said. "He'll swim part of the way." I took a couple of deep breaths and kicked hard with my legs, bringing my chest out of the water. I launched Lightning like a cannon ball.

He landed halfway between Pete and me.

"Swim, Lightning. Show your speed." I splashed water in his direction.

Lightning angled his approach to meet Pete who drifted with the current.

"Catch." Pete threw the rope at Lightning. This time it made the distance and in a couple of seconds, Lightning had it in his mouth. Pete reeled him in.

"There's no time to tie the rope on him," I said. "Throw him back."

Pete had moved past the tip of the island where the current moved faster. Using the backpack as a brace, Pete kicked hard and threw Lightning back at me. Short again.

"Lightning. Come on, boy." I motioned him closer.

Lightning's feet churned, making little bubbles on the surface. It wasn't enough.

I whistled. "I've got faith, Lightning. Do it."

He boosted his furious pace. Still too slow. He was about five feet away.

Without thinking, I swam further into the current and captured Lightning. I made a noose in the rope and draped it over one shoulder, leaving both hands free. When the current sucked me away from the island, I swam at an angle toward shore. I made steady progress.

Alex's light dimmed. There wasn't much time.

I had to rest, but my foot brushed bottom. I redoubled my strokes. Another few feet and I could walk. I staggered ashore, lugging on the rope to bring in Pete. He tried to shoulder Alex's backpack at first, but sank under the surface. He shrugged it off, and bent over, huffing.

"Pete, I'll take the backpack." I splashed toward him, grabbed it, and took his arm. We stumbled onto the beach and collapsed, Lightning tagging along.

A few minutes later, Alex and his dog, Jenna, Franco, and Izabella arrived. Alex handed me the headlamp. I stood, putting it on. But counting noses, I was one short.

"Has anyone seen Jonathan?" I swept the light over the beach, revealing patches of colorless grass and moss near the central hills. Driftwood lay on the beach.

Nobody responded.

"Stick with me," I said. "We need to save the batteries for our other headlamp and flashlights." We scoured part of the area for at least a half an hour, calling his name. He didn't answer. Eventually, we took our search over the hills.

On the opposite side of the island, a channel of rushing water wider than an eighteen-wheeler separated us from low rock shelves that jutted from the cavern wall. The inlet was to our right, and to our left, blackness. An unidentifiable noise rumbled in the background. The channel water flowed toward the dark void on the left.

"I'm tired," Jenna said. "If he were on the island, he would have answered our calls."

"Then where is he?" Franco said. "We need to keep looking until we find him."

"We're exhausted," Alex said. "Jonathan can't swim and he walked away from us. You know how he likes to be alone. He's here somewhere. We'll do a lot better if we get a little shut-eye first, then do a complete walk around the island when we get up."

"But we can't lose another person." Desperation tugged at me. "We have to…"

"No buts," said Alex. "We're done for now. Let's get some sleep." He led the group toward the hills to go to our landing spot on the island.

When I didn't move, he looked at me. "Gabe, drop it. If he wanted to be found, it would have happened by now. We can't see anything in this darkness."

"He is a loner," Pete said.

"It doesn't matter," Jenna said. "If he drowned, we won't find him. If he's hiding, we won't find him. I need sleep. Does anyone have a watch that works?"

Everyone checked. Franco's was the lone survivor. "It is 12:15 a.m."

"It's past everyone's bedtime," Alex massaged his forehead. "Let's go."

"All right," I said and marched over the hill to the other side.

We made ourselves comfortable, huddling together for warmth, and drifted off to sleep. Most of us, anyway.

Have we lost another friend? I tossed a little, trying to get settled in. I couldn't stand the thought of another death because of something Alex and I did, or didn't do. I imagined a horrible scene in which a helpless boy waved and shouted for help as the water drew him into its depths, never to return. A haze overcame my resistance. I sank into darkness with one thought. *Jonathan's dead.*

Chapter 39
~ The Island

I awoke to Alex's snoring. Had to be him. I had listened to that snore my whole life.

Where am I? I sifted through the sand, memories returning. We needed to escape.

"Alex, wake up." I slapped his meaty shoulder.

We slept in absolute darkness. I didn't turn on the headlamp—to save the batteries. When Alex didn't respond right away, I hoped I'd nudged the right person.

"What do you want?" Alex said.

"He wants you to rise and shine." Jonathan said, sounding rested and relaxed. "And get cracking. All you've done is sleep."

"Jonathan?" I said. "Where have you been?"

"Wandering around." Jonathan kicked me in the leg. "Sorry, I ran into someone."

"That was me. But…"

"I'm trying to sleep," Jenna said. "We can ask him where he went later."

"We need to get out of here." I fumbled around to find my headlamp. "What time is it?"

"3:00 a.m.," Franco said. "Go back to sleep."

"I'm too cold to do that," Izabella said. "Sleeping close to each other for warmth was a good idea, but with all of the tossing and turning, I can't sleep. I'm exhausted, and you all smell horrible."

"That bad?" Franco said.

Jenna nodded. "You guys smell like you haven't taken a bath in weeks."

Sand rustled as I found the backpack and put on the headlamp. I flicked it on Jonathan. "Where were you last night?" I folded my arms. "We searched half the island. We yelled and shouted. But you didn't answer." The headlamp started to dim.

"I already told you," Jonathan said. "And I hope you have more batteries."

"This total darkness." Franco stood and stretched. "I do not like it."

I clicked my flashlight on, but it didn't work. I fished around in my backpack and found a few used batteries that provided a weak glow. The headlamp also had another used battery, which gave off a stronger headlamp light than the original. I stored it for later even though the current headlamp light was feeble at best.

Alex checked his backpack for extra batteries, but he had little success—finding just one battery for his headlamp that wasn't fully charged. "We have to conserve power. Gabe, use your headlamp for now, then we'll use mine, and in the end we'll use what's left for emergencies."

The dogs loped in front of the group. We were hunting for anything that would float.

"Here's a broken plank," Jenna said. "A sorry excuse for a boat to get us across the lake."

"At least you can float." I trained my headlamp on it. "Anybody else hear that sound?"

Everyone stopped to listen.

"It's a huge waterfall," Pete said. "Like the one behind Neuschwanstein Castle."

"Maybe this lake flows into a river?" Izabella said.

"You might be right." Jonathan threw a piece from the broken plank into the channel. It spun, bobbed, and made rapid progress to our left. "See that move? A pretty strong current."

"The same current Pete fought on the other side," Jenna said.

"It's a lot stronger," I said. "Well, not much to see on this side of the island."

We changed course and plodded uphill.

"Gabe, we haven't finished on this side," Alex said. "Let's walk all the way around."

But Lightning zipped away over the top of the hill. Thunder chased him.

"Get over here, Lightning," I said.

"Why is your dog running?" Franco said.

I shrugged. "I don't know, but whatever's causing it has him excited. Could be an insect."

Franco tilted his head. "If they are excited, should we not go after them?"

"We need to follow the dogs." Pete hiked close to Franco.

We surged ahead, going over the crest of the hill. In the headlamp's dim beam, I could make out a rounded shape in the distance. With rapid strokes, the dogs tried to get underneath it. They alternated poking their noses into the ground and digging, sand flying everywhere. Hopping around each other, they worked to get the best spot. Thunder barked at us.

"Come on." Alex raced down the hill. "The dogs are going wild."

Chapter 40
~ Sea Rats

"What is it?" Pete peered at the dogs' flurry of activity. "Dry clothes?"

"Very funny." I took a deep breath. In the headlamp's fading light, an arched wooden frame broke through the ground. "Jackpot. It's a boat. Not in terrific shape, but it's okay." The backend had been ripped off. However, the rest of the wood appeared to be in good shape.

"But why are these dogs still going crazy?" Franco pointed at the sand spraying in the air.

My headlamp flickered and died. "Alex, your turn."

His light blinked on.

As we tried to turn the boat over, Thunder and Lightning dug even faster. They jumped into the middle of the boat the minute we'd flipped it over. They scratched at a wooden box about the size of a footlocker located near the stern.

"Useless." Jenna kicked the side. "The backend is a total wreck."

Alex stood, arms folded, one hand holding his chin.

"Think outside the box," he said.

Franco stared at Alex. "Is making a fire outside the box?"

"We might find a hundred different ways to use this boat," Alex said. "Burning the wood for warmth destroys all of those possibilities. We're not that cold, are we?"

"I'm freezing." Pete rubbed his arms.

"We can burn the wood later." Alex stepped into the righted boat.

I climbed inside to check it out. Detailed carvings and colored stones covered the outside. I couldn't open or move the box. Nails anchored it in place by a wooden brace on top. Using a broken piece of wood for a wedge, Jonathan and I wiggled the box loose. We wrestled it out and onto the floor.

"Pretty heavy," Jonathan said.

"I wonder what's inside?" Jenna said.

Jonathan brushed off the top of the box. "It must have been here for a while."

A latch held the lid shut. I opened it. "Food. Look at all these boxes." Some of it had been opened, leaving a rancid odor behind. "This is why the dogs went wild."

Pete rotated one of the cans. "I haven't seen food like this before."

Alex picked out one. "These are C-rats."

"Ughhh. Sea rats?" Jenna wrinkled her nose. "Who would ever eat rats?"

"Not sea rats." Alex smiled. "C-Rations. World War II stuff. Now they are called MREs."

"Em Are Ease?" Franco shook his head. "I am lost."

"Those are letters." I handed a can to Franco. "MRE stands for Meals Ready to Eat. Dad thinks they're better than C-rats."

"Even though the U.S. military officially phased out C-rats before the Vietnam war, you can still find them overseas." Alex handled a box, checking it out.

"All right, Mr. Scientist," I said. "That's great news, but it doesn't solve our new problem. "No can opener."

"There has to be a gadget here to open them. I think Dad called it a P-38." Alex inspected more boxes, dumping the contents.

"We could use a knife, yes?" Izabella said.

"It might not be as easy," I said.

We all dumped boxes of cans on the floor. A small clunking sound caused me to pause. A piece of metal, about as wide as a dime and an inch long, dropped onto the deck as we searched. One side was flat and rectangular. The other side had a sharp hooked edge on a hinge.

"This might be a P-38." I set it on the palm of my hand. "The sharp edge could be used as a can opener, but it doesn't have a handle."

"Let me see." Izabella stretched out her hand. She turned the object over several times. "It might work in this way." She opened the first can by putting the pointed edge on the inside rim and rocking the tool back and forth. She dipped her finger into the can and tasted. "Tuna. And it isn't spoiled."

The dogs jumped up on Izabella, but she held the can out of reach.

"Stop." Alex pulled the dogs away.

"Let me have a bite." Jonathan reached for the can.

"We will share." Jenna knocked his hand away.

"Cut it out." I stepped in front of Izabella. "There is plenty to go around. Look at all of these cans."

After finishing our tuna, spaghetti, and ham feast, we fed the dogs.

"You two deserve a treat for finding that food." Jenna's lips curved into a smile at the corners. She rubbed Thunder's thick fur and patted his side.

"Good work, Lightning." I rubbed his head.

Pete noticed something. "There's a date on my cans—1954."

"Dad ate C-rats in Okinawa in 1978," I said. "They were still using them during the typhoons that hit a few years ago. I guess the other stuff went bad because some of the cans were opened. We'll be fine." I was more concerned about the possibility of using the boat. "We need to fix this boat to see if we can get it to float." I walked to the hull and gave it a gentle kick. "But how? Without a backend, it's more like a raft."

"We need the right tools," Franco said. "We have no wood saw, no nails, and no boat to ride."

Alex's headlamp dimmed. He hit the lamp with his hand. The beam strengthened, but it wouldn't last much longer.

"Maybe that's a sign we should do what Izabella said." Jenna stood, brushed a few crumbs off, and narrowed her eyes at me. "Let's sleep. What time is it, Franco?"

"5:30 a.m."

"We've got to keep working." I reached for Alex's headlamp. "We already slept. You can sleep if you want, I'm going to work."

"Wait." Alex pushed me away. "We have the power left on your used battery after mine has gone out, then nothing."

Alex strode a few steps away from me and spoke to the group. "Listen. If you're tired and want to sleep, form a circle by the boat's stern within arm's reach of each other. If you want to plan, use the prow of the boat on the other side. But be quiet. Speak in whispers. No more work for now. I'll turn off the light to save power when we're all in place."

Jonathan, Pete, Alex and I went around the boat. Jenna, Izabella and Franco laid down to rest.

Alex's light cut out before I made it to the group.

We had started to talk when a light blazed into the darkness, cutting the conversation short. Like a spotlight, it moved across the water in searchlight pattern.

I leaped to my feet.

The faint edges of the brilliant beam revealed Alex sprawled in the sand. He elbowed himself to a sitting position. Jonathan sat cross-legged next to him. Pete had been lying on his side, but jumped to his feet when the light came on.

"Someone's found us," Jonathan said. "Maybe they're cave explorers. Let's call them over."

"Careful, they could work for Hans' boss." Alex got into a low crouch. "Move around to the other side of the boat."

"You're too afraid," Jonathan said. "These are huge caverns. That boat could be salt miners or an Austrian tour group. They could save us. Come on, Gabe. Help me call them over."

I looked at Alex. *Could Jonathan be right?*

"Don't be stupid," Alex said. "Get behind the boat."

"Over here." Jonathan jumped and waved his arms. He moved toward the edge of the water. "Over here."

"Tackle him. Keep him quiet and get down," Alex said.

Pete grabbed one of Jonathan's arms and I grabbed the other, heaving him backward.

"Over here," he said one last time from the ground.

The light was closer now and swung over toward the shore.

Izabella, Jenna, and Franco crawled to join us. We stayed low, huddled together behind the boat. The beam of light swept over the boat several times, and then faded.

I guess they didn't hear Jonathan or see him.

A shot rang out and splinters of wood showered us.

Chapter 41
~ The Landing

They are shooting at us," Franco said. "We have to surrender or they will come to kill us." He got on his knees, ready to stand.

I slipped a hand over his mouth as Pete tackled him. Franco struggled.

"Franco, listen to me." I clamped harder on his mouth. "We don't know what they'll do if they catch us," I said. "They can't be trusted."

His eyes, which had been wide with fright, relaxed a little.

I removed my hand and made him promise to be quiet. I worked my way next to Alex who had crawled to the front of our boat to check out the situation.

The boat's searchlight went out, replaced by a yellow glow. The bow of the watercraft scraped onto the beach's sand. A person stepped into the water, splashing and grunting as he pulled the boat on shore. He spoke to another man, but it was unintelligible.

Two men. On hands and knees, I edged past Alex's knee to steal a look.

The boat, larger than the one we hid behind, had a motor at the stern and two lanterns hanging from hooks at either end of a railing. The men wore blue coveralls, like they were workmen in the mines.

"Leuchte." The big man on the beach held out his hand. He had long hair like a rock star. The man in the boat obeyed instantly, jumping to grab the first lamp off the rail and placing it onto the outstretched hand. Rock Star walked toward our boat, raising the lamp for a better view.

"Get everyone to the back end of the boat," Alex whispered.

I pushed to get the group moving. Pete watched over Jonathan, but he and Franco grabbed our backpacks. The dogs, which were under the command of silence, stuck close to Alex and me. Alex motioned for me to take the dogs and hide. Jenna crouched next to him. I took the dogs and crowded in with the others.

"Halt." The lantern's light brightened.

"Don't shoot," Alex said. He and Jenna stood, brushing sand off their clothes.

What is Alex doing? Distracting the men from the rest of us?

Rock Star lifted his lantern to see their faces better.

Alex and Jenna held their hands in the air.

"Why are you here?" he said.

"We're lost," Jenna said. Her eyes were wide.

"I'm not believe you." The man advanced a step. "I think you are kids the boss is looking for."

"We've been wandering around for a while," Alex said. "I don't think anyone…"

"Stop the talk." Rock Star jabbed his finger at them. "Come."

Alex crossed his arms. He and Jenna didn't move.

Thunder tried to lift his head to see. I shoved him back toward the sand. His throat let out a low rumble.

I lifted his ear and whispered. "Shhh."

He stopped.

Over six feet tall, Rock Star looked strong. "Quit the stall. Either you will move or I drag you."

Alex's body tensed. His arms went to his side and he widened his stance, eyes narrowed. His lips were set in a straight line.

"Don't try to be a hero." Jenna reached out a hand to touch his arm. "I don't like this, but it might be better if we went with him." Jenna tilted her head toward the boat. "Remember what we learned in school about our actions making a difference for others."

Alex's neck muscles relaxed a bit.

"Others?" the man said.

"You know." Jenna stepped forward. "The others you captured."

"We have caught the rest?" Rock Star said.

"Uh, of course." Alex followed Jenna's lead and stood beside her.

"I think this is not right. We shall see." The man advanced, grabbed Jenna's arm, and shoved her toward the waiting transportation.

Alex hurried to stay beside her.

Thunder lunged forward, but I was ready. I clamped his muzzle shut, wrapped my legs on his hindquarters, and wrestled him to the ground.

"Not yet," I whispered. I talked to him until he stopped struggling. I loosened my grip on his muzzle and he rolled over, submitting to my command.

Rock Star kicked Alex, making him stumble. "Speed up."

When they neared the watercraft, I jabbed Pete.

"We've got to stop them," I whispered. I shouldered my backpack. "Grab Alex's gear."

"Got it." Franco crawled close. "You give the order."

"They're almost to the boat." Izabella wrung her hands.

"Get ready." I paused as we each prepared to move. "Go."

Chapter 42
– The Shooting

Pete, Franco, and I sprang to our feet. I darted past Jonathan toward the men.

The searchlight swung in our direction, hitting Franco in the eyes. He stopped.

"I cannot see," Franco said.

Pete and I kept moving. The dogs raced toward Jenna and Alex, distracting the guard.

Alex spun around, kicked him in the knee, and punched him in the nose, sending him to the ground. He and Jenna broke into a sprint toward the hills.

"Scatter," Jenna said to the rest of the gang. "Get away."

The searchlight's beam revealed the beach and hills in glaring brilliance. I shielded my eyes and caught a glimpse of Alex's guard—his hand pinched his nose as he got on his feet.

"Halt. Don't move," said the man in the boat. He was small and wore a red collared shirt that matched his red hair. Red seemed like the boss. But I had missed another man earlier.

The third guy sat on a bench, leaning on his elbows and watching from the rear of the boat. He wore clothes meant for a yacht. His collared pink shirt sported a blue striped golden tie. Pinky's close-cropped hair matched his clean-shaven cheeks.

"Spread out wider," I said. "They can't catch us all." I scrambled up the hill past the broken boat. Jenna and Alex were at least a fifty feet behind me.

The two dogs had split apart, Lightning in front of me. Thunder bolted toward Alex. The rest of the group went in different directions, the majority toward the top of the hill.

A shot rang out and faded into the immense cavern space.

"Halt," Red said. "If you run, this next round will not miss."

"Ignore him." I waved everyone to continue. I dashed ahead. To my left, Alex and Jenna were making good time, but lagged behind. Rock Star had stopped chasing Alex.

The second shot brought a cry of pain. Alex went down.

"My leg," he said.

I hesitated. *If I keep running, they might shoot me. If I stay, they might not. But if I run back, maybe the others can get away and fight later.*

"Come on, Lightning. Let's go." I sprinted to my brother.

"Keep going." I waved the others away. Franco and Pete crested the hill and disappeared. Jonathan decided to walk back. Izabella made a beeline toward Alex and Jenna.

Red holstered his pistol and stayed in the boat. Pinky got out and joined Rock Star. They came after Alex and Jenna, but didn't seem in any rush.

Alex, flat on his back, held his left leg to his chest.

"Let me see," Jenna said. "I can't help if I don't know how bad it is." She coaxed him to release his hands on his leg.

I arrived a few seconds later, tossing my backpack on the ground.

Thunder lay next to Alex, licking his cheek.

Alex clenched his teeth when Jenna picked at his pants leg. He grimaced, rolling over.

"Stop moving," Jenna said. "I can't get your pants leg up to see the bullet hole."

"Use his Leatherman." I dropped to my knees and brushed the sand away while examining Alex's bloody pant leg. Lightning sniffed and licked Alex's face.

"Get...dogs away." Alex waved his arm.

"Not now." Jenna dragged Thunder back from Alex, then snatched Lightning.

I searched Alex's belt, found his Leatherman case, and popped out the knife.

"Hold his leg still," I said.

Pulling his pants away from the skin, I slashed along the seam and peeled them off.

A steady flow of blood came out of the wound, but it wasn't pulsing.

"At least the bullet didn't hit an artery." I kept working. "Jenna, keep his hands off his leg. They're dirty."

"Okay," she said. Her skin was pale.

"Alex." I adjusted to look him straight in the eyes. "This may hurt, but it's gotta happen. Don't touch your leg and do what I ask. Help me out, bro."

I twisted his leg a fraction to get a better look.

He nodded and clenched his fists.

Izabella and Jonathan arrived, but stayed with the dogs a couple feet away.

"The bullet hit you in the calf," I said. "You're bleeding more than I like."

I cut off the lower part of his jeans and sliced the material into strips.

"Izabella, can you find a stick about a half-inch thick?"

She nodded and left.

By this time, the two men had arrived. Pinky took the lantern from Rock Star, who bent over to lift Alex. But I shoved him away.

"Not yet," I said.

The man snarled, inches from my face.

"Don't hurt him," said Pinky.

The drying blood on Rock Star's upper lip told me where Alex's punch had connected. He hung close.

I tied one of Alex's blue jean strips below his knee. I tied a second strip about three inches lower, but above the wound.

"What are you doing?" Jenna sat near Alex's head. "That's not going to help much. The blood hasn't slowed."

"I need that small stick," I said.

Izabella arrived, set three sizes of sticks by me, and drifted toward Jonathan and the dogs.

Rock Star moved from Alex's feet toward his head.

Thunder growled and bared his teeth. He got to his feet, ready to lunge. Jonathan put a hand on his collar, but not enough to hold the dog if he attacked. Izabella had Lightning.

The man pointed toward Thunder. "Call him away."

"Come here, boy," I said.

Without taking his eyes off the long-haired man, Alex's dog shifted next to me.

"Hold him tight." The guy motioned for me to grip the dog's collar.

"Why?" I said.

"Do it." Rock Star leaned over Alex toward Jenna.

I clenched both hands on the leather.

The thug grabbed Jenna's hair and pulled her head back, sending her toward the ground.

I let go.

Jenna braced for the fall, eyes opened wide. She gasped.

Thunder roared and leaped across Alex.

Rock Star let go of Jenna and smashed his fist into the attacking canine.

Thunder fell on top of Jenna, sliding off. His sides heaved, but he didn't move otherwise.

Izabella held Lightning in her arms, preventing him from leaping to his buddy's side.

"You killed him," I said.

"Not yet." Rock Star removed his brass knuckles and dropped them into his pocket. "Maybe later. Now, do what I say."

Jenna had gathered herself to a sitting position. She regained her balance and the man's hand clamped onto her hair. He yanked her head again.

"Stop. You're hurting me." Jenna's eyes were wide.

"Ja, Ja." Tightening his grip, the man shifted his unshaven face closer to her ear. "Yes, you nice looking girl, really nice."

Jenna's face became paler in the lantern's light.

I jumped to my feet to pull the guy off.

"Don't." Rock Star's face broke into a broad grin. He pulled out a black object that flicked open into a gleaming switch-blade.

"Enough." Pinky acted like he had full control of the situation. In spite of the fighting, his face showed no emotion. "Let the girl alone. Put your knife away and get the boy into the boat. We'll gather the rest of them when we return. They're not going anywhere."

"You can't take him yet," I said. "If he loses his leg he'll be useless to you."

I picked up one of the scattered pieces of wood and laid it on top of the knotted jean strip closest to Alex's knee. I tied another knot over the piece of wood and twisted the stick in circles several times until the blood quit flowing. I tied the lower jeans strip into a knot to anchor the wood in place. *My first real life tourniquet. Hope it's right.* I looked at Pinky. "He's ready."

Rock Star knocked me away. He jerked Alex to his feet by his shirt and shoved him toward Jenna, who supported him. They hobbled toward the boat.

I scrambled over to Thunder.

Lightning sniffed his buddy, and whined. Thunder was still breathing, but had a huge swollen bruise below his right ear near the eye. And his swollen muzzle still had claw marks from the wildcat fight.

Izabella joined me. "I'll watch him," she said.

I nodded and edged near the shore.

Red helped Alex's guard to lift both Alex and Jenna in the boat. Then he threw a few ropes to Rock Star, who tied Jenna's hands behind her and plopped her onto a seat. She was shaking. The long-haired man wrapped his hand under her jaw, wiggling it. "Pretty blonde hair." He laughed. "And cute."

Jenna shrank away, but the man patted her on the leg.

"Halt." Pinky tapped Rock Star with a swagger stick. "Keep your hands off. Find another girl we've kidnapped. This one is off limits. Protected." He caught her attention. "For now."

The man glanced sideways at his boss. He shook his head slightly and approached Alex. Rock Star tied Alex's hands and tossed him in the seat next to Jenna. Alex yelled in pain. Rock Star climbed out of the boat to push it into the water. He grunted a couple of times before he finally got the craft afloat, then hopped aboard.

"We'll see you soon." Pinky gave a thin smile and waved, amusement in his eyes. "Enjoy your food. Stay healthy."

Lightning ran into the fringe of the water, yipping at Jenna and Alex.

"Don't hurt them," I said above his noise. "You're not gonna get away with this."

"Say goodbye to your brother." Red chuckled. "And your friend. You won't see them again—at least alive."

Rock Star laughed. Then he kicked Alex's wounded leg.

Alex yelled, writhing in pain.

Chapter 43
– Izabella's Swim

The boat carrying Alex and Jenna sped away. Their light faded. I raced up the island's central hill to see where the boat would dock. At the crest of the hill, I noticed several new spotlights across the channel. They illuminated the inlet. And the cavern wall lights lit the low shelf. I sprinted along the backbone of the hill to get a better view.

The boat slowed, steered into the inlet and slid behind the wall guarding the dock. The boat's spotlight, about twice my height, was the single visible part of the boat. It became still.

The two henchmen carried Alex and Jenna out of the dock area, up wooden stairs to the flat rock shelf, and behind a brick wall attached to the wall of the cave. Pinky climbed the stairs, pausing on the rock shelf. He waved in our direction before he disappeared inside.

The lights went out. The blackness wrapped around me like a blanket.

"Did you see where they went in?" Franco tapped me.

"Into a hidden entrance behind that brick wall," I said. "Is everyone else here?"

Jonathan and Pete joined us, informing us that Izabella had stayed with Thunder. Pete had Lightning with him.

"My headlamp and batteries are in my backpack by Thunder and Izabella," I said. "Let's make a single line and Lightning can lead us by smell."

"Or, we could use this glow stick," Jonathan said. "I borrowed it from your backpack."

"Did you take that when you took my flares?" I said.

"Earlier. When Hans died, I thought I'd better be prepared if worse things happened."

I heard the familiar crack of a bent glow stick. The red glow became brighter when he shook the stick to mix the chemicals.

What else has he taken? Pete's warnings not to trust Jonathan flashed through my mind.

When we got back to Thunder and Izabella, I shouldered my backpack and strapped on the headlamp. The last set of batteries didn't have a good charge. "I'm not turning the headlamp on while the glow stick's still working. The food is still at the boat. Let's head there."

We hiked several minutes to reach the boat. Pete laid Thunder on his side.

"He hasn't moved in a while," Izabella said. "Is he unconscious?"

"I can't tell." I knelt and shook him.

Alex's dog stirred, but didn't sit up or open his eyes. Lightning nuzzled him. When Thunder didn't move, Lightning whined and curled up next to him.

"Since those thugs have Alex and Jenna, we don't have much time." I took a seat inside the boat and we discussed our next move.

We had to swim the channel to steal the kidnappers' boat.

"I can do it." Izabella stepped forward. "I placed in the European Swim League competition for homeschoolers at the Munich Olympic swimming pool."

"Cool." I motioned toward the channel. "Can you swim against a current?"

"But of course. I trained in the Mediterranean when living in Spain."

By the channel, Izabella waded into the water. "I'll bring the boat to the other side if the current, she is too strong on this side, yes?" She clamped the glow stick between her teeth.

"You can do it, Izabella," Franco said.

"Angle into the current and you'll make it," I said. "It's not that far."

She swam halfway before trouble began. The current was too strong.

"Izabella, go more to the right," I said.

We jogged on shore to stay with her as she drifted, tripping in the darkness.

She changed her angle, faltering again, losing ground. The glow stick disappeared.

"Hang in there," Franco said.

Seconds later, a faint red glow waved in the air.

"She made it to the other side," I said. "Now she has to climb that shelf to get to the boat."

The red glow began rising in steady stages, the light zigzagging higher in the air.

Franco's hand brushed my shoulder. "Should she not be at the top by now?"

"Anytime." I strained to see.

The glow stick fell, bouncing near the water. It didn't move.

"Izabella, are you okay?" I shouted, but got no response.

"I think she's hurt," I said. "Jonathan, do you have more glow sticks?"

"Just one."

"Give it." I switched on my headlamp, hand out.

220

"We might need it later." Jonathan hauled out the stick. "What are you going to do?"

"Watch. I'll use this." I tapped a flat piece of driftwood plank with my foot. I cracked the glow stick and shook it hard. The blue light made eerie shadows on our faces.

"Franco, if I don't return in an hour, fix the broken boat on the other side." I grabbed the board. "You'll need to take care of Alex's backpack for now. Use anything you need in either of our backpacks. I'm sure *Jonathan* knows where things are."

Jonathan frowned.

"Be careful with the current," Franco said.

I undid the headlamp's straps and gave it to Jonathan, trying to make amends for the mean comment. "Point the light where I should go, then turn it off. Save the batteries. Five minutes later, turn it on to show me where I am. Keep doing that until I get to the other side."

"Sure," Jonathan said. He strapped on the headlamp. "I'll make sure you don't get lost."

I put the board in the water.

"Lightning." I slapped my thigh. "Get on board. We're going to help Izabella."

"Good luck," Franco said.

I jammed the glow stick into my mouth and used the wood like a paddleboard, lying on my stomach with Lightning on the forward edge. In minutes, my arms ached. I couldn't see the small cliff in the blue glow, but the headlamp's light let me see how much headway I had made.

Lightning wiggled toward me. He put his cold, wet muzzle against my nose.

"Not now." I fought off fatigue and plowed forward. A faint light flickered overhead. I glimpsed the cliff and saw the current had taken me even farther to the left than Izabella. I changed my angle, but was losing ground too fast. *Don't panic. Don't quit. You can make it.*

The light behind me went out. I surged, but couldn't go much farther. Weariness settled over me like a fog. *Just swim.* I heard faint sounds of water crashing onto rocks to my left.

Was it the waterfall? I dug deeper. Lightning wobbled to his feet. Barking. Swaying.

The sound of the water cascading down the cliff muffled his barking. I struggled to keep the board balanced, clutching it with both hands. I stretched a hand for Lightning.

The board smacked into something, pitching Lightning and me into the water. I snatched the glow stick out of my mouth for a quick breath before going under. I banged into rocks, struggling to surface, gasping for air. The current sucked me farther into the rushing torrent.

"Lightning?" I placed the glow stick in my mouth again, fingers clutching for anything solid. I found a handhold, but the current ripped it loose. I tried again, and this time was able to hang on. I kicked my legs hard enough to get a solid grip with both hands. After an eternity, I lodged myself on top of the eroded rock. I clawed into a safe position, legs dangling in the water.

The blue glow showed a back eddy area in front of me, leading to an alcove in the wall. The current was weaker there. My feet located a nearby rock. With a shove, I abandoned the safety of the rock to push through the current to the eddy. After a short crawl, I lay on my stomach, sides heaving. Minutes later, I waded in the direction I had come from.

"Lightning, where are you, boy?" Nothing. I called and searched, but only the roar of the waterfall answered. *When will this end?* I counted the tragedies.

Lightning? Gone. Alex and Jenna? Taken. Izabella? Unknown. Hans? Dead. Dieter? Broken. Erik? Eaten. And Thunder? Unconscious.

Sobs wracked my body. *It's not fair.* Then I got mad. *God, why aren't you helping?* When one wave of guilt passed, another one washed over me. I choked and coughed, trying to keep it together.

After some time had passed—I don't know how long—I approached the cave wall. As my glow stick faded, I took a deep breath to stop trembling. Even with Lightning gone, my friends were counting on me. Dad didn't raise me to be a quitter.

We're getting out of here, or I'll die trying.

Chapter 44
– Search for Lightning

At the wall, I discovered a path on the edge of the alcove that ended near the crashing sounds. Gushing water, foamy from the turbulence, sailed into pitch-black space—a massive waterfall. A pit opened in my stomach. If Lightning got this far, he couldn't have survived.

I returned to the alcove. The water lapped against the path by the wall, swirling in the center. I waded across toward the boat dock. A small ledge guided me into the main cave. Squishing ahead, I kept calling into the dimming bluish light.

"Lightning?" I wasn't going to believe he had been swept away. My shoulders slumped a little each time he didn't answer. "Izabella? Lightning?" Nothing broke the softening sound of the waterfall while I wandered in the direction of the dock.

In ten minutes, I saw the outline of a pier. I eased down a short incline, snuck past the brick wall, and found a motorboat tied to the dock. Hidden from the island behind the brick wall stood a metal door—an exit. Next to the door was a grey electrical box. Inside were switches and buttons below a clock. I tried to read the legend, but the writing was unreadable.

I tapped the box, contemplating my next move. I flipped the first switch. Lights came on at the dock area. I flipped a few more and low cavern lights lit the waterfall where we had flown out of the lava tubes. Lights came on for the ledge where I stood.

I darted out from behind the brick wall, signaling I had made it. The guys waved. Franco pointed to my right. *What's he doing?* I raised my hands. He motioned to my right again, so I obeyed. After a few minutes, he motioned the way I had come. Several paces later, he crossed his arms like a ground crew telling a pilot to halt. Then, he pointed downward.

I stepped to the rim of the cliff. Below me, Izabella lay partially sitting on a small flat rock, with her head to one side and her palm pressed against the side of her bowed head.

"Izabella, are you all right?" I crouched to get a better look. "Can you climb?"

Izabella leaned back. She frowned. "What you say?" She seemed groggy.

I glanced at the cliff to find a path to the base. I noticed a large crack a couple of feet away. Testing each step, I climbed down the rock face and rushed to Izabella.

Scratches on her arms and head showed the injuries from her fall. She kept moving, though, bending her neck and holding a bruised spot on her temple.

"Let me." I lifted her hand to check out the bruise.

Her lips pinched tighter. The bleeding had stopped on her temple. A large lump bulged under her black locks.

"We have to climb." I sat and gazed into her eyes. "Can you make it?"

She gave a slight nod. *Concussion?* I'd have to keep an eye on her.

I explored to find the best place to ascend. The slanted rocky outcropping we were on ended a few feet in either direction, leaving a six-inch ledge that was submerged underwater. To our right, two feet beyond the water-covered ledge, a climbable 'chute' zigzagged to the top.

"Izabella, can you focus on climbing instead of your pain?"

Eyes closed, she tipped her head forward in agreement.

I got behind her and helped her upright.

"Face the wall."

She turned around.

"Your feet are going to go into water, then you can climb." I tugged her shoulder enough to get her to move. "It's going to be slippery in the water. Hang on to me."

Hesitating, she used delicate movements. Her toes searched for firm footing in the water before she shifted her weight.

I coached her as she made her ascent.

Part way up, she swayed.

"Don't stop," I said. "Lean forward." I wedged myself into the chute to stabilize her.

She faltered, but finished the climb. She crawled onto the ledge's widest area, curled into a ball, and placed her head in her palm.

I finished the climb and knelt next to her.

"We have keep going to the boat dock." I touched her arm, speaking in gentle tones.

"Okay."

I strained to hear her response. I raised her and put one of her arms around my neck, pretty much carrying her to the landing.

"I've got bandages and Tylenol when we get to the island. That will help you feel better."

"Thanks," she said.

I helped her into the boat and eased her into the co-pilot seat. Casting off the rope, I hopped in. The starter was right by the wheel. I pushed it. No sputter or roar. Nothing.

I paced to the rear, checking for a gas switch. There wasn't a gas tank or valve to turn.

At the helm, I hit the red button again. A background hum ceased. I pushed it once more and the hum started again.

Ahh. Electric. I turned on the spotlight, steered out of the harbor, and into the channel. The current pushed the boat right, but full throttle kept me gliding on course.

I picked up Franco and Jonathan and zoomed to the other side to get Alex's dog and Pete.

Thunder trotted toward me, massive tail wagging, thumping the side of the boat. He seemed fine. His right eyelid drooped and his muzzle puffed out, but he had a little energy.

"Nice boat." Pete loaded both backpacks and the leftover C-rats.

I rummaged through my backpack, pulling out bandages and Tylenol. Izabella took the pills and drank some water. I dabbed antibiotic ointment onto her cuts and bandaged them.

"Did you find Lightning?" Pete said.

I shook my head.

"Then we need to find him." Pete pointed to the long way around the island.

"There's a waterfall over there." I shook my head again. "I don't want it to pull us over."

"We will not go over." Franco patted the motor. "I agree with Pete. Find your dog."

Jonathan shrugged. "Give it a shot."

I steered the boat the long way around the island. When I cleared the bottom tip of the island, the waterfall's crashing noise swallowed everything else. I gunned the boat toward the middle of the channel. The current pushed the boat toward the waterfall.

"I've got the spotlight," Pete said. He tilted the beam across the water.

"Closer, Gabe." Franco motioned me toward the small cliff opposite the island.

"Angle more upstream," Jonathan said.

"I see him," Franco said.

The nose of the boat started to drift downstream.

"More power," Jonathan said.

I pointed the boat straight upstream, but the current dragged us toward the waterfall.

"Yes, that's him." Pete pointed at a rumpled clump of hair half-in, half-out of the water.

"Get the boat out of the current, or we'll go over that waterfall," Jonathan said.

I gunned the engines, nosing the prow at a forty-five degree angle. It wasn't working. The noise of crashing water made my blood run cold. In ten feet we'd be over the falls.

Chapter 45 – The Solution

The current swept the nose of the boat crossways. The water hit us broadsides.

"Try again," Jonathan shouted. He hung onto a seat in the rear.

I hit the power boost next to the throttle.

The boat lurched forward. The force of the current slammed us into rocks near the edge of the cave, five feet before the waterfall.

The cavern wall was a foot away. The bottom of the boat scraped a section of rocks that held us at the edge of the current. The torrent carried us closer to certain death.

"Push against the wall," I said.

Pete, Jonathan, and Franco strained against the wall, scrabbling for any grip.

Two feet until we plummeted over the waterfall.

Izabella tapped my calf. When I ignored her, she pinched me.

"Oww. What?"

Izabella held the boat's emergency oar out to me. She motioned for us to change places.

I grabbed the paddle, giving her the steering wheel. I scrambled to the rear and wedged the oar's blade into the last crack in the wall, shouting directions and shoving at the same time.

The boat scraped forward.

We dug in. Sweat poured off our bodies.

First inches, then feet. With peak throttle, the engines overcame the current. Izabella drove us toward a side pool. A wan smile spread across her face. She exchanged places with me.

"Thanks." I touched her shoulder. *Incredible. She felt horrible. But never gave up.*

We tied up at the dock. I left to get Lightning. On this side we were closer to him.

"Wait." Pete signaled me. "Where you going?"

"I think I can rescue my buddy. Now that I can see."

"We should do this together," Pete said.

"Okay. Hurry."

Thunder, Pete, and I got to Lightning's location near to the eddy in a matter of minutes. I tied rope around my waist, descended the cliff, and walked upstream. Pete, holding the rope, coached me to the right place as the current carried me to the chunk of rock holding my dog.

"Lightning?" I wiped the hair out of his closed eyes. "Can you hear me?"

He stirred.

I brought the rope up under my arms and tightened it. I cradled Lightning in one arm, wrapped the other arm with the rope, and jumped into the water.

The current's force sucked at me. But Pete wedged his heels in and reeled me back.

I climbed the cliff near where Izabella and I had scaled the rocky face. Back on top, I rubbed Lightning's head, wet hair and muzzle pressed against my cheek. His little tongue caught the side of my nose. He shivered.

"We need to get this little pup dried off." I slapped Pete's back. We set a brisk pace toward the dock. Franco had unloaded the backpacks from the boat by the time we got there. I asked him to carry Alex's backpack until we reconnected with him.

"Now what's the plan?" Jonathan asked minutes after we reached the dock.

"Go through that door, find Jenna and Alex, free them, and escape," Pete said.

"What about the kidnappers?" Franco said. "They have been trying to catch us. This is too easy. Maybe the door, it is a trap."

"Why do you say that?" Jonathan asked.

"We have the lights on for a while and no one comes for us," Franco said.

"I'm not sure they monitor this cavern," I said. "I haven't seen any cameras here. But if we're not here, they'll know we've escaped."

"Either that or we've drowned," Jonathan said. "Where else can we go?"

"I guess we have to move through this door." Franco stroked his chin.

"Maybe we can find a side passage when we get inside." Izabella sat with her arms around her legs, chin on her knees. Her face had relaxed. She seemed comfortable. "The Salt Mines, they are such a maze of passages. We might get lucky, yes?"

"Right," I said. "We go through the door, see if there's a side tunnel and try to find Alex and Jenna. If we run into the bad guys, we have to take them out or hide. Then escape."

"Too simple. I don't think it'll work." Jonathan rubbed his nose.

"Got a better plan?" I asked.

Jonathan eyed the door. "Not really, but we'd better get going instead of talking all day."

I slammed my hand against the door and rattled the handle. "We're not going anywhere until we pick this lock. Any takers?"

"I will try." Franco worked on the door for five minutes with no success.

"You can stop now." Jonathan yawned. "We might as well wait for the kidnappers to come."

"I'll do it," Izabella said. She pulled a bobby pin out of her hair and took off its tiny rubber tip. "I've made this work at home." She jiggled and poked the lock with her makeshift tool.

Pete approached me and sat against the wall. "Did G send anything other than the song? Seems that G would know…"

I slapped a hand on my shirt and sprang toward the door.

"What are you doing?" Pete followed.

I lifted the 550-cord from my neck. The first of the seven mystery keys shone in the light.

"You have a key," Pete said.

"Yes, but does it work?" I rushed to Izabella with the milky-white key and tapped her on the arm. "Let me."

She stepped aside.

The key slid in and rotated. I pushed, but the door wouldn't budge.

Chapter 46 – The Cell Block

The key turned okay. It's gotta work." Pete pulled the handle, but no luck.

"Maybe it is stuck." Franco slammed his shoulder into the door. It didn't budge.

"Did we finish the song?" Izabella asked.

I thought for a second. "We didn't do the last couple of lines. What were they?"

"You're the only one who knows," Jonathan said.

I thought about it out loud.

Blank for the clock, *blank* the key when it talks,
Way, Hey, Blow the man down

"That's the last two lines."

"Where's the clock?" Jonathan asked. "I've only seen one and that was at the bridge."

"I don't see one here," Izabella said.

We all looked at the walls, on the boat, and on the brick wall.

"Oh, I remember." I darted to the gray box that had the light switches, revealing a digital clock inside. "But this thing doesn't talk." I shook my head.

"Did you read what is left of the label inside the box?" Izabella focused on the words. "This label, she has German writing that mentions a key. And there's a button here."

"Press it," Pete said.

Izabella pushed, but nothing happened.

"Guess that wasn't it," I said. "We're not going anywhere."

German chanting filled the air.

"Hey, the clock's counting down in German," Pete said. "Try the key."

I did, but no results.

"It's still talking." Pete said. "Two. One. Zero."

"Anschalten," the clock said.

"That's it," Pete said. "Turn it now."

I twisted the key and heard a click. The door swung open. "We're in." I grinned.

"Yes." Franco pumped a clenched fist. "We are going to our home."

"Don't celebrate too soon," Jonathan said. "We have to get past a few bad guys." He put his hands on his hips. "That's not going to be easy."

"Quiet." I motioned for them to sit. I leaned against the door to keep it open. "We can't make a lot of noise moving through these tunnels because of the guards. I'll teach you a few basic hand signals to communicate with each other in silence." In two minutes I had shown them the sign for stop, spread out, forward, and charge.

Pete shut off the lights in the cavern. We entered in a single file.

The tunnel seemed like an ordinary hallway in an office building with a few exceptions. Though the floor had been smoothed out, stalactites hung from the ceiling. A cable on the wall to our right connected lights at equal intervals.

I tested the wall. *Still salt.* I got on my knees and patted my thighs. Thunder and Lightning padded close. Thunder's bump on his head had receded, but the gash made by the brass knuckles formed a jagged scar.

"Boys, let's find Alex and Jenna." I stroked their fur, clicking leashes onto their collars.

Thunder made a high-pitched whine.

"Yes, buddy." I hugged his neck. "We're going to find them. Shhh."

I lifted Lightning and scratched his ears. "Sniff out their location." I tapped his nose.

The dogs took the lead, sniffing the ground, walls, and air. I signed for the rest to keep ten paces between each other. Izabella fell in line behind me, followed by Franco, Jonathan, then Pete. We reached a curved stairway leading to the level above. I motioned for the rest to wait at the bottom of the stairs. At the top, all seemed clear. I tiptoed down in a rush. The gang followed me back up.

The dogs stopped at a T-intersection. Thunder's hackles rose.

I stayed low and snuck up to their position.

To our left I heard kids talking. To the right, two car lengths away, stood a guard. Dressed in the blue coat and pants of a miner with his blond hair half stuffed under a cap, he marched back and forth into a side passage. His rifle lay propped in the corner by a stool, but he carried a pistol clipped to his belt. The guard looked at the corridor on his left. He sighed, made a few arm gestures, and ambled out of sight into the branching corridor.

I motioned for everyone to join me. Finger to my lips, I whispered that we were going around the corner to avoid the guard, but I would check it out first. The T-intersection to our left curved out of the sight of any gunman on the opposite side. I told the dogs to wait, handed their leashes to Pete, and stuck my head into the intersection. No guard.

I scooted around the corner to our left. The noise of children talking grew louder the farther I crept along. The tunnel intersected with a long hallway, the width of a school hallway. The passage to my left contained rooms on either side. To the right, the hallway went into the distance with no breaks that I could see. The rooms were hollows in the rock, metal bars forming the wall between them and the walkway. I saw boys and girls in a couple of cages. They were dirty, and their clothes were torn. Several had rags wrapped around their hands.

"Psst." I made that sound four or five times before one of the kids heard. She came to the bars and looked at me.

I put a finger to my lips and locked eyes with her.

Her hand went to her mouth. She ran to the others, finger over her lips and pointed.

One of the bigger boys came to the bars. A shorter boy crowded next to him, saw me, and shouted. A large hand clamped over his face. The big boy spoke to the loudmouth, their noses almost touching. The shorter boy nodded, skittered away, and whispered to the others.

The larger boy made motions toward the other side of the room, which I couldn't see. His whispered English was difficult to understand because of a heavy accent. "Be still. A visitor comes, not guard. No yelling." When the boy finished, he came to the corner of the cage.

I looked all the way round the corner.

He pointed at the ceiling.

At the far end of the room, in the left hand corner, a camera made a slow sweep of the room, from left to right.

I nodded. I'd have to kill the camera. As it panned away, I started to race across the room.

The boy threw both hands out to stop me, pointing upward.

Above the entryway door, another camera covered the room.

After pointing at myself, I acted out leaving and returning, and smiled.

The boy gave me a thumbs-up.

I returned to the group, called Franco forward, and whispered the plan to him. He followed me to the room of cages.

Opening the largest blade of my Leatherman knife, I tapped Franco to go.

We rushed inside the entryway. Franco bent down. I leaped on his shoulders, knife between my teeth, steadying myself on the wall. Franco grabbed my lower legs and stood. Knife in hand, I grabbed the wires and cut them. The green light on top of the camera flickered to red. I glanced behind me.

The other camera swung in our direction.

Chapter 47
~ The Guard

"Quick," Franco said. "Get down."

I folded the knife. Jumped. And stumbled to my knees.

The camera's lens would catch me in an instant.

Franco, who was in the lead, reversed direction and hauled me out of the way.

We continued to our right, staying out of the camera's view. We angled to the far end of the room, staying under the working camera. I sucked in some air and let it out. *Out of danger.* I slashed the wires on the second camera and its light turned red.

"Franco, go tell the gang to stand by." I pointed with my thumb. "I'll talk to some of these kids to find out where the kidnappers took Jenna and Alex."

The taller boy in the cage who was nearest to the room's opening motioned me forward. Other kids leaned closer, faces framed by metal bars. A collection of four cages filled this area, each holding eight or nine boys and girls of varying ages. I touched the bars and stared.

The tall boy might have been my age. But deep in his eyes, he looked much older. Ripped clothing hung from a gaunt frame. Bags like charcoal smudges under his eyes betrayed his lack of sleep. A bruised left eye, a jaw that looked like it had been broken at one time, and holes in his shoes completed the picture. He smelled like laundry that had been worn for weeks.

"Help." He reached through the bar and tugged on my arm.

"You speak English?"

"Some."

"I'm looking for my brother and his friend, a girl." I wiggled out of his bony grasp.

"New boy and girl." He nodded, pointed back the way I had come. "That way."

I turned to go.

"Wait," the boy said. "You open door. Let us out."

"Later. After I get my brother and friend." I spread my hands. "They're first."

"Too late." The boy sat. "Soon guards change. You don't know…"

"Go on."

"…how they change. We surprise them." He smiled.

I surveyed the place. All of the children in the cells tried to hear us. They crowded into the corner of each cell closest to where I knelt.

The tallest boy in the cell watched from the corner. He broke in with a strong Australian accent. "That bloke's not gonna help us. Call the guard."

"Don't." I sprang to my feet. "Can you control everyone if we let a few of you out?"

"Of course, mate. I control the lot of the prisoners in these cells." The older boy crossed his arms. He was about six feet tall, lean and had dark-tanned skin—maybe sixteen or seventeen.

"Can you get us out?" He drifted closer.

"I don't know the way out of this maze." I shook my head.

"Not the maze, Yank, the cells." He swept his hand to indicate all of the cells. "We know how to get out of these tunnels. Can you take down the guards?"

"We have to be careful," I said. "There's a guard in the hall."

"That's Anton." The dark-skinned boy lifted his chin. "He's probably on a smoko—that's a cigarette break to you. He'll bring us food soon. The guards change sometime after that."

"But he might come early. I killed the cameras. Wouldn't that set off an alarm??"

He ignored the question. "How many of you?" The older boy put his hands on the bars.

"Four in the hallway." I scratched my wrinkled forehead. "And they captured my brother and his girlfriend."

"That's not good." The boy's knuckles grew white from clenching the bars. "Their business is kidnapping boys and girls."

Hmmm. He seems to know what's going on.

"Get your mates," the Aussie said. "Quit mucking around. We need to plan our escape. We have about fifteen ticks on the clock. Be quick." His face pushed against the bars.

"What about the cameras?"

"No worries. They won't notice that until the late shift. Go on, then. Back to your mates. We don't have all day." He shooed me away.

The guard hadn't returned. I sprinted to our group and explained the situation. One by one, we darted into the corridor that held the caged kids. When we gathered again, I spoke to the same two boys. The other kids in the cells listened as well. We prepared the plan for execution.

Ten minutes later, Anton pushed the rumbling food cart into the center of the room.

"We're hungry," a large boy said from the farthest cage on our left.

"We want food." All of the kids rattled their metal cups against their cages.

"Shut up." The guard banged the lid off the container on the food cart. "Or I'll give you something to whine about."

Most of the kids backed up against the wall.

Perfect.

When the guard reached over the cart for a serving spoon, I sprang from the wall. Placing a hand on his back, I tugged on the handle of the pistol to pull it free, but it didn't come out.

Stupid safety strap.

Chapter 48
~ The Aussie

The guard knocked me down, flipped open the holster's security strap, and drew the weapon in one swift motion.

Thunder burst out of his hiding place, knocking Anton over, snarling in his face. The gun went off. The guard held Thunder by the throat while his other hand raised the pistol to fire.

Lightning dove at the man's face, paws scratching his cheeks, and teeth nipping whatever he could reach. Anton slashed at the dog with his gun, but missed several times.

I rolled to my feet and leaped to Thunder's side. I gripped the guard's wrist with both hands and bent his pistol hand down and back underneath his wrist.

"Drop it," I said.

The guard clenched his teeth, trying to free himself from my grip.

"You asked for it." I pressed his hand and wrist closer together, causing his bones and cartilage to crack and grind.

He dropped his gun, yelling in agony.

"On your face." I kept the pressure on his wrist until he obeyed.

"Lightning, fetch Pete." I increased the pressure and toed the gun toward the wall.

Pete and the gang arrived.

"Gun." I directed with my head. Pete grabbed the gun and hurried to join me. He pointed it at the guard, but his shaking hands put me in danger of getting shot as well.

"You take over from me," I said.

"I'm not sure I know..." Pete lifted his shoulders.

"It's easy. Put the gun where the guard can't touch it. Apply strong pressure. If Anton does anything you don't like, squeeze like this." I squeezed harder and the guard ground his teeth, grunting in pain.

Pete clamped onto his wrist and maintained the hold I taught him.

I grabbed the gun and pointed it at Anton.

"Thunder." I motioned with the free hand. "Guard."

Alex's dog poked his nose into the man's face, baring his teeth.

"Franco," I said. "Use those zip ties on the guard's belt to tie his hands behind him."

In minutes, Franco had finished, dragging him to a sitting position by the wall.

"Quick." The Aussie rattled the bars. "Let us out. That shot could bring other guards."

"Where are the keys?" I stood and scratched my forehead.

"Right pocket," he said.

I lifted the keys from Anton, stuffed the pistol into my belt, and rushed to the boy's cell. I stared at him—my face inches from his. "Remember your promise."

"No dramas. I'm easy."

I unlocked his cage first, then the other three.

The boy gathered the freed group of children together and barked out orders in German. In groups of three or four, the kids began to separate.

"Stop." I rushed toward the Aussie. "You said we'd all cooperate. Franco, guard the door." I pointed toward the entryway.

Franco stepped in front of it.

"Right, mate." The boy smiled at me. "We're cooperating. Most of these teams will make it to the surface, get to their parents and the police, who will then rescue the rest of us."

"But we have to get our friends first before an alarm locks this place down. Then we can all leave." I crossed my arms. "You said if we helped you, you'd help us."

"And we will, mate. But you don't need the lot of us. Besides, if all these tin lids get to the surface, the scum that dragged them here will scurry to find holes to hide in."

"But I don't want those thugs taking my brother and his friend with them." I stepped out of his reach and drew the pistol, aiming at one of his shoulders.

"Yeew! Don't get wobbly on me. I'm the bloke that can get you out of here alive. We're on the same team." He gestured at the gun. "Guv'nor, would you mind pointing that someplace else?"

"You're not doing anything unless I agree." I held the pistol steady.

"I reckon not." His arms swept out to the other kids. "These tin lids are my mates. They'll do as I say. And if you shoot me, they'll tear you apart like fairy floss."

"I want to make sure my brother and his girlfriend won't be punished for their escape." I dropped the pistol's muzzle a few inches.

The Aussie stepped closer and with cautious movements, pushed the gun barrel toward the floor. "You're pretty high strung, aren't ya?" The boy shook his head, moving closer. "She'll be right. We've got it covered, mate. Relax." He guided me by the shoulder, leading me to where the groups were assembling.

"Listen." He clapped his hands together. Every face focused on him. He spoke in English, then in German. "The Yank's given us our chance to escape. If you're captured, don't talk or you'll ruin it for everybody else. No contact with guards. Absolute quiet. Understood?"

Heads bobbed in agreement.

"Brilliant." The boy stepped away. He guided me to a corner and faced away from the crowd.

"Well, mate? You need to let them go." The boy pointed over his shoulder.

I tilted my head and narrowed my eyes at him. *Why so calm?* I studied the groups. One group of three had gathered near the security guard. *We're outnumbered. I could make this difficult, but I have to trust this guy—and he does seem to have a plan.*

"I guess you're right." I waved Franco away from the door.

"Thanks, mate. When they're gone, we have work to do." The Aussie sent them out, two groups at a time. Afterward, he gathered the remaining three kids and our group to discuss the battle plan.

I let the Aussie speak first.

"The name's Willie." He smiled and stuck out his hand. "Let's talk about the next step."

Chapter 49
– Level Five

I see some unfinished business." Willie pointed at Anton and motioned at a cell. We stripped the guard of the rest of his equipment. I had the pistol. Willie took the rifle. Others took the zip-ties, a boot knife, a switchblade, and a Leatherman knife. We forced the guard into a cage and one of the captured boys stayed behind to watch him. The rest of us gathered to talk.

"There are only a few guards." Willie threw a handful of dirt on the ground, spreading the pile to draw diagrams. "They have five on duty here. The rest are away, *recruiting.*" He demonstrated, tugging the collars of two kids, acting like he would toss them back into their cells. He let them go, scrunching his face like he had eaten a lemon. "You get the meaning. They snatch tin lids and sell them to the highest bidder." He knelt next to his drawing. "These lines are tunnels on this level. We're on Level Five."

While he drew, I glanced at Thunder. He lay next to me, head propped on my leg. Lightning sat on his haunches on the other side of me. His head moved every time the Aussie's finger made a motion in the dirt.

"Level Four," he pointed toward a line above the one for our level, "is where the supplies come in. And this is where The

Dagger lives." His finger traced a box around a corner of Level Four. "The Dagger has his own special guards—a personal body guard and at least two others."

"The Dagger? And who is that?" Franco said.

"You've seen his people, right? They have a dagger with lots of little grapes tattooed on their left forearms and hands. The more grapes, the higher you are. The guards claim that each grape stands for the number of people they've killed on their recruiting runs."

I glanced at the guard. "He doesn't have a dagger on his arm." I motioned with my head.

"Anton joined the guard force a few days ago. He hasn't gone out on his first raid to capture boys and girls."

"Where are the controls for the video cameras?" I asked. "There must be a control center here. And why hasn't anyone come to check on us?"

"Right. The Level Five control office is here, opposite where we are." He looked at Anton. "The chief of the guards left the three most incompetent guards behind to take care of us. The other two have been here for years. I reckon they aren't all that bright. Since we're scared prisoners, I bet the other guards sleep while they let Anton do all the dirty work."

The Aussie went back to his diagram. "Here's where we need to go. Level Four's control room is next to the boss's office and sleeping quarters." He pointed. "And Level Three is where they bring in the new recruits."

"You keep saying recruits. You mean kidnapped kids ?" I raised my eyebrows. "Why?"

"Bang on. You're looking at one of them, mate. Once we're sold, we're transported to other countries. Then we become slaves forced to do whatever our *owners* want. It's an ugly business."

We talked for another couple of minutes, then the Aussie led the way out of the cell holding area. He moved to the corner where I had first seen Anton. After a pause, Willie waved me forward.

"No guards," he said. "We have to get to the control center. They must be there."

I nodded.

Like shadows, we hugged the walls en route to our next destination. Small tunnels branched off the main passageway. After a few zigzags, Willie held up his hand. When we all stopped, he waved me forward.

Pressing against the wall, I eased one eye to where I could see the whole layout. Two men sat at a table playing cards. One wore a plaid shirt, jeans, and work boots. He had blond hair and a thin mustache. The other man had on a grey shirt, black belt, and khaki pants with work boots. He had a bald spot, but his sideburns snaked down to his jaw.

There were a few other tables, all made of wood large enough to seat four people. The two men focused on their game, oblivious to us. Our tunnel came in at an angle to the side of their table. We were three car lengths away.

Willie pulled me back. "Distraction?" A big smile lit his face.

I shrugged and smiled. "Sure."

We moved from the break room and set our plan. The last cross tunnel went to our right. Partway down the hall were two bunk areas, across the corridor from each other. Pete found an older alarm clock with two bells on top, set it for five minutes, and handed it to me. I gave him my backpack. Everyone except Willie and me crammed into the sleeping area on the left side of the tunnel. The two of us snuck across the hall. Willie hid behind a chest by the door, cradling his rifle. I put the clock on a side table and went to the break room entrance to watch the show.

The alarm went off.

The man in the grey shirt stood up.

His companion mumbled and laughed.

"Gott in Himmel," the first man said.

"Yes, God is in heaven," the blond man tipped his chair on its rear legs. "Go turn that alarm off."

The guy in the grey shirt slammed his cards down, shoved his chair back, and headed toward me.

Fleet as a gazelle, I reentered the sleeping area and sat on a bed, ready for action.

The man swore as he approached the room. He rounded the corner, stepped inside, and spotted me.

248

"What are you…?"

Willie sprang from the corner and smashed the butt of the rifle against the back of the man's head.

He collapsed.

"That's for Cassie." Willie stood over the man, sides heaving. A tear bulged in the corner of his eye.

I swung around the corner of the bed. "We still have to take care of the other guard."

The kids across the tunnel had swarmed into the room. They lugged the unconscious guard across the hallway into their bunk area.

I went into the hall as the alarm continued to ring.

I peeked inside the control room. The other guard was nowhere in sight.

Cold steel pressed against my temple.

"Pretty funny, kid." The guard's hand grabbed my shirt and yanked me into the dining room. "How many of you are here?"

"Eight." I spoke without thinking and my heart sank into my gut.

"I'll take that." The man lifted the gun out of my belt and set it on a table. "Knives?" He latched onto my hair and yanked me to within an inch of his face.

"A Leatherman." I tugged my head away and took out the knife.

He tossed it onto the table. Grasping my hair even tighter, he turned me around to face the tunnel where I had hidden a few minutes ago.

"Tell your friends to come out." He poked the gun's muzzle in my ribs. "And don't be a brave boy. I've alerted other guards that you're here."

My mind scrambled to figure out how we were going to escape. "Come on out everyone. We've been caught," I said. "Time to give up."

One by one they came out of the hallway. The gunman motioned them against the wall, jerking me around by my hair.

"That's six. And the seventh one is…?"

"I don't know." I tried to move my head away, but couldn't break his steely grip. "I met the kid a few hours ago. He might have escaped on his own."

"You released the prisoners, I see." He pointed at the smallest new kid. "Bad boy." He slammed the gun into my right ear.

It sounded like an explosion. I flinched, but his other hand had a firm grip on my hair, which prevented me from dropping to the floor. My hand went to my injured ear.

"I'm telling you, missing friend, if you don't come out on the count of three, this young man will die."

"One…" He pressed the muzzle into my temple.

"Two…" He pulled the hammer of the gun back. It clicked.

The lights cut out.

Chapter 50
~ Level Four

The crack of a gunshot split the air. Dogs snarled and kids yelled. The alarm clock's bells kept clanging.

I fell to the table and into silence.

"Wake up." A hand jiggled me. "Come on, Gabe."

I blinked a few times. "Pete?"

"That's good. Now…"

I spluttered when Willie splashed water into my face. I pushed to a sitting position. "Why'd you do that?" I dried off the water and touched my bruised ear. A reddish tinge covered my fingers.

"Come on, mate. We don't have time to muck around. Can you stand and walk?" Willie's strong arms lifted me.

"Other than a splitting headache and a little bleeding, I'm okay," I said.

"I've checked it out and you'll be chipper in no time." Willie patted my shoulder. "Now, off we go."

I tugged on his shirt. "I thought you'd left us."

"I'll never leave you or forget you, mate." Willie smiled.

I stared at him, mouth open wide.

"Close your cakehole," Willie said. "It's bad manners. Here's your weapons. We've got to run."

We left both guards zip-tied, face down, and spread eagle, on separate beds in different rooms. Taking a different tunnel out of the dining area, we reached a corner cave. A diagram of the level hung against one wall and had a control board at waist level. Video feeds showed different sections of Level Five.

"Here's where I cut the lights off." Willie placed his hands on the control board.

"I can see the two sleeping guards," Pete said. "Those two black screens must be the cages."

"Right, mate." Willie said. "Now we have to get to the next level and past The Dagger."

"How big is his operation?" I took my backpack from Pete, and shouldered it.

"Tell you in a second." The Aussie made a few changes to the control board. "That ought to do it. Now we can go."

"The Dagger's got southern Germany, nothing else?" I pestered him while we took a path slanted upward. The rest of the group followed.

"This human trafficking business consists of ten operational headquarters. The Dagger owns the European center, but not the largest." Willie held up his hand. He slunk ahead by himself and vanished around a corner.

I signaled the others to stop. I tiptoed toward Willie when he called me. We rounded the corner and dropped to our bellies. Inching past a wall to see the control room of Level Four, we caught a glimpse of the room and moved backward.

"The next part of this escape is tricky going," Willie said. "Do exactly what I say. Can you do that?" The Aussie grinned again.

"You haven't told me yet." I crossed my arms.

"Sometimes, you have to trust first." Willie leaned against the wall.

All my friends below me on the trail depended on me to get them home. *Can I depend on this stranger? He seems to know everything about this place, but the kidnappers captured him, too. Still, he did save me once when I thought he'd left me. And he returned my weapons.*

"Sure." I shrugged.

"You're going into The Dagger's headquarters. I'm sure he's expecting you. You and Pete go in alone. In the outer office, when you want to fight, don't. When you want to cry, laugh."

"That's weird."

He nodded. "But it'll get you out of this dog's breakfast alive."

I blinked.

"Dog's breakfast—the mess we're in."

I looked at the ceiling and shook my head. *I'm trapped in a German cave and can't even understand the Australian who's trying to rescue me.* "What about Thunder and Lightning?"

"Leave them here." He patted my shoulder again. "You'll see them at the right time."

"And the rest of the gang, including the kids we released?" I asked.

"Don't get fussed about that. You take care of this. That will give us the cover we need to get the rest of the lot out. If I can help you another way, I will. But you and Alex have to win this one." He gave me a few more tips and sent me to the others.

I called them all together to reveal our plan.

"What do you mean, we are not coming with you?" Franco raised his hands in the air. "You would not be here without us. We have worked like a team to make it this far. I have done all you wanted, including lugging Alex's backpack for miles."

"I know, but…"

"How can you let a person you do not even know tell you what to do?" Jonathan said. "We have known him less than three hours."

"We should have faith in Gabe." Izabella squeezed past the two boys and put her hand on my arm. "He has not perfection, but the heart is right." She crossed her arms, lips a firm line.

"Your right, he's not perfect," Jonathan said. "I remember…"

"You try to remember his faults," Izabella said. "Have you perfection?"

Jonathan gave her a sideways glance and stepped away.

"I haven't known Willie for long, but he saved us on Level Five," I said. "He's asked us to take action and we've succeeded. He knows this place—I don't know how, since the kidnappers brought him in three days ago. And, this is kind of wild, but I sense that he's okay. I'm going to have confidence in him. And I want you to follow him out. Once you are free, alert the police and our parents. We'll be all right."

"If you think he can be trusted, let's give his plan a try." Pete sighed.

"Go for it," Franco said.

"Pete, follow my lead. Jonathan, take this backpack." I handed it over. "Lightning, Thunder. Listen to Willie." I ruffled their heads.

"Izabella, thanks for the support." I smiled.

"Be careful." She gave me a hint of a smile. She knelt to stroke the dogs and looked back up at me.

"I will." I tucked the pistol in a little further and hurried to Willie's side.

"You won't need that." He opened his hand.

"What?"

"That handgun."

"How do I defend myself?" I backed away. "They all have guns."

"Didn't you listen?" Willie raised his eyebrows and cocked his head, his hand still extended.

"Yes, but I didn't think I would have to go in without a weapon." My gut tightened.

"No worries, mate. You can do it. Give it a go." Willie remained calm. And waited.

"How do you expect me to win?" I surrendered the gun.

"By trust. Have faith. They'll be looking for weapons." Willie took the gun, put it in his belt, motioning Pete and me out into the corridor.

We entered an ordinary looking office with the exception of a control panel in one corner, but it was empty. Noticing a door inside, I cracked it open to sneak into the next room and was met with a rifle barrel pointed at my chest.

Chapter 51
– Outer Office

Did I lead us into a trap? Have I been scammed?

"Come in," the rifleman said. "The Dagger is expecting you." He motioned us to enter. Closing the door behind us, the rifleman backed up a step. "Meet Slagle, the chief of security."

A muscular man with a military style haircut reclined behind the desk. His crisp uniform mimicked the German Polizei, with a few alterations in patches and nametapes. His tan short-sleeve shirt, black pistol belt draped over the back of a chair, and his olive colored pants were an exact imitation of a policeman's clothes. He toyed with his revolver, opening and closing the cylinder. Click. Spin. Open. Shut with a click. Spin.

"You like the pistol?" Slagle lifted it higher for me to see. "It's old fashioned. A Colt 45 from the western United States of America. Not very accurate." He eased to his feet. "But in this small office, it's deadly." He pointed the gun at me, cocked the hammer and pulled the trigger.

I ducked.

"Oh, it's not loaded. Yet." The security chief chuckled. "Welcome." He gestured to a couch on our right that faced the wall opposite the entry door.

Why doesn't it face the chief's desk?

A wooden coffee table sat in front of the couch. Over the coffee table, a window containing German rolladen, rolling blinds between two panes of glass, closed off the view.

"That wall in the front of you has equipped with a two-way polarized mirror. The normal one-way setting allows the seeing into the next room without the guests seeing us. The two-way function, now operated from either room, changes the mirror to allow The Dagger's seeing into this office. The rolladen provides The Dagger with privacy in his personal retreat center during difficult interviews. Those events can be a little..." He sat. "Disturbing to our visitors."

Pete and I sank onto the couch.

"Where's my brother?" I said.

"And my sister," Pete added.

Slagle opened a switchblade with a click. He leaned forward in his chair with a slight rocking motion. "Wait outside, Lieutenant."

The man stepped out.

When the door closed, Slagle looked at us again. He opened a drawer in his desk and retrieved a silver whiskey flask. He unscrewed the lid, took a long pull, and recapped the flask. He set it on his desk.

"Your father." He pointed at me with the blade. "He has a critical piece of informations we want." He started to trim his fingernails with the knife. "We have been patient, but you have not been cooperating with us." A smile came and went on his face. He glanced at the flask.

"I think you will cooperate in this time." He touched a switch on his console and the rolladen lifted. "Now you can see and hear the happenings in The Dagger's inner room."

I jumped up. "Alex?"

"Sit," Slagle said. "And don't come near that glass. It's too expensive."

Alex and Jenna sat across from The Dagger in high-backed wooden chairs. Clamps held their arms and legs against metal plates in the chairs. Wires ran behind the chairs to a machine. The Dagger's massive mahogany desk occupied the right corner of the room, setting at an angle. The Dagger lounged in his chair, his personal assistant standing behind Alex and Jenna.

"Ah-h-h-h." The Dagger looked right at us. "Slagle tells me that your brothers are here. Let me show you." The Dagger pushed a toggle on his desk panel.

Alex and Jenna struggled against the shackles on their hands.

"Pete, run." I leaped out of the seat, but Slagle crushed me into the couch.

"Don't try anything funny." Slagle held the revolver against my head. "You're here to watch first. You'll be having your chance at interrogation later."

"Enough," The Dagger said. He punched a switch on his desk, switching the window to one-way, and chuckled. "Children are most amusing."

Alex and Jenna's eyes searched for us, darting in our direction.

"Here." Pete waved.

"They are not seeing you anymore." Slagle walked to his desk. "You can see and hear, but they are cut off."

The Dagger folded his hands and spoke to Alex and Jenna. "I can see your brother and his friends have been busy. When the new guards arrive in a few hours, they'll clean up this little catastrophe and I'll punish the guards they tricked. Perhaps I'll let you watch."

Alex shook his head.

"No? You don't like discipline?" The Dagger's smile was more like a sneer. He wrinkled his nose and drew his lips back, almost snarling. "Well, I did enjoy the beginning of our adventure together. You showed remarkable ingenuity in the water chamber."

"More like a death chamber," Jenna said.

"Not for you." The Dagger rose, walked around the front of his desk, and sat on the far corner of it. "I didn't realize how much fun my Egyptian maze would be. I modernized some sections and added a peril of my own, which, you have to admit is a technical marvel—the treacherous tentacles, I liked to call them, full of heat and light sensors."

"But we destroyed that horrible machine," Jenna said.

"Oh, I haven't forgotten. You'll pay for breaking my pet project." He adjusted his perch. "But first, I'll get more pleasure watching one of you die. As you let my latest apprentice die."

"Hans?" Alex said.

"He had such great potential."

"That wasn't our fault," Alex said. "We tried to warn him."

Jenna nodded. "His bull-headedness got him into trouble." She held her chin high.

"For that little indiscretion, one of you will give your life. For now, take this." The Dagger twisted a knob on his desk and a series of green lights glowed at the bottom of a gauge on both chairs. The light went up a quarter of the scale.

Alex and Jenna jerked and shook, screaming in pain.

"Stop." I attacked the glass, fists pounding. "Turn it off."

Slagle set down his whisky flask and raised the revolver. A shot rang out and he laughed.

I dropped to the table and rolled onto the floor. When I raised my head, the security chief's polished boots filled my view.

He hooked a hand onto my belt, slinging me onto the couch like a sack of potatoes. "Sit."

My stomach churned. I was close to tears.

Slagle went to his desk. "That's the last one," he said. "I have no more blanks. The next firing will be with a real bullet." He pulled out an apple and started peeling it.

The phone rang. Slagle picked up and swiveled away from us.

"What are we going to do?" Pete whispered. You're not giving in, are you?"

I handed my weapons to Willie. I trusted him. All he gave me were those ridiculous instructions to laugh when I'm sad.

"Do what I do," I said.

Pete gave me a squeeze.

"This passing of time is for me tiring when I should be getting your informations." Slagle had finished his phone conversation. He slugged down another gulp of alcohol.

I laughed hard, grabbing my stomach. "Passing time. Funny."

"You are amused, little boy?" Slagle said.

I elbowed Pete.

"That's hilarious." Pete chuckled.

Slagle grabbed him by the ear.

"That's too funny." I laughed as hard as I could, bouncing on the couch.

"Ow-w. Oh." Pete alternated between yelling and guffawing. He wasn't a good actor.

Slagle's hands seized our necks. I forced more laughter, trying not to choke. I kicked the glass while I struggled. A moment later, The Dagger's personal assistant entered the room.

The mirror disappeared. Alex and Jenna could see us. I kept up the comedy routine.

"Gabe, you're laughing at us?" Alex's forehead shone with sweat.

"I can't believe it." Jenna's body was still twitching.

The Dagger activated the switch again, bringing the mirror back.

"Stop this now," the personal assistant said. He grabbed Pete's shirt and slapped him. Pete's chuckling ceased, hands going to his face. The personal assistant dragged him through the entry into The Dagger's office like he weighed less than a bag of feathers and slammed the door.

Slagle turned toward me. I balanced on the end of the couch, rubbing my neck. When The Dagger's door had crashed shut, the door to the outer office cracked open. I stiffened.

Willie glanced in, acted out laughing motions, and pointed at me. He made a circular motion with his hand that told me to keep it going.

Slagle paused, watching me.

I slapped my legs, and let out a party howl. "Awesome. What a game this is. Now you have to catch me."

Slagle lunged at me, arms closing in on empty air.

I bounced backward off the couch into a corner that contained a small armless wooden chair. I held it like a lion tamer would if he were trying to keep the lions away.

Slagle collected himself. "You wish to be funny? I'll be shooting you with my favorite pistol. A first time for me." He started to turn toward his desk.

I gasped. Willie wasn't behind the desk yet, so I rushed at Slagle with the chair.

He caught a leg and ended my charge, forcing the chair into my gut and ramming me into the wall.

The blow caused me to lose my breath. I grunted and fell onto my side.

Willie gave me a thumbs-up and hid.

"I'm beating you black and blue, you little..."

"Slagle?" The Dagger's personal assistant swung the inner door wide. "What is going on? That boy is The Dagger's personal guest. Don't hurt him. He is boss' business, not yours."

"He has no visible damage, Craven." Slagle said. "The young man is feeling no pain, correct?" He hauled me over by the shirt collar.

"I'm okay." I doubled-over and groaned.

"Get him in here," Craven said.

Slagle obeyed, kicking me through the opening. "Good riddance." He looked at The Dagger. "Boss, you must kill this one first. He cannot shut the mouth."

Chapter 52
~ Inner Sanctum

The door banged shut behind me. I stumbled into The Dagger's inner sanctum—his torture room.

"Bring that one here." The Dagger pointed at me.

Craven, a man with no fat on his frame, pulled my arms behind me and thrust me into the desk, not letting go.

I leaned forward, waist smacking the desk's edge. I could see most of The Dagger's office, including Alex, Jenna, and Pete, who had been tied to a metal chair a few feet from Alex and Jenna. Weapons of all sorts hung on the walls, like a trophy room. Behind Alex and Jenna, a strange looking table sat with pliers, needles, and dentist drill bits.

"Why aren't we laughing now, Mr. Hero?" The Dagger poked my nose with his finger. "You're not afraid of me are you?"

I swallowed and studied the overweight, bald man. He wore an open-collared black shirt with short sleeves. Both arms displayed tattoos of daggers with several bunches of grapes surrounding the blades. *He must have killed a lot of people*. The colorful ink filled every inch of his arms.

I felt Craven pushing my elbows closer together. I'm double-jointed so it didn't really hurt, but I faked a groan.

"You know, in this business when we take a child, no one outside of us knows if we use them or dispose of them." The Dagger sat and waved me away. "However, I know I will get more out of your father if you both make the telephone call together."

"I won't make any phone calls," I said.

"We won't talk." Alex jerked at his metal cuffs.

The Dagger touched a control on his desk.

Jenna shrieked.

Alex writhed in his chair.

"If you won't call your father, perhaps you would like to sign a few papers?"

"You're hurting them," I said.

"I believe that's the point." He rotated a dial and Jenna screamed even louder.

"What kind of papers?" I leaned forward. "I don't know what you mean."

The Dagger twisted the dial one more notch. The green lights on the chairs began to rise.

"I'll sign them. Just stop torturing them." I hung my head.

"If you insist." The Dagger dialed down the juice and tapped his console, leaning into his chair.

Alex and Jenna groaned.

"New technology is critical for this business," The Dagger said. "It's why we need the information your father knows. The electro-shock isn't the latest invention, but it isn't like the crude tools I used in the old days. I had to educate myself and find better ways to inflict pain. Young friend, if you think this is bad, imagine when I had to make my point with this."

In a flash, he pulled a knife and drove it into the desk. The blade quivered when he let go. The knife matched the dagger design on his forearms.

"Should you or your brother waver in signing your confessions, I will resort to cruder methods."

"Craven, let him go."

His personal assistant released me and I slid away from him.

"Notice Craven's left hand." The Dagger took the hand of his assistant and put it on the desk. It was missing a little finger. Craven's remaining fingers looked permanently bruised and broken.

"It took Craven several lessons to learn obedience." The Dagger pushed away his assistant's hand. "But I think he understands now."

A thud startled me. The polarized window shook.

"Craven, see what's happening out there." The Dagger's hand pounded the desk in fury. "If Slagle is drunk again, I'll teach him a permanent lesson in obedience. That window cost a fortune. No one disturbs this sanctuary of solitude." He looked at me and smiled.

Craven elbowed me on his way out.

"That Craven doesn't miss a good opportunity to do a little damage." The Dagger chuckled.

As the door shut, I placed a hand on the desk, glancing at The Dagger's console. He had each switch labeled.

Seconds later, the office door flew open. Thunder and Lightning bounded through, past the struggling forms of Willie and Craven.

I lunged onto the desktop and hit the third toggle on the top row.

Click.

I reversed direction and fell out of The Dagger's reach.

Alex and Jenna collapsed from their electro-chairs to the floor. Though they tried to move, their muscles didn't cooperate.

I dashed for the closest weapon hanging on the wall, a throwing knife.

The Dagger yanked the blade out of his desktop, and took aim at me. As he was releasing it, Lightning leaped on him, spoiling his aim and causing the steel blade to whiz by me.

I grabbed the throwing knife from the display mount and rushed over to free Pete.

Thunder darted behind the desk, biting The Dagger and doing his best to avoid the man's fists. Lightning did his part as well.

The Dagger punched several buttons before the dogs forced him from behind his desk. An alarm went off in the outer office and corridors.

264

While the dogs bit and clawed him, I slashed through Pete's ropes. We half-dragged, half-lifted Alex and Jenna behind the chairs. I scanned the walls for a better weapon.

Willie and Craven continued to fight.

Crash.

Several shots rang out. *Who's got the upper hand?*

The Dagger glared at me with narrowed eyes, jaw clenched. He planted a nasty kick to Thunder's jaw, knocking him away. Though Lightning flashed at his face, The Dagger brushed him aside with a jab that sent the dog to the floor.

I grabbed the first thing I found on the table behind the chairs—a huge set of pliers, and threw them at him. He fended them off with his thick forearm and laughed.

In a few quick steps he reached his desk's middle drawer, drawing out a black pistol similar to Dad's 9-mm military handgun.

Pete ducked behind an electro-chair.

"Sic 'em," I yelled at the dogs and dove for one of two throwing hatchets on the wall beside me.

The Dagger's shot nicked my left forearm, tearing open the skin in a flesh wound.

The blood streaked my shirt as I jerked the arm back. I closed a hand on one of the hatchets, feeling exposed without any cover. *Why hadn't the dogs attacked?*

The Dagger chuckled and paused. "You will die last, watching your friends go first." The Dagger trained the pistol on my heart. "Drop the hatchet."

In shock, I surveyed the mess. Thunder had retreated to Alex, lying on the floor and whimpering. His right jaw was bloody and swollen and his right eye was a slit. Lightning limped near his partner, unable to attack anything. Alex and Jenna still couldn't move and Pete seemed unable to budge. The hatchet slipped from my hand.

Thunk.

The Dagger kept his eyes on me. "Craven, get in here. You've got a lot to do." He didn't wait for a response. Instead, he resumed his place behind the desk and rolled his chair underneath himself. He sat.

"Your little escapade has failed. Guard reserves should be here in a few minutes to mop up." He silenced the alarm. "My other European operatives and cells know of this disturbance and will hide until I give the signal. And I will gut the guard force of the imbeciles who let this occur."

He thumped his hand on the desk. "Craven, what the…"

The sounds had slowed in Slagle's office, but the door that had automatically shut earlier burst open.

I tensed.

The Dagger's reflexes kicked in. His weapon swung toward the door as Craven's body fell into the room, gun clattering onto the floor near me.

In that split second, I grabbed the hatchet and threw it at The Dagger.

He fended it off with his shooting arm.

I dove low, snatched Craven's gun and rolled behind the empty chair that Pete had occupied, yelling as my wounded arm brushed the floor.

Two shots rang out in rapid fire.

A red spot spread on The Dagger's right shoulder. His shooting arm dangled at his side.

The chair had been knocked back into the wall by The Dagger's bullet.

I crawled to my feet, gun and eyes focused on my target. I leaned against the wall. The weapon shook as I aimed at The Dagger's heart. "Don't move."

Willie appeared in the outer office door, clothes in disarray, but he leveled his gun at The Dagger. "Good on ya, mate." He limped into the room. "Looks like you've captured the big man. But you've been shot."

"Yeah. Left arm."

"The reserve guards will wipe out all of you." The Dagger sneered.

"Get stuffed, boss-man. Not on my watch," Willie said. "While you tortured his brother and girlfriend, I took out the lieutenant, called the Polizei on your telephone lines, and then disabled communications. All thanks to this bloke's actions." He waved his free hand toward me.

"He saved his friends and put you out of commission."
Willie gave a big thumb's up. "He killed it."

Chapter 53
~ Next Assignment

"You don't look too bad after a shower." Mom ruffled my hair. "Mom, I just combed it." I sighed and headed back to the mirror.

"Don't you look sweet," Alex said. "Gonna see someone special?" He winked and gave me a playful punch as he limped out of the bathroom.

"You look fine yourself, gimp." I slammed the door a little harder than I wanted.

"Gabe, let's go," Dad said. "This ceremony's been in the works for three weeks. We'll be late if you don't hurry."

We arrived at the Polizei Station on time. Several people applauded for us and waved.

Chief Bruno Barr met us and ushered us to their Polizei van. An hour later, with police motorcycle escorts, we arrived at the International Congress Center in Stuttgart, Germany for the official ceremony. The auditorium seated about three thousand. The Polizei walked us into the building, pushing reporters and photographers away. The German Chancellor's deputy represented him. Several senior officials of other nations attended.

The Deputy Chancellor of the Federal Republic of Germany, the main speaker, sat on stage. The commander of our military base, our town's mayor, and all our friends from the salt mines were there. Many of us still had bandages. My bandaged left arm sported a sling, Alex had a crutch and walking cast, like his friend Dieter Klein, and Erik Eberstark had bandages on his arms from his battle with the gray tentacle machine.

I slapped each of their raised palms when the Polizei seated us. We all grinned.

When it came time to recognize us, Chief Bruno Barr and Herr Bauer, the mayor of Goeppingen, assisted in handing out our awards and medals, then posed with us for the photos.

The Deputy Chancellor discussed Hans Becher's death, mentioning his parents' lack of involvement. When he spoke about how Germany would take steps to fix these types of issues, I wondered about the skateboard bully. *Would his parents have changed anything? Maybe when he was little. But he wouldn't have listened—to me or anybody else when he was older. If he had, he would be here today.*

The girl who had been kidnapped from Goeppingen six months before our salt mines adventure came by and shook our hands, glad to be home again.

After the ceremony, we left in the Polizei van to return to Goeppingen for the local celebration. The mayor spoke, more photographers snapped shots, and I wanted to head home. But Chief Bruno insisted that we enjoy a meal first in the Polizei headquarters.

After we entered the party room, Pete found me. "How can you stand it? Pictures, handshakes, and all this nonsense? All because thugs kidnapped us."

"I guess we're heroes." I stabbed a piece of cake with a fork. "At least Erik and Dieter survived. I'm glad the Egyptian maze sections The Dagger modernized weren't death traps."

"Yeah. And the dogs look like they've healed okay. How's Alex?" Pete made sure no one was watching and slid two large slices of cake onto his plate. He stuffed the food into his mouth.

"He still limps and uses a crutch, but he's okay. They cleaned out the gunshot wound pretty well." I shoveled in a mouthful of cake. "And we're taking martial arts training again."

He nodded. "You know, Jonathan seems to think he solved the entire mystery."

"He can be a snot, but he had a bad upbringing. I feel sorry for him sometimes." I scooped another piece of cake into my mouth. "He's different, that's all."

"He's headed for jail. He stole things out of your backpack."

"Who cares?" I swallowed. "We don't see him often— only at the castle playground."

"Yeah, I guess." Pete left to get a soda and my brother limped over with his crutch.

"Dad wants to talk with us for a minute." Alex tugged me in his direction.

I snapped my fingers.

Lightning, who had been lying near the door with Thunder, came toward me, toenails clicking on the tile floor. He was back to normal, but his canine buddy wasn't as lucky. We had to keep Thunder's muzzle wrapped tight, feed him soft food for six weeks, and give him sedatives to make him drowsy until he healed. He padded along and brushed against Alex's leg.

"Boys?" Dad waved us over. "Into the police chief's office."

Chief Bruno waited with a cup of steaming liquid in hand.

"Coffee?" He lifted his cup in the air.

Dad picked up a cup and let Bruno pour.

"You will be celebrated for years to come, boys." He nodded at us. "You have broken the European human trafficking ring."

"We couldn't have done it without a little help," I said.

"God answered our prayers." Alex nodded.

"Yes," I said, trying to be humble, "and we had others who helped, like Jonathan, and…"

"And Hans," Alex said. "He did help a little, though we forced him to do it."

"Yes, and the strangest of all—a kid named Willie." I paused. "He…"

270

"Yes?" Chief Bruno said.

"Well, he helped us, but he left before I could thank him." I frowned. "He seemed cool."

Willie walked into the room wearing a sport coat, collared shirt, tie, dress slacks, and dress shoes. "Wow, I'm cool."

"Boys, I'd like you to meet special agent William Gretzke, from Australia." Chief Bruno gave a grand wave of his arm. "He led the undercover police effort to find the weak spot of the human trafficking operation, but your sacrifices created a way to take it down."

"Nice to meet you." I extended a hand and instead Willie engulfed me in a hug.

"You're like a rellie—that's a relative in Yank-speak. Part of the family." He let me go and ran his eyes over me. "You clean up pretty well."

Willie hugged Alex and stepped back. "This brother of yours isn't all that bad, is he mate?" He laughed and punched Alex in the shoulder.

"William specializes in hard to solve crimes." Chief Bruno motioned for all of us to sit. "We have another one we need some help on." The chief glanced at Dad.

"Bruno, you haven't asked me yet," Dad said. "You know how Rachael and I hate to put the boys in danger. And they have school, homework, and..."

Chief Bruno went to the coffee pot for a refill. "All I am asking is for a little intelligence work. That's what you do for a living and you know most of it isn't dangerous."

"And look where it got these boys." Dad got to his feet. "Kidnapped twice, almost killed on the road, and gone from home for days without any idea where they are. It's too dangerous."

"Eli, Eli," Chief Bruno said. "Calm down. I will not involve them in anything dangerous. This is mere fact finding." He gave us a thumbs-up. "They are great at finding out the facts."

Dad paced. "Rachael needs to know. And I must warn you, Gabe hates doing research."

"Oh, she has to know." Bruno sipped from his mug. "I'll tell her myself. I hope she won't mind going to Austria for a weeklong, all expenses paid trip to Salzburg." He grinned. "And," Chief Bruno put his arm on Dad's shoulder, "Willie will be the special agent on the case. He'll look after the boys."

I nodded my approval.

Alex smiled.

"It's all settled?" Bruno raised one eyebrow at Mom.

"I guess. You'll ensure the boys aren't kidnapped?" She sipped her glass of water.

"Quite." Chief Bruno puffed out his chest. "This is information gathering. I'm sure the boys will love it."

"When do we go?" Mom asked.

"In about six months." Chief Bruno looked at Dad. "Would that work?"

Mom glanced at Dad, who nodded. "They'll examine odd occurrences in Salzburg—special musical paperwork that might be missing." He put his hand on my shoulder.

"Yes, I guess that will work." She gave Bruno a big smile. "Thanks for offering a project I can use to teach our music homeschool lessons. In particular, I'm happy this includes the European Master Musicians." She raised her eyebrows and looked at me.

I gave her a sheepish grin and shrugged.

That night a bitter storm blew in. I was cold even under the covers. The wind shook the windows, waking me up. I got up to get a glass of milk and a cookie from the kitchen. On the way, I heard a rattle coming from the stairwell.

I unlocked the door, cracked it open, and peered out onto the landing. I didn't see anything, but the rattle continued. I went down the stairs to check out the front door and found the door latch a little loose. *Why?*

I opened the door and glanced outside to make sure someone had not tried to pull the door open. Since I didn't see anyone, I made sure the latch closed properly and trudged back up the stairs. Halfway up, I paused. *What if G dropped off another gift?* I raced back down the stairs, two at a time. When I got to the bottom, I unlocked the door and yanked it open.

Light poured out of the doorway into the windy cold. I stepped outside. My bare foot touched the freezing marble stone. The chill made my leg ache.

A white box leaned against the top step. I snagged it. *It's about the same size as the others.* A large, handwritten number two covered the brown paper on one side and a note card dangled at the top from a curled gold ribbon.

Once I was back inside, I stomped my feet until feeling returned. I slammed the door shut, then locked and jiggled it to ensure it was tight. I rushed upstairs, locking the inner door behind me. Inside, I ripped open the envelope holding the note card and read it several times.

Mystery Lies in Lands Afar
Paintings, Artistry, Music, and Charm
But Not All is Sweet and Full of Good Cheer
For What Remains Hidden Some Wealthy Men Fear

Open This Package
A Surprise You Will See
For an Austrian Trip
It's a True Necessity

G

I raced to the bedroom to wake Alex.

About Aaron M. Zook, Jr.

Aaron M. Zook, Jr. loves his Lord and his family. He and his wife live in Belton, Texas, and have two married sons with children. He enjoys any Grandpa time he can get.

Writing adventure stories energizes Aaron. He created many stories for his boys while driving them on weekend vacations in Germany and has now developed those ideas into a twelve book series.

Aaron embraces music, sports, studying the Bible, and mentoring other young Christians. He runs, plays golf, and hits the gym several times a week. He likes to devour life, one big bite at a time.

Community is important to Aaron, so he is involved in many aspects at his church, including leading the Praise and Worship. He gives regularly to charitable organizations.

Aaron's published books include the first two books of the Thunder and Lightning series, *The Secrets of the Castle* and *The Salt Mines Mystery*. The third book, *The Phantom of the Fortress*, is already working and is next on the publishing horizon.

Find out more at Zookbooks.org.

Like Aaron on Facebook-FaceBook.com/ZookBooks.

Follow him on Twitter: @ZookAaron.

Pintrest: /aaronzookjr/

Made in the USA
Columbia, SC
14 April 2019